ACROSS DEATH VALLEY

The Pioneer Journey of Juliet Wells Brier

A Novel

Mary Barmeyer O'Brien

TWODOT®

GUILFORD, CONNECTICUT
HELENA, MONTANA
AN IMPRINT OF THE GLOBE PEQUOT PRESS

Dedicated with love to the Sibs Club

A · T W O D O T® · B O O K

Copyright © 2009 by Mary Barmeyer O'Brien

Project manager: Julie Marsh
Layout: Joanna Beyer
Text design: Sheryl P. Kober
Map: M.A. Dubé © Morris Book Publishing, LLC

Library of Congress Cataloging-in-Publication Data
O'Brien, Mary Barmeyer.
  Across Death Valley : the pioneer journey of Juliet Wells Brier : a novel /
Mary Barmeyer O'Brien.
    p. cm.
  ISBN 978-0-7627-4505-0
  1. Brier, Julia Wells, 1814-1913—Fiction. 2. Women pioneers—Fiction.
3. Overland journeys to the Pacific—Fiction. 4. Death Valley (Calif. and
Nev.)—Fiction. I. Title.
  PS3615.B76A25 2009
  813'.6—dc22

                                                                2009002361

Printed in the United States of America
10 9 8 7 6 5 4 3 2 1

God help thee, Traveller, on thy journey far;
The wind is bitter keen,—the snow o'erlays
The hidden pits, and dangerous hollow ways,
And darkness will involve thee.
No kind star
To-night will guide thee, Traveller . . .

—Henry Kirke White

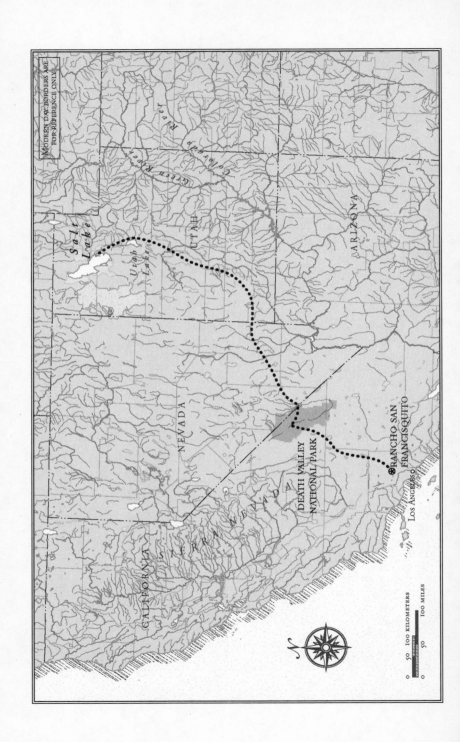

PREFACE

Death Valley National Park and the surrounding deserts comprise one of the harshest landscapes in the United States. It was here that Juliet Brier and her family nearly perished on their 1849 journey to California.

Before I visited the unforgiving expanses of Death Valley and the adjacent Panamint region, I knew that Juliet's courage in crossing the vast deserts of Nevada and California with her family was exceptional. Yet it wasn't until I followed a long portion of her trail, saw the enormity of the parched distances she walked, and experienced the severe environment for myself that I realized her journey was nothing short of miraculous.

As my companions and I descended from a windswept ridge onto the stark salt flats below, the dangerous (but beautiful) landscape sobered us. We, however, drove paved highways in an air-conditioned vehicle filled with emergency supplies. Juliet Brier passed there on foot without food, water, a wagon, or even a map. Our trepidation at the area's harshness was real, and we could only imagine how much more extreme Juliet's foreboding must have been, particularly since she and her husband were traveling with their three young sons.

Her historic trip west—and her extraordinary response to it—inspired this work. Although these pages generally follow the westward journey of James and Juliet Brier, there are numerous descriptions of that memorable trek, and they contain dozens of different interpretations. No matter where her exact trail may have taken her and who her companions were each day, I have endeavored to stay true to Juliet's inner story and her remarkable personal reactions to the party's desperate situation.

It is important to note, however, that this is a western historical novel. As such, many of the circumstances, events, and details are fictional.

ACKNOWLEDGMENTS

Special thanks to the following people:

Juliet Brier, whose remarkable story inspired this book.

The forty-niners who recorded the details of their grueling journey, including William Lewis Manly, Sheldon Young, James Brier, and, later in his life, John Wells Brier.

Poet Henry Kirke White.

The historians, researchers, park rangers, librarians, writers, and curators who have studied the Brier family's journey and provided many insights into their story.

My editor, Erin Turner, and the rest of the staff at The Globe Pequot Press for their expert editing and publishing skills.

Melissa Guyles and Katie O'Brien, who accompanied me to Death Valley and beyond to research this novel's setting.

Dan Burnett of Ridgecrest, California, who graciously provided detailed information, photographs, and insightful interpretations about the landscape and natural history of sections of the Briers' trail; his assistance was indispensable and greatly appreciated.

C. John Di Pol of the Historical Society of the Upper Mojave Desert for his very helpful packet of information and thoughtful comments about the Briers' route.

Friends and family who painstakingly read parts or all of the manuscript and made their valuable suggestions, including Maggie Plummer and Dan, Jennifer, Kevin, and Katie O'Brien.

Trudé and Paul Hunsucker and other ranchers who shared their knowledge about cattle to help me re-create the behavior and appearance of the oxen in this story.

Donna Olson for her help with Spanish wording.

Library Director Marilyn Trosper and the staff at Polson City Library for their support, interest, expertise, and help, as always. Special thanks to KayCee Smith for her persistence in locating research materials.

CHAPTER 1

It looked impassable, this immense rift in the land. Juliet Wells Brier stood on the edge and stared at the stark clay outcroppings that lined the drop-off. Below, a green river pushed through a deep, rocky gorge. It was a welcome sight after these past days of traveling without much water, but a cruel trick as well, for no one could reach its cool depths from here. As far as she could see, the wide chasm, lined with massive boulders and dotted with scruffy sagebrush, sliced the landscape. In the distance, angular mountains lifted from the brown desert.

She wondered if this would be the end of their attempt to reach California without slinking back to Captain Hunt, confessing their folly and admitting they had met an obstacle too formidable to cross.

She turned from the edge and took a deep breath. The air was scented with faded sage and dry dirt. She and James were in the lead today, so the dust wasn't bad. Yesterday, when they had taken their turn bringing up the rear, the wagons ahead of them had riled so much powdery earth that she had been forced to breathe through her handkerchief all day. By evening, the gathers of her long, gray wool dress

Juliet and James Brier and their three sons.

were streaked with dust. Her fine brown hair, which she wore pulled back and secured at her neck, was dull with grit, and she could taste the flavor of clay.

Now, as she watched, the other wagons lumbered up and gathered into a haphazard bunch nearby. Their tired canvas covers hung limp between the bows, smudged with grime and gray campfire soot. Alongside trudged the women, too weary to bother with conversation. A few dogs scuttled beside the children, and, out behind in a cloud of dust, the extra cattle followed, driven by the older boys and a few hired teamsters.

Juliet watched as the men jumped down from their drivers' seats and gathered in a perplexed line along the gorge's rim, scuffing their boots in the dirt and calling out to each other.

"This looks like the end of the road to me."

"What? Turn around, you mean?"

"Well, we can't get the wagons across, and look for yourself. This drop-off goes on for miles in both directions."

"We need to send the scouts to find a place to cross."

"These cliffs can't go on forever." It was Juliet's husband, James, speaking now. "There must be a route across. I'll take a couple of men and look for a way down. The rest of you can set up camp for the night."

"We can never get the wagons down there, Brier. Those boulders are the size of small cabins. Even if we could scramble down ourselves, we couldn't get the gear down. Or the animals. We've no choice but to turn back."

The others began deliberating among themselves. Juliet stepped closer to them and bent to collect a few pebbles from the reddish ground. She glanced back at her three young boys sitting on the wagon tongue where she had instructed them to stay. They were still there: four-year-old Kirke, quiet six-year-old Johnny, and Columbus, who, at eight, could barely contain his energy and was pegging stones at a nearby rock. The three of them, dressed in plain brown trail clothes, looked minute under the immense gray sky. Even the bulky wagons were dwarfed by its enormous span stretching overhead in a huge, cloudy dome.

"I believe we should do whatever will hasten this venture," Mr. Arcan was saying. "And going back to Hunt isn't getting us to California."

"But gentlemen! We must remember that we have no map." One of the older men was speaking now. "Need I remind you there could be death out there in those uncharted lands?"

"There could be death with Hunt's wagons, too, if we run out of provisions," James Brier spoke up. Juliet watched her husband's straight mouth tighten. "We've been following him for seven weeks now and we're just a fraction of the way to the settlement at Los Angeles. We should be near the end of the trip. I don't know about you folks, but back in Salt Lake,

I bought just enough food and supplies for nine weeks, as he instructed us. It's already November. I believe we need to make a dash for California by the shortest possible route—and Hunt's route doesn't seem to be the way."

"I say we listen to Reverend Brier," Mr. Wade spoke up. "He knows what he's talking about, which is more than we can say of Hunt."

"Those who want to go back and follow Hunt can do so," interjected a thin man with a white beard whose last name was Isham, "and the rest of us can take the shortcut."

"A sound idea!" James Brier agreed. "Whoever wants to return to the old company can turn back now, but you'll need to hurry. The rest of us will scout a way across this blessed river, and, when we find a suitable crossing, we can head straight for Los Angeles—due west, I believe. I, for one, expect this shortcut will save us hundreds of miles."

Juliet straightened up in relief and retied the strings of her old black sunbonnet. She couldn't bear the thought of returning to the taciturn Captain Hunt and the others they had left behind. Her patience with the captain, whom she had trusted and respected at the beginning of the trip, had turned to alarm and disappointment. The men had been gathering in covert circles to discuss the frightening possibility that the man did not know where he was going. He had taken their hard-earned money—ten dollars per wagon—to lead them across the Great Basin to the pueblo settlement at Los

Angeles, a distance of about 700 miles. Ever since, he had been stumbling around this country, clearly unsure about the way to reach the Old Spanish Trail. Now they were only about a third of the way to safety—not even 250 miles southwest of Salt Lake—and seven of the nine weeks were gone.

Today, at long last, they had veered from the route that felt as though it led nowhere. Although her own desire was to return to Salt Lake for the winter, anything would be better than plodding day after day behind the Captain's stern back, feeling her trust in him evaporate like rainwater on this arid soil.

She scattered the pebbles she had collected, brushed off her dusty hands, and turned back to the wagons. Her boys were tussling on the rough, slanting wagon tongue now, tired of sitting but obedient to her command. Johnny, especially, would do as she told him until tomorrow's sun came up. She marveled sometimes at his dogged obedience. A warm wind blew from the south or the day would have been as chilly as an autumn morning back home in Michigan. Back home, though, brilliant red and gold leaves would have lighted up the rolling countryside and cold rains would have freshened the air. Here, the dry air blew discouragingly between the waist-high, spiny cacti and across the scorched expanses of blue-green sage.

There would be no complaining, she reminded herself firmly. Michigan was in the past, and she had forced herself to acknowledge that she would never see it again. Now the chore was to put it out of her mind and not dwell on old possibilities. She had a choice: She could pine for a cultured life that she would now never have, or she could straighten her shoulders and embrace this trip west as best she could.

"Boys, you may begin your chores. I'm pleased by your obedience."

Columbus jumped to his feet and bolted away, but Johnny scampered a few feet and then turned and waited for Kirke to catch up.

James emerged from behind the wagon. After more than ten years of marriage, Juliet's heart still lifted when her husband appeared. His solid height and broad shoulders contrasted with his boyish personality. His face added to his look of strength, carved as it was into a series of pleasing, even planes. Dark eyebrows frowned low over his eyes even when he smiled, but Juliet thought they served to intensify the impact of his preaching. Back home, his dark hair was always neatly parted and combed; out here, it blew in the wind and settled across his high forehead in long strands. He looked down at her now, searching her eyes for a reaction to the news. "I'm sure you overheard the decision just now. What are your thoughts?"

It was unusual for a man to seek his wife's opinion, but James almost always included her in decisions. Most of her friends were expected simply to abide by their husbands' wishes.

"If we can't go back to Salt Lake, James, then I believe taking this shortcut is the right course." She noted the small creases that had begun to show recently around his eyes and the abrupt new angles of his cheekbones.

"Good, then. We'll head straight to California as quickly as we can. Those travelers we met last week thought there might be springs along the way, so we should have plenty of water for our needs. We'll hunt for food. I don't believe we'll have much trouble. A map would help, of course, but we have good levelheaded men and enough weapons for any emergency."

"Yes."

"I'm leaving now to scout the route. Bennett, Manly, and I will go south and we'll send a few of the others—probably a few of those young Mississippians or maybe a small group of the Jayhawkers—to scout the north rim. Stay safe, Juliet, and watch the boys. One misstep in this country could . . . well . . . " He looked off into the distance. "I doubt I'll be back by dark. You'll be all right?"

"I'll be fine, James. Let me pack some biscuits and jerked beef for you to take along."

One misstep. The words repeated themselves in Juliet's head like an unwanted song as she wrapped food for James in a clean cloth. How well she knew their truth.

CHAPTER 2

J uliet watched as half of the wagons rumbled out of sight, rocking and swaying over the rough ground. Her stomach fluttered, perhaps in gratitude that her own wagon was not among those turning back—or with unease at the sudden quiet and the smallness of the group left behind. James was gone, scouting with Mr. Bennett and Mr. Manly. Mr. Doty and four of his fellow Jayhawkers had gone north.

She scanned the landscape, checking for the children. They had gathered only a small pile of twigs for the campfire, preferring instead to test their skills at jumping over the highest clumps of sagebrush. Finding fuel was a neverending job out here, but she pretended not to notice when they turned it into a game.

It was a motley group of travelers stalled here above this wild and remote abyss. They were only a fraction of the wary strangers who had flung themselves together at Salt Lake to undertake the 700 backbreaking miles to California. Now that they had split up, there were fewer than 100 of them in all. Juliet thought they seemed as insignificant as a thimbleful of seeds scattered on the hard-packed landscape of this immense Great Basin.

Like the Briers, they came mostly from the Midwest, but some hailed from the East Coast, the South, and even from England. No matter where they had started, they all knew the same stories about California. There, the air would be healthier, the soil miraculously rich, the water abundant, and of course, there would be gold—real gold—that could be plucked from mountain streams in nuggets. News of its discovery had electrified the country.

The breeze quickened, and Juliet wrapped her arms around herself as she watched the children. She could feel her ribs poking through her faded wool dress. The waistline she had fitted so carefully last year hung loosely now, and she cinched it tighter with her apron strings.

She had never had weight to spare and she often wished for more height. She was too small, for example, to reach into the wagon without perching on the wheel spokes. When she scolded Columbus for some misdeed, she found herself looking straight across into his blue eyes, since, at eight, he was already as tall as she was. He weighed more, too. His bones were heavy and solid while hers were petite and light. James often teased her that she was like a songbird, almost delicate enough to fly.

Although they laughed about it, James's description was accurate. She flitted about her life, seldom sitting, always moving. Even her gray eyes traveled quickly, missing no detail. Her small hands—a bit clawlike in their slenderness, she admitted—were rarely idle. And, she thought wryly, as hard as she tried to stay unruffled and calm, she sometimes pecked at those around her.

Besides James and Juliet and about sixty-five or seventy single men, there were just three other families in the party now: the Arcans, the Bennetts, and the Wades. Juliet knew the Bennetts better than the others—good, hardworking Asahel and his delicate wife Sarah. Their two little daughters and fair-haired son were close in age to the Briers' boys. Juliet gravitated toward Sarah in motherly fashion, for Sarah was fragile and easily upset. Her fine features and porcelain skin were marred only by the crooked front teeth that protruded in a jumble when she smiled. Out here, where hardship was the only thing that never changed, Sarah cried into her handkerchief when the others lifted their chins and carried on.

The Arcans traveled with the Bennetts. Abigail Arcan wore stylish, pastel silk dresses that were long-since stained and tattered. She put on a different one each day and piled her hair fashionably on her head as if defying the wind and grit and campfire smoke. The other women wore calico or serviceable wool and stuffed their long hair into buns kept smothered by sunbonnets. Abigail rarely took her eyes off her little Charley as he played under the wagon, sometimes alone and sometimes with Kirke. Her abdomen swelled slightly under her gown, telling the world that Charley would have a playmate soon, although she never mentioned her condition to anyone.

Henry and Mary Wade had gathered their four children and followed the lure of California all the way from London. Juliet marveled that Mary had sailed across the ocean, spent a short time in Pennsylvania, and then struggled this far west—and was still in good spirits. She had a level, thoughtful gaze that spoke of her intelligence and capability. Although she kept to herself much of the time, Juliet had found her to be a kind, practical listener when the journey's worries grew too much to bear alone. She could trust that Mary's sturdy shoulders would help carry the load.

The men who made up the bulk of the party were a collection of small westward-bound groups that had merged for protection and expedience. Mostly young, dirty, rambunctious fellows, they included a few older gentlemen and two experienced western explorers whom Asahel Bennett had befriended back in Salt Lake. The largest group called itself the Jayhawkers, a name Juliet had not yet figured out. A second was named, more sensibly, the Mississippians. They chafed over delays and embraced this shortcut as the quickest way to the gold fields.

Juliet took the last hard biscuits from their cotton wrapper. As she made her way toward the children, skirting the tough sage that poked up from the hard ground, she stumbled and caught herself. The limited rations were beginning to tell upon her. The children, too, had shrunk to skin and bones from the long days of walking and the meager provisions. She hoped James would find a quick route to the settlements. So far, her little family had fared reasonably well on this trip, but she knew they couldn't last forever.

James was correct. One misstep—or too much delay—could change everything. She knew it was too soon to expect the scouts to return, but the daylight hours were, once again, slipping away while the wagons remained at a standstill.

CHAPTER 3

Across the circle of wagons, Sarah Bennett was banking her fire for the night. Juliet waved. Sarah was indeed a sweet-natured new friend. More than once, Juliet had purposely distracted her from overhearing the men's conversations about the perils ahead. The trail's strain and fear of the unknown had worn Sarah down to a bundle of jitters and tears and, when she was especially tired, unhappy complaints. Tonight her face was pale and she kept glancing at the gorge they would somehow have to cross.

Juliet perched on the wheel hub as the evening shadows inched across the landscape. She should mend the tear in Columbus's shirt before the light failed, but her strength was flagging. She could hear the boys whispering behind the canvas, as they always did before falling asleep, and the occasional bawl from the cluster of cattle.

"It's unusual to see you resting, Juliet. Are you all right?" It was Sarah.

"Yes," Juliet replied. "I'm just gathering the strength to finish the chores."

"I could help. I finished mine early tonight and I need to keep busy with Asahel gone."

"Do you want to help me pick some of those juniper berries to take along? My remedy book says they're a good cure for stomachaches and digestive upsets," Juliet said. There wasn't an apothecary within 200 miles of this far-flung spot. If someone needed doctoring, she wanted to be prepared.

"Yes, I'll help. It will get my mind off my thoughts."

"Are you worrying again?"

"No . . . I've just been imagining hitching up the wagons while the men are gone and taking the children straight back to Salt Lake!" Sarah gave a grim little smile. "It's an outlandish idea, but I wish we could."

"I'd come, too," Juliet said, more seriously than she intended. "We could be there in two weeks."

"I've begged Asahel every day to turn around," Sarah said. "I just know it's the best thing to do, but he won't hear of it."

"I've asked James, too."

"We women should run the wagon train." Resentment crept into Sarah's usually gentle voice. "If we did, we wouldn't be dragging our children across the continent in November!"

"You're right about that."

"Those men think they know best—but they don't. They don't even have a map or enough provisions, for goodness sake! It's madness, I know it is."

Juliet looked at her friend standing there in the evening light. The color was high in Sarah's cheeks now, and her voice quavered.

"I want to go back, too, Sarah," she said. "But you're right about another thing. The men absolutely won't hear of turning back."

"No. Which means that we women have no choice but to carry on. It's dreadfully hard."

"That's why I want to be prepared, as best we can. Every little thing—like juniper berries—might make a difference later." Juliet bent and poked a stick into the fire.

"We know best about the children, Juliet. The men don't always consider that."

"I agree." After a thoughtful pause, she tried for a lighter tone. "I always wondered why James wanted to name Columbus after Christopher Columbus. Maybe he wanted Col to explore the world. California in particular."

"Well, it looks as though he's going to get his wish." Sarah took a deep breath. "It's getting dark. Shall we find those berries while we still have some light? What is this remedy book you're talking about?"

"Just a little book I brought from home. It tells the cures for all kinds of ailments." Juliet lifted the wagon cover and peeked at the boys. They were asleep now, a sweet tangle of arms and legs and dark tousled hair. "Back home I used to fill in for the doctor when he was gone."

They stayed near the wagons picking the pungent berries until their apron pockets sagged.

"I'm nervous at night with Asahel gone," Sarah said
softly in the darkness. "It's awfully hard to fall asleep."

"At least we'll be in the wagons, up off the ground."
Juliet tried to be reassuring. "They'll be back in the morning, don't you think?"

In truth, Juliet dreaded crawling under her own blanket
when darkness came. With James gone, she knew she would
spend a fitful night. She would jolt awake every time a horse
snorted or someone in a nearby wagon coughed. No matter
how many layers of clothing she wore, the crisp night air
would creep underneath and she would be cold. She was
glad she wouldn't be in the tent. She felt safer up off the
ground, even if it meant being crowded in with the boys.

"I hope so. Good night, Juliet."

"Good night."

Juliet rubbed her eyes and passed her hand over her high
cheekbones. Her face was gritty. She wished for an ounce or
two of water with which to scrub away the dirt. Mr. Isham
and Mr. Wade had taken buckets and scrambled down an
animal trail to the river, but there was barely enough water
for drinking, and none for washing. At least she had succeeded in brushing most of the day's dust from her dress.
The functional charcoal-colored cloth hardly showed the
soot and grease that she was sure must be splotched all over

it. Granted, wool was too warm sometimes when summer lingered here in this odd country, but her slight body was easily chilled, so most times its warmth felt good.

Later, crowded next to little Kirke on the hay-filled mattress, she thought about the times she had spoken with James about turning back. She would try again, even though she knew what his response would be. He was far too eager about reaching California to consider reversing direction. There were thousands of forty-niners pouring into every part of the gold country there, he said, and they were a godless sort. They needed good preachers.

Back home, his boyish enthusiasm and brash confidence had outweighed her own trepidation about going west. Persuasive words were the tools of his trade, and he used them skillfully. Eventually, she had been caught up in his exuberance and excited sense of duty when he convinced her to share his dream of carrying the Methodist gospel, their marriage, their hard-earned household—and the boys—to California.

Now, the miles they had yet to travel piled up in her mind like stones, and unpleasant possibilities edged their way into her thoughts: accidents, sickness, clashes with the Paiutes, even starvation. What right did she and James have to put the boys in the way of those dangers? If she had posed the question to her husband, he would have answered that they were taking the boys to a better life in California, an end that justified the means.

She didn't want to drift off to sleep. Inevitably, her dreams took her back to the little farm in Vermont where she grew up, or to the hand-hewn log cabin she shared with the rest of the Wells family after they moved to the Michigan wilderness. When she awoke and made out the sagging canvas overhead, the disappointment was crushing. It was hard enough out here combating fatigue and uncertainty without torturing herself with longings for home. Lying there in the dark, she could recall it all so vividly. Her parents. Her much-loved brother, Hiram. Her childhood.

She remembered the fresh wood smell of the one-room school she started attending when she was just four years old. Hand in hand with her mother, she walked the woodsy mile to the schoolhouse where the young teacher, Miss Van Brunt, greeted her with a kind smile. At first, Juliet stayed by Teacher's side watching the older children play hide-and-seek, but soon she skipped off to join them.

Gentle Miss Van Brunt, Juliet realized now, recognized her smallest pupil's quick mind and aptitude for memorization. She skillfully guided Juliet's lessons until her tiny student could read fluently and figure sums in her head.

By the time Juliet was fourteen, her parents had enrolled her in Vermont's Bennington Seminary. She spent the next happy years studying reading, spelling, mental arithmetic, and geography. She remembered fondly the young teacher who insisted that they study hard but who turned a blind eye to his students' mischief and merriment. At noontime she would sit with her two best chums, the governor's blonde-haired daughters, under the spreading shade tree in the schoolyard, whispering and giggling until the teacher's bell called them indoors again.

There was no end to the hard work back home. Staring into the darkness, Juliet recalled that picking rocks from the Vermont fields was a never-ending task for the Wells family and their overworked neighbors. As she grew older, she helped her mother with the countless indoor chores, as well: spinning and weaving the wool her father sheared from his small flock of sheep, milking the cow, churning butter until her arms ached, sewing clothes, piecing quilts, and knitting. She learned to make soap and candles and to keep the fire burning in the massive cookstove her father purchased to save his delicate wife from tending a kettle suspended in the fireplace.

In the evenings, after hauling firewood and helping with the day's cleaning and mending, Juliet studied her lessons. By firelight, she memorized poetry and entire Bible chapters and practiced her elocution. She could still see the pride in her father's face when she recited verse after verse of the pieces she easily committed to memory on those long winter evenings.

Young men began to call at the cabin, boys from surrounding farms and from the growing congregation at the picturesque Congregational church where Juliet spent her

Sundays. Juliet greeted them with grace and politeness, but encouraged none of them. Hiram, she remembered, teased her about the trail of dejected suitors that streamed from their door, but Juliet good-naturedly assured him she would know her mate when she saw him. By the time she was in her early twenties, Hiram had quit teasing. His sister was obviously in no hurry to marry.

The Wells family prospered in an austere way, but life in cold, stony Vermont was exacting, and the winter snows were deep and ferocious. In the mid-1830s, when news of the open frontier in Michigan circulated, her father began to talk of going west. By the time Juliet was twenty-three, he had decided to move. After months of preparation, the family left Vermont for what they hoped would be a better life in Michigan.

Lying in the wagon now, with the children sleeping beside her, Juliet recalled how backbreaking it had been to hack out a meager new farm in the Michigan wilderness. If Vermont had been difficult, at least it was settled and civilized in contrast with the frontier. Juliet helped clear timber and pile slash, plant new fields, and haul water until her arms and legs were wiry and strong, and, despite her tiny build, she could easily lug a full bucket of water or a bushel of potatoes.

When a tall, raw-boned young Methodist circuit rider named James Welsh Brier rode through their clearing one day to visit her father, Juliet found herself captivated by his natural eloquence and his straightforward manner. As the months went by, he sometimes joined the Wells family for supper in their cramped new cabin. Soon, it was clear that he had his eye on slender, twenty-five-year-old Juliet, whom he had learned was levelheaded and intelligent with a sensible, calm demeanor, dark hair and sparkling eyes, and a strong faith to match his own. They were married on September 23, 1839.

For the following decade, James and Juliet moved from cabin to cabin while he rode the circuit and she began raising their babies. Christopher Columbus Brier, their first child, came into the world red and squirming and had not stopped moving since. Johnny followed, and she gave him her old family name—John Wells Brier—that now matched his quiet, thoughtful demeanor. A few years later, little Kirke came along—Kirke, whom she named on a whim after her favorite poet and who worried her with his feeble health. During those long days spent alone with her boys in their cabin, Juliet tried to duplicate the warm atmosphere of her rustic girlhood homes that smelled of venison stew and, when wind sent gusts down the stick-and-mud chimneys, the fragrance of wood smoke she had always loved.

And then James began talking about California.

Now, in this desolate desertlike place, she tried to put the past out of her mind. Thinking of home and family could fill her with longing until she could no longer bear the loss.

CHAPTER 4

Before dawn lightened the black sky, Juliet stepped barefoot from the wagon and rekindled the fire to warm her hands and boil a little water for coffee. She sat on the ground beside the small flames, ignoring the smoke that blew in her face and the sparks that landed nearby while she laced her worn-out black shoes. The soles were beginning to crack from the many miles she had walked in them.

There was no sign of James and the other scouts, although it was still too dark to see along the rim. It wouldn't be long before the camp began stirring and the children asked for their meager breakfast of dried apple and the biscuits she had made at the last camp. And coffee. She never dreamed she would allow the boys to drink coffee. People back home said it interfered with a child's growth. But the boys so despised the taste of muddy creeks and soured springwater that mealtime was miserable for them. While James could stomach water straight from its source, she and the boys did better with coffee to mask the flavor of silt and minerals and old leaves.

Waiting made Juliet restless and edgy, but the children found a new amusement at every dusty place. A few days

ago, it was the long-eared hares that hunched behind clumps
of sagebrush. The boys had spent hours trying to catch one
of the scruffy creatures that darted away at the first sign of
movement. Today, no doubt, the three of them would continue making their miniature landscape of overland trails
using small stones as covered wagons. Columbus had dug a
trench in the hard-packed dirt to represent the river gorge
that stalled them. Juliet wanted to sit in the dust with them,
jump the tiny wagons across the gap, and put them on a road
to Los Angeles so straight and true they would be there in
a minute.

By mid-morning, she had done every task she could to
keep herself busy. The day's biscuits were ready, the wagon
was tidy, and her mending was done. The juniper berries
were drying in the sun. Maybe she could find the tatting
project she began back home or work on the thick socks she
was knitting for James. When preparations for going west
began to use up every second of her time, she had been
forced to set her handiwork aside. Her half-finished projects
were packed in the wagon somewhere, along with the rest of
her old life. If she could find them, she would ask Sarah to
join her in the weak November sun while she worked.

Sarah's eyes were puffy this morning, and the same wisps
of blonde hair that had broken loose from her bun yesterday
still framed her pale face. Her shoulders hunched as she
bent over her smoky cook fire and poked the coals with a

stick. One of the young Jayhawkers had fanned last night's embers into flames for her, since Asahel was gone. Even her dress looked limp, and she shooed her children, George and Melissa, away from the fire in a listless voice. Little Martha clung to her mother's skirts.

A little bird with an azure head and back flitted in and out of the dull vegetation, like a bright sapphire in a bed of dirty gravel. There had been other unfamiliar birds out here—falcons or hawks of some sort and yellowish green insect eaters. This one, though, was like nothing Juliet had ever seen before, and she watched it for a moment before it disappeared into a thicket of low junipers.

They had seen animals as they traveled, including a tortoise and an odd snake that slithered sideways. She'd grabbed Kirke away instinctively. There were also large black-and-rust-colored lizards that sunned themselves on the nearby boulders. Juliet had seen one that was nearly two feet long. It looked vicious with its sharp claws and a horrible bluish tongue that licked out of its mouth like a gruesome finger, and she wished never to see another. She wondered if it could climb into the wagon at night.

The little things needled her out here. Foreign-looking reptiles and insects. Constant dirt. Smoke in her eyes. No privacy. Where on a treeless flat desert could a woman be alone to take care of her bodily functions? It had been a rude shock that first day on the trail to realize that wherever she might be, she could be seen plainly for miles from all directions. The other women, virtual strangers at first, were too polite to speak of the dilemma, and they suffered in silence. It was Juliet who broke the social taboo and suggested a solution. The long, full skirts they all wore must be good for something. If they surrounded the woman who needed privacy, discreetly turned their backs to her and held their skirts out from their sides in fluttering half-circles, they could shield her from view.

The men, too, had their hands full with the hardships and logistics of wagon travel. It was more than one man's work to oversee a family's animals, drive and repair the wagon, clear the trail, haul water, and perform a hundred other tasks. Now that they were a smaller train—only twenty-seven wagons— they had added hunting and scouting to their chores.

"I wish Asahel would hurry up and come back," Sarah said, as Juliet walked near. "What if . . . " She glanced down at the children and stopped.

"They must be near," Juliet broke in. "We'll wait together. The moment we see something, we'll get Mr. Wade to take a look through his field glass."

An hour later, Juliet scanned the canyon rim for the hundredth time and finally saw a small party on horseback following the edge of the precipice in the distance.

"There they are, Sarah." She secured her knitting needles and looked around the circle of wagons until she spotted

Mr. Wade. "Would you watch the children? I'll ask Mr. Wade to look."

She made her way to the Wades' wagon. Its old canvas cover flapped in the light breeze. A butter churn was strapped underneath. Mr. Wade sat on the wagon's extended tongue, oiling his harnesses. He rose and fetched his field glass when she asked.

"Yes, I believe I can see your mate out in front," he affirmed in his British accent as he peered through the lens. He was a scrappy man with a wild tousle of red hair and hawkish blue eyes. Juliet wondered if his vision was good. He had a hard time with small jobs like buckling harnesses. "They're moving our way. I should think they'll be here in less than half an hour."

"I hope they've found a route," Juliet replied. "We're losing time just sitting here."

"Well, I for one wish I'd bought more provisions than I did in Salt Lake. We'll run out before we reach Los Angeles at the rate we're going. Of course, we can always use the cattle for food, but . . . " He stopped and glanced down at Juliet. She was relieved to hear him say what she had thought to herself many times. She knew that James would balk at the idea of killing the cattle for meat, though. The animals were their investments. He brought along a small herd of seven draft animals, as well as the four tough oxen that pulled the wagon, to sell when they reached their destination. The big, copper-colored animals would provide them with the means to start a new life in California. They followed along behind the wagons, lowing and raising dust—and getting thinner and bonier and less glossy by the day. Two young men, Patrick and St. John, watched over the train's herd day and night. They seemed like pleasant fellows, and they took their jobs seriously.

"Could I look?" Juliet asked. She needed to see for herself that it was the scouts and not a party of Paiutes headed their way. She had seen enough old trails and dead fires to know that the Paiutes were near, and from the stories that circulated she knew that they weren't pleased with the wagon travelers who traipsed across their country.

Mr. Wade handed her the field glass, and she focused on the riders. Yes, that was James. Even from here, she could see his shock of too-long brown hair getting in his eyes. Normally he sat up tall on his horse, but now he was slouching.

They would be hungry. She gave the field glass back to Mr. Wade and went to tell Sarah. Then she returned to her wagon to warm a biscuit for her husband. His tin cup stood full of the water she had saved from last night's allotment, and a generous strip of the dried meat was waiting on his plate. He would probably be in too much of a hurry to sit down. Instead, he would gulp the food, thank her politely as he always did, and begin urging the others to ready their wagons. Sometimes he was like a child in his eagerness to reach California.

She looked over the camp, assessing whether the company could be ready to pull out soon if James had found the route. The wagons were angled into a tight circle surrounding a trampled area cluttered with cook fires, sprawled dogs and children, pots, pans, bedding airing in the fresh breeze, and men cleaning guns or fixing ox yokes. Outside the circle, the Mississippians approached, carrying buckets of water hauled from the river for the cattle. The animals milled about them, tossing their horns, excited by the smell of water.

She loaded the cookstove into the back of the wagon and cinched up the wagon cover. She would be ready to go whenever James gave the word.

CHAPTER 5

J ames rode up with a sober face and slid wearily from his bor-
rowed horse. Asahel Bennett and Lewis Manly followed.

"No," he answered when the others crowded around
him. "There's no way across to the south. We went at least
thirty miles."

Lewis Manly stepped down from his horse. His direct
gaze and reasonable, thoughtful manner told of levelhead-
edness. He looked slightly younger than thirty years old,
slender but muscular, and tanned from his weeks in the sun
and wind. He kept his shaggy brown hair out of his eyes with
a faded tan bandana knotted around his forehead. Juliet had
heard talk about his trip from Michigan to Salt Lake City, an
adventure that taught him friendship with the native peoples
and a cautious respect for the wilderness. He seemed like
a principled man whose confidence and skill in overland
travel were well-honed. When he hunted, his carefully spent
ammunition connected with its target nearly every time, and
he brought the meat for the others to share. He was almost
always the first to notice the thin lines of smoke from Paiute
campfires, or a subtle change in the weather, or a hidden
patch of green that could indicate a water hole.

"Are the Jayhawkers' scouts back from the north?" he asked.

"Not yet," Juliet replied.

The Jayhawkers were a group of about thirty-five gold seekers, a hodgepodge of men from various places and backgrounds. Boisterous and noisy, they annoyed some of the other travelers, but Juliet found them entertaining. A few were barely past adolescence, and their boyish features and thin new whiskers made her realize that they were not more than eight or nine years older than Columbus. She struggled to call the youngest among them "Mr." as tradition and proper behavior demanded, but James sometimes slipped and used their first names, as if they were children.

They were rough and haphazard and yet an adept group of forty-niners, and she was grateful for their presence, which substantially swelled the number of able-bodied men out here with her family. There was vigor about them, a raucous energy that manifested itself in loud voices and quick actions. Their clothing was dirty but functional. Whenever they tied back the covers on their light wagons, Juliet could see jumbled heaps of bedding and clothing and greasy cooking gear piled inside.

When their group of five scouts finally returned, it was mid-afternoon, and they whooped into camp as fast as their worn-out horses would move. Juliet looked at their eager faces as they gathered around the wiry leader of the scouting party, Ed Doty. Their captain, Asa Haynes, stood with them studying the ground. He was a quiet man, older at forty-five than nearly all of the others, with a farm and a family back home. He had a deliberate manner of speaking that was often interrupted by his impetuous company.

"We had to go quite a distance," Doty told them as he jumped down from his bay horse. He turned and looked at them with gray eyes fringed with surprisingly long black lashes. "The canyon sides are too steep for miles, but we finally came to the head of the gorge. It's possible to go around there without too much trouble, although it will add more days to the trip."

"I think we should go immediately." James spoke in relief. "Shall we pack, everyone, and move out while we still have a few hours of daylight?"

"Uh, Reverend Brier . . . " Captain Haynes began carefully. "With all due respect, we Jayhawkers have come to a decision. We're unencumbered, and we can travel much faster because of it. We'd like to go on at our own pace— by ourselves." Ragged, unshorn, and dirty, his party stood together in an eager knot.

"You'd split us up again?" James was aghast. "Men, there's safety in numbers and our numbers are already small enough."

"I agree with Brier," Mr. Arcan said. The color rose in

his cheeks. "We're a company. Those of us with families will not be left behind like extra baggage."

"Gentlemen, we see your point. But there's gold in California waiting for those who are fast and clever enough to reach there first. That's why we're taking this shortcut. We've seen no serious threat to your families if you travel without us."

Ed Doty spoke up. "No offense intended, but we simply don't wish to be slowed down by your babies and women-folk." He winked at his fellow scouts.

Juliet stiffened. She stared at the faces around her. On one side were the single men, full of youthful energy and unseasoned, bold confidence. On the other were the family men, experienced, cautious, angry, tired.

Asahel Bennett stood up from his seat on his wheel hub.

"I can't agree that there's no danger in traveling in a small group out here!" Asahel rarely raised his voice, but when he did, those around him paid attention. Now he raised it a notch. "By leaving, you'll be putting our children in harm's way."

"Sir, we have no desire to do that. We don't believe harm will come to you, and we need to move on quickly. Getting to those southernmost gold fields is the entire reason we're making this trip." Doty shifted his weight.

"Let them go, then!" cried Henry Wade, his British accent clipped in anger. "Who needs them? They'll only fester with resentment if we slow them down."

"He's right, men," Lewis Manly agreed. "We're strong and capable without them. Let them go."

"There's nothing that says you can't try to keep up with us," Doty remarked. "If you can travel as fast as we can, you're welcome to come along."

"Go, then." James's face was flushed. "Go. You won't be as quick as you think. You'll have to break the trail every day."

Juliet knew there was no way for the families to keep up. For one thing, their wagons were heavier, filled as they were with household goods and children. For another, the single men could be up and on the road before daylight and travel until after dark, and they cared little for a routine of building cook fires and eating regular meals. Give them a strip of dried beef and they would eat it on their jostling driver's seats. At night, they would throw their bedding on the ground to avoid the time it took to set up camp. If the trail got too rough, they could abandon their wagons and continue by foot—something not possible for families with young children.

"We'll be with you, Rogers and I," Lewis Manly spoke up again, looking around at the families. His pants were frayed at the knees and his old boots gaped open at the seams. "We're committed to seeing this party through to Los Angeles. Since we're both single, it should be simple for us to scout or hunt, whatever is needed." He smiled at the group. "John Rogers is a skilled hunter; I can vouch for that. I suggest we all pack up immediately, as Reverend Brier suggested, and leave now. We still have four or five hours of daylight. Let the Jayhawkers go at their pace, and we'll go at ours. If we're unable to keep up, at least we'll know they're somewhere ahead of us. Rogers and I can go fetch help, if need be."

James looked at the others with raised eyebrows. Mr. Arcan nodded his agreement as did Mr. Bennett. Juliet caught her husband's eye and lifted her chin. The dishes and cooking things were in the wagon, the children were near, and she had made sure the canteens were full and not leaking. She was used to walking long distances now, and she was ready to step out briskly with the wagons. No one was going to accuse her of slowing them down.

CHAPTER 6

They traveled until the orange sun inched below the western horizon, and then stopped to set up camp. In a pocket of smothering smoke, Juliet was coaxing a reluctant campfire into flame when Sarah Bennett called from the next wagon.

"Juliet! Quick! Come here!" Juliet's head snapped around at the frantic, shrill tone. Sarah's honey-colored hair was coming undone and the color of her face matched the grayish wagon cover. "I can't find our laudanum flask, and I think Martha has gotten into it. I can't wake her."

Juliet grabbed her skirts and ran to her neighbor's wagon, casting a quick glance at her boys and Sarah's other two children playing inside the circle of wagons. They were safe for the moment with Abigail Arcan's little Charley. Abigail would have her eye on them. Juliet clambered over the splintery wheel and into the wagon's dim interior. Three-year-old Martha was asleep on the bedding. Her face was flushed and her white-blonde hair was damp with perspiration. Sarah's voice rose and her hands trembled as she shook the little girl and called to her, but the child did not open her eyes.

Juliet laid a hand on her friend's shoulder and bent to smell Martha's breath. There was, indeed, the faint odor of laudanum. If the child had swallowed more than a small amount, it could be deadly. It was potent enough to dull the worst of pain—or kill a child.

"Water. We've got to give her water right away." Juliet made an effort to keep her voice soft and low. "And the flask, Sarah. Do you know where she left it? We need to see how much she swallowed."

"Oh, Juliet. This is my fault entirely! I took it out of the trunk to give Asahel a dose for his knee pain. I meant to put it away again, but something interrupted me. It was lying here on the quilt for a few moments." Tears streamed down Sarah's thin, blotched cheeks and fell onto her blue cotton dress. "And Asahel's gone again. Hunting."

"Do you have any water left?"

"No, we've run out."

"I have just enough. I'll be back." Juliet scrambled to the back of the wagon and jumped down. She ran for the reserved water in her canteen and poured it quickly into her own battered tin cup. As she hurried back to Sarah's wagon, she caught sight of the small silver flask lying on the ground beside the front wheel. The dirt around it was wet and dark.

"Sarah, here's the water. I'll come up and help you. We're going to have to sit her up. But look! The flask is here on the ground. There's liquid spilled around it, so we know she didn't swallow it all."

"Oh, thank God! Can you tell how much she drank?"

"No. But there's a good-size wet spot here. Was the flask mostly full this morning?"

"No. Asahel has been taking a spoonful now and then."

Juliet climbed back in beside her friend. "We must get some water down her throat to dilute what she's swallowed. That should slow down the poisoning. Then maybe we can make her retch." She kept her voice low. Nursing was almost as natural to her as walking or eating. She had had no formal training, just plenty of steady practice with her children and neighbors. Back in Michigan, people up and down the creek used to call for her when they had tooth-aches, broken bones, open wounds, and, worst of all, the deadly cholera that sometimes took their lives before she could get to them.

Sarah lifted the child's head while Juliet poured what little water she could into Martha's small mouth. The little girl stirred enough to swallow a few sips, and then a few more. Then they turned her over onto her stomach. Juliet gently thrust her finger to the back of Martha's throat, without result. Sarah tried then, but although her daughter stirred and choked, nothing came up.

"Maybe there's not enough in her stomach to vomit," Juliet finally said. "We need to get her to take more water."

They tried again to dribble sips of water down Martha's throat, but nearly all of it leaked down her chin and darkened the front of her brown calico dress. Between attempts, Sarah kept trying to rouse her daughter and leaning down to check her heartbeat. She was sobbing openly now, and Juliet handed her the handkerchief from her own apron pocket.

Finally, Juliet drew a deep breath and set the cup down. "There's nothing more we can do, Sarah, except wait and see. I'll stay with you. Let me tell James and the children where I'll be."

Juliet jumped again from the back of the wagon praying silently. If Martha had swallowed just a little laudanum, she would be all right in the morning. Cases of overdose were common, though. She took a long, steadying breath and ran her hands over her face. Could there be a worse thing than losing a child?

The hardest part of nursing children was the terrible possibility that her best efforts wouldn't be enough. She remembered when her own little Kirke came down with whooping cough in the dead of last winter. It was a day-and-night struggle to keep him alive. She read her remedy book until it was dog-eared and torn, and she offered Kirke every possible herb that might overcome the hacking and wheezing that plagued him for weeks. Common sense told her to keep Columbus and Johnny at a safe distance, but it was hard in the little cabin. Still, she flooded the small rooms with fresh air every day and kept the older boys busy outside as much as the weather permitted. Finally, the cough weakened and disappeared.

She'd always fretted about Kirke. He had been small since the day he was born. She had named him after the English writer, Henry Kirke White, whose poetic works she loved and could recite by heart. The young man died of illness when he was just twenty-one, leaving behind hundreds of melancholy verses. Now she wondered if she had foretold little Kirke's disposition and physical condition by giving him the poet's name.

Kirke was different from the older boys in so many ways. Columbus and Johnny took after her husband's side of the family with stocky builds, solid boyish muscles, and straight dark hair. Their skin tanned readily, giving them the look of perfect health. Kirke, though, had always been pale, and it was clear by now that he resembled Juliet.

She found the boys where she had left them near the Arcans' wagon.

"I'm hungry, Mother," Columbus said when she told him she would be in the Bennetts' wagon for the rest of the evening. "Could we eat something?"

Abigail Arcan spoke up. Juliet knew she had missed no part of the overdose incident. What happened to one member of the wagon train happened to them all, and the families were in such close proximity that Sarah's frantic call for help would not have gone unnoticed. Abigail knew that the best way to assist was to leave the nursing to Juliet and watch the children.

"Let me feed them some beans, Juliet. Sarah needs you."

"Thank you, Abigail." Suddenly, Juliet was too tired to think about supper of any kind.

Lewis Manly strode around the side of the wagon. His forehead was creased in concern and his eyes searched Juliet's face.

"Is everything all right with the little Bennett girl?"

"It's too soon to tell. There's nothing more we can do. I'll go back and sit with her, but we'll just have to wait."

"Sometimes smelling salts can bring them around."

"Thank you, Mr. Manly."

"I'll fetch some firewood and go down to the river for a bucket of water. Anything else I can do, you let me know, Mrs. Brier."

CHAPTER 7

Juliet sat in the Bennetts' cramped wagon as the evening light faded, listening to little Martha's measured breathing. Sarah slumped beside her with red eyes fixed on her daughter's rising and falling chest and flushed face, and she didn't speak.

An hour passed, and another. Juliet leaned over, placed her ear on Martha's chest, and listened to the heartbeat. It was rapid, like Johnny's and Kirke's, and strong. She straightened up. Surely, the laudanum would have had its terrible effect by now if Martha had swallowed too much. Juliet had never taken the potent medicine herself, even in childbirth, but she felt sure the opium had run the worst of its course.

She eased her stiff, straight back and unclenched her hands as she looked again at Martha's freckled face.

Sarah stirred beside her and whispered. "Do you think she'll be all right?"

"I do. I was just thinking so. She'll sleep the through the night, but I think she'll be fine in the morning."

"Thank you for staying with me, Juliet." Sarah's eyes filled with tears again, and she used the sodden handkerchief to wipe them.

"You're welcome, Sarah. I'm grateful it turned out this way. If you need me again, just call."

Juliet stepped out of Sarah's wagon and drew a deep breath. She knew her face would be drawn and white from fatigue, so she pinched her thin cheeks to bring color to them. She might be as skinny and small as a child, but she was strong. No use looking utterly drained in front of the others.

Abigail greeted her with a helping of brown beans on a tin plate and a cup of hot coffee.

"Here's some supper for you, Juliet. Mr. Manly went all the way down to the stream again just so we could have coffee. Is little Martha all right?"

"Thank you, Abigail. She's fine now. She's still sleeping, but the effects will wear off by morning. Would you spread the word?"

Juliet accepted the simple meal with gratitude and took the boys back to the wagon. She needed to sleep, but baking tomorrow's biscuits had to come first. She rekindled the cook fire. Even in fatigue—and with her nagging worries about the dwindling food supply—cooking was one of her favorite chores. More often than not, her campfire biscuits were smoky and charred on the bottom, but her family ate them ravenously without complaint. Trying to create perfect, golden biscuits on the fickle flames was another of God's challenges to make certain this monotonous trip didn't bore her, she thought with a weary smile. He certainly had His ways of keeping her in line.

She mixed the dough with her small, agile fingers, scraping them clean afterward. Her hands always felt crusty with dried flour these days since water was so scarce. Earlier in the trip, she had hated the stiff, dry residue on her fingers, but now she barely noticed.

Questions that she had never considered were forcing their way into her mind. If she took some of her warm biscuits to Sarah, was she endangering her own children? Shaking her head, she pushed the thought from her mind. Of course, sharing was the best course. She couldn't imagine selfishly hoarding biscuits when her neighbors were hungry. A human being was little more than an animal without carefully cultivated beliefs and the courage to carry them out. Yet, she had just told Kirke that he must wait until breakfast when he asked for one.

James came out of the darkness and sat on the ground by the fire.

"Is she better?"

"Yes."

"Good." He nudged a stick into the fire. After a moment he said, "Well, we've begun covering some miles again—but in the wrong direction. The Jayhawkers are already far ahead." He lowered his voice. "That Doty annoyed me to no end. I'm certain he was the one to suggest splitting off from us. He's determined to get to the gold fields at the expense of everything else."

"We're much fewer in number now, but we're still strong, James."

"We needed their company for protection. They've got the best rifles, among other things."

"At least we still have Captain Towne and his Mississippians."

"Yes. They're a small group, though, and they're impatient with the delays. I won't be surprised if they take off after the Jayhawkers."

"Maybe we should reconsider our decision not to turn back, James. We could reach Salt Lake by the time the weather turns bad and start out again in the spring."

"No, Juliet. We've come this far. It would be useless to turn around now. We'll make it to California. So far, we've seen nothing to fear."

"I'm loyal to you, James, you know that. I just think the children would fare better if we made a new start in the spring."

"Nonsense. They've done well every inch of the way."

"Without enough to eat."

"We'll bring in plenty of wild game. I know you think we could butcher the cattle, Juliet, but we can't. They're our only hope for making a start when we reach Los Angeles. Besides, the oxen pulling the wagons are starting to wear out, and the ones behind the train are getting thin. They wouldn't make good eating. We have to get them through as quickly as we can. And we will. We'll make it through quickly."

Juliet sighed, and the words of Henry Kirke White flashed through her mind. *And Thou wilt turn our wandering feet, and Thou wilt bless our way.* Of course. Was she doubting that God would see them safely through?

CHAPTER 8

They pulled out before dawn and made five miles by sunup. Juliet let the boys sleep in the wagon. After the laudanum incident, tenderness for her children was foremost in her mind, and she welcomed a few hours of their peaceful sleep.

She would have expected that Kirke would be her biggest responsibility out here. She'd found, though, that he tagged along wherever Johnny went and she could trust Johnny not to get into trouble. Col was another matter. While the younger two were content to play by the wagon, watch for rabbits, and even work at their simple lessons, Col was drawn to peer over precipices, wander farther from camp than he was allowed, and mimic the Jayhawkers' rough behavior. When he grew tired of tramping alongside the wagons, he would lag behind until the two older Wade boys caught up with him. Then the three of them would tease and shove and toss each other's caps into the sagebrush. So far, they had not come across any serious mischief, but Juliet tried to keep a close eye on Col whenever he was awake.

"Whoa!" James called from the wagon seat, interrupting her thoughts. Up and down the line, the yokes of cattle stopped, and the grinding of iron wheel rims on stones and hard-packed earth turned to silence. Sarah and Asahel were in the lead today, and their back wheel rested at a rakish angle. Under their wagon, a splintered axle dug into the ground.

James let out a long sigh. "This will take a while."

Juliet glanced around at the stunted junipers moving in the soft breeze. "Do you think any of these trees is suitable to fix it?"

"I don't know," he replied. "Either we'll have to combine wagons or find a tree big and straight enough to work. It will take most of the day to replace it."

Lewis Manly walked up from behind. "Looks like trouble," he commented quietly. "Bennett can't go on without that wagon. Not with those three children."

In the end, it was Manly who found the tree rooted deep near the riverbank where access to water had enabled it to grow straight and strong. Juliet watched from the rim as he cut it. Perspiration soaked his dirty shirt. The Mississippians clambered down to help drag it over the boulders and up the rough animal path. It would need to be cut to size, trimmed, shaped, and installed on the Bennetts' wagon before they could be back on the trail.

Juliet busied herself making another scant batch of biscuits, concentrating on turning them golden brown this time instead of too dark. Johnny ran up to her out of breath.

"Mother, I went by Mrs. Bennett's wagon, and she's weeping again. I asked George what was wrong with his Ma, but he didn't know."

"I'd best go see. Thank you, Johnny."

The boy waited, scuffing his toe in the dirt. "She cries a lot, doesn't she, Mother?"

"Yes, she does. But it's just her way of working things out, I suppose."

Juliet pulled the biscuits off the fire. They weren't quite done, but it was clear Sarah needed her. Tonight they would just have pallid white biscuits instead of black. It seemed she never could get them right.

The wagons were scattered across the landscape today like ships on a windy sea. Sarah was sitting on a boulder nearby. She had her back to the men, and her hands were idle in her lap.

"Sarah?" Juliet approached and knelt in front of her friend, shivering slightly. She had changed her gray wool dress for her old blue calico, and it wasn't warm enough without a shawl. "What's wrong?"

"Oh, Juliet." Sarah ran a chapped hand over her face. She sat hunched over with her feet pulled up under her skirt and her faded sunbonnet hanging on limp strings down her back. "Just when I think we're finally making progress toward California, something else comes in the way, like this broken axle. I know I'm not supposed to use the word 'hate,' Juliet, but I do *hate* this horrid trip. I wish Asahel had never wanted to come. It's nothing but hardship and worry and delays until I want to scream! And I feel as though I'm going to fail Asahel by being too weak and frightened to make it all the way to California. How much farther do you think it is?"

"I think we'll be there by Christmas. That's only about five weeks."

"And what will we find when we get there? I've heard that plenty of families have to live in leaky tents or in their broken old wagons until they can build a cabin. I can't imagine spending the winter in a tent with the children."

"Let's not borrow trouble, Sarah. We might find a nice hotel or a cabin in the settlements. And remember, they say that winter in California is like summer back home. Warm and sunny. It won't be like the winters we're accustomed to. There might even be gardens and flowers."

"I just don't believe that, Juliet. Whoever heard of a land like that? Flowers in winter? I can't imagine that can be true."

"Why don't you bring your mending back to my wagon? We'll work together and watch the children while the men fix your axle."

But she wondered if Sarah's assessment of the journey was accurate. This ill-conceived shortcut was already beginning to feel interminable and more difficult than she had imagined. The unthinkable distance was enough to bring anyone to his knees, and the landscape's barrenness a chilling contrast to the fragrant Michigan forests. Perhaps this cutoff route to golden California was really the road to disaster.

CHAPTER 9

Juliet lifted her pounding head from the straw tick. Its shooting pain told her that her stomach would be roiling until the sun was high overhead. Slowly, she sat up and closed her eyes to the morning's bright light. Her long brown hair was knotted and untidy, but she didn't have the will to brush and tie it into its usual smooth bun.

It was a routine malaise that occurred regularly with her cycle, so she couldn't mention it to anyone, not even Sarah or James. A woman wasn't to talk about such things, although she wished she could. Maybe it would help if James understood why she couldn't always finish the chores on days like this. When they were first married, he used to ask why she wasn't eating, why her face looked so white, or why she was sitting down at her work. Nowadays, he was used to those quirks and simply accepted them.

She stepped slowly from the wagon and stood for a moment, then took a stick and stirred last night's coals, hoping for a glowing ember that would ignite the dry twigs the children had gathered. If the embers were gone, she would have to use the flint and steel to make a spark. The men had another, easier way to start a fire, but Juliet wasn't certain it was safe. They put a small charge of powder in a rifle and then shredded a cotton rag and put it loosely in the barrel. The flash of the powder set the rag afire, and the men quickly nudged it underneath their prepared kindling.

If only James knew how much it would help if he would start the fire. She was concerned about him, though. His shirt hung on his lanky frame like an old coat on a scarecrow. Several times over the past few days, he had asked Juliet to take the reins while he stepped from the wagon seat, disappeared over the ravine's edge for a few minutes and then hurried to catch up. His face was gray after his brief forays, but when Juliet asked if he was ill, he said he was doing as well as expected without much food or water. Over time Juliet came to the realization that he was suffering from dysentery or inflammation of the bowels. She said nothing, but quietly adjusted his diet, offering him herbal tea and a few light pancakes in the place of heavier biscuits.

In the east, the sky glowed faintly above the black mountains, but the light had not yet touched the wide plain that stretched northward along the canyon. James said they would reach the head of the gorge today where they could cross and finally turn west again. She looked out over the chasm, which was indeed growing shallower. Tonight, perhaps, she could make her way down to the stream and wash at least her face and arms. She would fill the tin canteens and the water kegs, as well, for when she looked to the west, there was nothing to indicate the possibility of streams or springs. The men said there would be water, but Juliet had her doubts. It looked as though the land stretched to eternity without any relief at all. She tried not to think about the monotonous long days that they would spend inching over the hostile landscape.

She knelt to blow on the ember she saw glowing in the gray ashes. A wisp of smoke curled up, and she quickly laid her sagebrush twigs across it. Usually she found the pungent smoke fragrant, but today it made her choke. Her stomach churned, and she leaned back. Holding her breath, she added more small sticks and twigs and waited for the flames to flicker upward. Before the fire was ready, she put the blackened coffeepot with a few ounces of water on to boil.

Sarah was making her way to Juliet's wagon, tying her pale blue sunbonnet over her brushed and braided hair.

"The men are finished with the axle," she reported in her usual soft voice. "We'll be able to travel again today. I feel badly that we've held everyone up."

"Oh, I'm glad the axle is ready. Is little Martha still all right?"

"She's fine, thanks to you. In fact, she was a bit of a challenge yesterday. She won't stop scratching her insect bites no matter how often I tell her. She bothers them until she bleeds. But I'm so thankful we didn't lose her to the laudanum that I can't bear to be too cross with her." Sarah's eyes flickered over Juliet's pinched face and disheveled hair. "How are you today, Juliet?"

"I'm all right. A little tired, but I'll be better once we start walking." Juliet ran her hands over her hair, trying to smooth the loose strands, and straightened up a little taller.

"Good. If I can help with the boys today . . . " Sarah fumbled in her apron pocket and pulled out a dried purple flower with a narrow red ribbon tied around its stem. "Here, Juliet. I brought you a sprig of lavender from home. Did you see it hanging from the wagon bows the other day? It is said to bring serenity. I thought it would be a fitting way to thank you for your help with Martha."

Juliet took the little spray and held it to her nose. Its fragrance did seem to soothe her edgy feelings. "Thank you, Sarah."

"If we were back home, I'd give you more than a sprig of lavender to let you know how grateful I am. I honestly do not know how you stay so calm and helpful, Juliet. We all watch you and marvel at the way you manage things out here."

Juliet tilted her head and looked at her friend.

"Why, I don't do anything differently than the others." Didn't they notice the times she was sharp with the children or James? The times she was dead-tired, thirsty, and annoyed? Maybe biting her tongue when she felt irritable was working, after all.

"They say you're strong, inside and out," Sarah said. "I know what they mean. You have a way of seeing what's essential and important—and then acting upon it."

Juliet tucked the lavender into a buttonhole. "How kind of you, Sarah. But I'm not certain I deserve such a compliment. After all, I just plod along like everyone else. I have such a hard time some days."

"I've seen it for myself, Juliet. You have a lot of courage and determination."

CHAPTER 10

here's water ahead!" Juliet wasn't certain whose voice lilted through the wind, but the news traveled down the line of wagons like a melody. Water. Imagine being blessed with a drink. Three days had passed since they crossed the shallow stream at the head of the chasm. It ended up being a simple crossing. They navigated the slow, gentle grade to the shallow stream, jostled the wagons over the stones in the narrow streambed, and hauled the load up the other side. Juliet had made her way downstream to a secluded spot to bathe gratefully in the cold trickle, and then filled the kegs and canteens to the brim. There hadn't been a creek or spring in the long distance they had covered since, and the water she'd collected was nearly gone. She had saved just enough in the bottom of the last keg to give the boys and James one more drink. James, especially, needed water. The dysentery left him weak and shaky and worsened his dehydration. He made an effort to keep up with each day's chores, but Juliet began helping him hitch and unhitch, lift the heavy wooden provisions box, and set up the tent.

She glanced up. The wagons snaked out behind her on the sandy soil like the crooked tail of a kite. Dust billowed up around them. Some of the men fanned out to the sides, picking their way through the sage and juniper. As usual, the women and children straggled alongside. The children wore dirty clothing, and their wind-snarled hair blew into their eyes. They were no longer barefoot because of the spiny cacti, but instead wore tough, hand-stitched cowhide on their feet—crude, amateur moccasins their mothers had hurriedly constructed.

Juliet watched Columbus and Johnny lift their heads as they heard the cry about water. The meager dribbles in the bottom of their cups never quenched their thirst. Who could have dreamed that the thought of a mere drink of water could brighten their faces like that? Johnny looked as if it were Christmas morning. His cracked lips broke into a grin that revealed a gap where his two front teeth had been.

She snapped to attention. Where was Kirke? He had been here a few moments ago, lagging behind his brothers. Juliet scanned the group, but she couldn't see his tousled head anywhere. A knot formed in her stomach as she hurried toward Columbus and Johnny.

"Boys, where's Kirke?"

Columbus turned and looked behind them. "He was here just a moment ago, Mother. May I have a drink now that the men have found some more water?"

"Yes. . . . Did you see where he went?" Juliet answered distractedly.

Johnny spoke up. "He stopped to look at a dead beetle. Could I have a drink, too?"

"Yes, Johnny." Her eyes, frantic now, scanned the line of wagons and the straggling walkers beside them. The landscape was so flat here that he couldn't have disappeared into a crevice or hole.

Johnny and Columbus ran to the wagon as Juliet strode toward the back of the line. What if Kirke had stopped long enough for the loose cattle in the rear to overtake him? Their hooves could trample a small child.

"Kirke!" she called out. Her high, thin voice carried well if she put enough force behind it. Up and down the train, the others looked up from their driving. James gave one glance at her and immediately halted the wagon and secured the reins. He stepped down as she began to run to the rear of the train. The other wagons, too, lurched to a halt.

She stepped on a sharp stone that felt as though it cut through the thin sole of her shoe, but she kept going, lifting her long blue skirts and dodging clumps of bunchgrass and sage and cacti. She glanced under each wagon as she ran but saw only swinging buckets, and an occasional churn— no small dark shape that could be Kirke.

Then Asahel Bennett called down to her from his wagon seat.

"He's here with us, Mrs. Brier. No need to worry. He's safe up here."

Juliet stopped, gasping for breath, as relief and then anger choked her. Her small frame was rigid. She drew a few breaths, struggling with the impulse to shout at Mr. Bennett. She couldn't imagine what had possessed him to lift Kirke up beside him and not ask her permission or let her know. She heard James stumble up behind her, breathing hard.

"Kirke. Get down from there immediately and come here." James spoke first. "Do you know how worried your mother and I were when we couldn't find you?"

Asahel handed the boy down and jumped down himself.

"I'm sorry. I never thought. Poor little Kirke here was looking so tuckered out that I thought I'd just give him a little ride."

Juliet tried to bite her tongue, but it was no use.

"I'm sure you meant well, Mr. Bennett, but you scared us witless, you know."

Sarah poked her head from behind the wagon cover. She looked as though she had been napping. "Is something wrong?"

"Just a lost child," Juliet replied grimly. "Your husband is to blame, I'm afraid."

Back home, she would have rather died than be so rude. Out here, though, exhaustion and layers of fear and despair made her say things she knew were ill-tempered. Seeing Mr. Bennett's surprised and contrite expression, she knew she should be thanking him instead of speaking icily as if he were a stranger.

She grabbed Kirke by the hand and started back down the line of wagons. Her knees felt weak, her hands were trembling, and her heart was beating too fast. Suddenly she stopped. Ahead were Columbus and Johnny, happily drinking the rest of the water from the last weather-beaten keg. There was a wet spot on the ground where they had spilled the precious water while they poured, and the keg was on its side in the dust, obviously empty.

CHAPTER 11

Juliet stopped short, and her hand flew to her mouth. Columbus and Johnny hadn't noticed her approach.

"You spilled it, Col! Mother's going to be cross."

"It doesn't matter, Johnny. Mr. Arcan saw some water up ahead. Look for yourself."

Johnny's anxious eyes searched the horizon and then stopped. "Oh, there it is. It looks like a lake, doesn't it, Col?"

"Yep. I'm going to jump right in and drink so much I'll never be thirsty again."

"I'm going to splash you." A grin crept over Johnny's face. "And dunk you under." He glanced over and saw Juliet, still holding Kirke's hand. "Oh, hello, Mother." The grin vanished and his gaze faltered. "We spilled the water. By mistake."

"I see that." Juliet said briskly. "You boys must never touch the kegs again until we reach California. Is that clear?"

"Yes, Mother. But you said . . . "

Kirke's flushed face crumpled. "You didn't save me any," he wailed. "I'm thirsty, too!"

Columbus glanced at his little brother and nudged the empty keg with his foot. "We can get more, Mother. See the lake over there?"

"Col, you're old enough to have remembered that the rest of us need water, too. And that lake in the distance— even though it looks close, it could be a long way off. Maybe a couple of hours away."

Columbus scrubbed the dirt with the toe of his moccasin. "I'll run ahead and get you and Kirke a drink," he said.

Juliet forced herself to smile at his childish solution. "No, Col. You stay right here with us. Go and ask Mrs. Bennett for a drink for Kirke. It's not much to ask, seeing as they can refill their kegs later today."

"Rolling out!" someone hollered as Col scampered off. He caught up a few minutes later with a half cup of water for his brother.

While Juliet walked beside the wagons, she could see the Jayhawkers' wheel tracks in the dirt. She tried to figure out how long ago they had passed. They should be far ahead by now, but it didn't appear as if they were. The sharp cuts made by their iron-rimmed wheels were plain in the dust, and it was easy to see where their animals had been. Their few remaining horses, once glossy and strong but now gaunt and tired, would be in poor shape at this point, but the oxen that pulled the wagons would be plodding along as ever. By now, the miles behind them—the distance back to the safety of Salt Lake—felt like infinity, and the ones ahead still stretched to eternity.

Seeing evidence that the Jayhawkers had traveled this way was like spotting a familiar constellation in the black night sky. It was comforting to know that those strong young men were up ahead somewhere, still within tracking distance. At least something was familiar out here where even the air felt different than it did back home.

The lead wagon stopped suddenly, and the others piled up behind it. Juliet looked ahead to see what caused Mr. Wade to call another halt. Far off, she could see a horse with a rider—or was it two riders? Behind it trailed a second, smaller horse. Mr. Wade propped his elbows on his knees and trained his field glass on them.

"That front horse—the black one—has two riders, but no one's riding the one behind," he told the others. "The second rider is sitting crooked."

"Can you see who it is?"

"No. Well, maybe. It looks a little like Doty in the front. A couple of the Jayhawkers, perhaps. Nothing threatening."

Juliet stood in the wagon's shade and kept her eyes on the riders as they came near.

"Ho, there." It was, indeed, Ed Doty who pulled up on the reins beside the wagons. Slumped behind him was another of the Jayhawkers, a young man named Bill Robinson. A bloodstained gray cloth was bound across his forehead, and below it, his thin face was white. Dark hair streaked with blonde hung to his shoulders.

"Robinson here had a bit of an accident," Doty began. "We wondered if perhaps Mrs. Brier could do some of her nursing."

Juliet's heart began to thump. Surely these boys hadn't ridden all the way back for her meager nursing skills! But then, where else could they find help in this lonely wilderness? She drew a long breath and smiled at Robinson. Her head felt fuzzy from thirst, and there was an odd hissing in her ears.

Robinson was leaning against Doty's back. Mr. Arcan and Mr. Bennett helped him slide from the horse and laid him on the sandy ground.

Juliet knelt beside him. She didn't know him well, but he looked to be about nineteen or twenty years old, a skinny lad with a few whiskers across his upper lip and wearing worn-out, dirty clothing. She checked his frightened eyes as she greeted him. One pupil was a pinprick in the December sunlight, but the other was large and dark.

The boy looked up at her. "I took a nasty spill, Mrs. Brier. Doty says I hit my head on a rock. Horse got spooked." His words slurred and his eyes drooped as if he were fighting off sleep.

"Well, Mr. Robinson. You're going to be all right." Juliet spoke with confidence but wondered if she was wrong. "Did the blow knock you unconscious?"

Above her, Doty spoke up. "It sure did. Scared the lot of us. We thought he was dead at first."

"And I imagine you've got quite a headache."

"Yes, ma'am, I do."

"What else are you feeling?"

"My . . . my stomach is queasy."

A tall shadow fell across the young man, and Juliet looked up to see her husband and Columbus. James knelt beside her and gave Robinson an assessing look.

"James, I'll need my garlic. It's wrapped in a flour sack in the food box. Bring my little pestle, too, so I can mash it into a poultice. And Col, I'll need some more water from Mrs. Bennett. Carry it carefully in two cups so it doesn't spill—one for Mr. Robinson to drink and one to use for washing his wound. Tell her I need some clean strips of flour sacking, too."

Juliet untied the crusty bandage covering Robinson's forehead, aware of the young man's eyes searching her face for her reaction. She composed her features. The gash was ugly, swollen, and purple. There was an egg-size lump, but at least the bleeding had stopped.

"Mr. Robinson, here's what we're going to do. You'll need to drink some water, just a sip at a time. Then I'm going to mix up a poultice to keep your wound from becoming poisoned. You'll have to stay here with us and lie still for a few days. You must stay off your horse."

Doty spoke up. "I need to take him back with me. We're a day up the trail. The men want to get going again."

"Mr. Doty, jostling Mr. Robinson on horseback will only cause more problems. We'll put him on the bed in our wagon and bring him up to you Jayhawkers. It will be a little slower that way, but safer for Mr. Robinson. You ride back and tell your men . . ." she tried, but failed, to keep the irritation out of her voice, "to imagine this gash in their own heads. See if that doesn't cure their hurry for a day."

CHAPTER 12

T hat's what we thought, too," Ed Doty said to the men clustered around him. "It looks just like a lake. But I swear to you, it's nothing but a figment of your imagination."

"Not *my* imagination," insisted Mr. Wade. "I can see that water plain as day and it's less than an hour's travel away."

"It looks that way, I agree," Doty countered. "But as you get close, it disappears entirely. It's some sort of hateful trick of the eyes."

"A mirage," James stated, coming up on the conversation. "It's a mirage. I was afraid of that."

Mirage. Juliet had heard the word, but nothing had prepared her to expect such a cruel, elusive thing out here. It meant no cool drink, no bathing, and no filling the kegs.

Kirke was crying from thirst again, and young Mr. Robinson, who was sprawled out on the straw tick in the wagon, asked for another drink as well. Juliet's own thirst was so intense she could no longer ignore it. James had cracked lips and leathery skin, and when he walked, he stooped over, as if to ease a pain in his abdomen.

"There's a little mud hole where my men are waiting," Doty offered. "It's possible to gather about eight ounces of water every half hour."

Juliet swallowed. Just the mention of water made her need even greater. But two cups an hour for a whole party of parched travelers and animals? It seemed as hopeless as slicing a boiled egg to feed a city. Whatever small drink they found there might be mostly mud, as well.

The wagons started up, crushing the pungent, scattered bushes in their way. Mr. Wade, not listening to Doty about the mirage, insisted that any fool could see there was a lake, right ahead on the desert floor. It even shimmered in the sunlight. He was determined to reach it in as short a time as possible. At least they were closing the distance to the Jayhawkers' camp, as well.

Juliet carried Kirke on her hip, but he was too heavy for her to lug more than a few minutes. To take her mind off his weight, she tried to imagine what this group of travelers would look like from the heavens—an insignificant train of graying wagon tops winding through a land so vast that it put the Great Plains to shame. This was the West, with its unimaginably massive features. In her mind, she could see the hundreds of miles of arid flats behind them interrupted by whole ranges of rocky hills and rough mountains that fanned out onto the brown flats again. Here, distance was measured more by endurance than by miles, and endurance was measured by sheer tenacity and perseverance.

Never in her worst imaginings had she thought that thirst would be their fiercest enemy. It was such an insidious, invisible adversary. Lack of water shaped this harsh country that completely lacked the cool streams one took for granted back home. How many times had she dipped her bucket into a Michigan creek without thought or appreciation? How often had she complained about the puddle that formed at their doorstep or the drips of pure rainwater that leaked through the roof? During the long winters back home, she had yearned for the sun's warmth; now she'd give anything for relief from its harsh white glare.

She took Kirke to the moving wagon. James halted the drooping animals for a moment. Earlier in the trip, he would have reached down and easily swung Kirke onto the wagon seat, but today he waited for the little boy to climb the wheel spokes himself. "Just for a few minutes to rest your legs, Kirke," he said. "The oxen are worn out and they're already pulling Mr. Robinson, so you'll have to walk again in a little while."

Juliet resumed her pace beside the wagon. Her foot was sore where she had stepped on that sharp rock. She had taken off her shoe to look, and there was a long, maroon bruise along her arch. If she walked on the side of her foot, it didn't hurt so much.

Johnny and Columbus were following along. Johnny's pace was lagging, but even at six years old he had an uncanny ability to bear up under these harsh circumstances. While little Kirke would cry and Columbus disobey, Johnny could sense the group's discouragement and fragility. He plodded along, already old enough to know that the best way to help was to carry on without complaint. He pushed his dark hair out of his eyes with his fist and looked at his brother on the wagon seat. Most children would ask to ride too, but Juliet knew Johnny wouldn't.

"Johnny, come here a moment," she called, reaching into her apron pocket. When he got close, she told him, "Try sucking on this bit of dried apple. Give one to Col, too, will you? They'll help you not feel so thirsty."

"Thank you, Mother." He popped one into his mouth and looked up at her, squinting in the sunlight. "Should I give one to Mr. Robinson when we stop? He needs one, too, I guess."

"These are for you. I have another for Mr. Robinson."

"Are we almost to the lake, Mother?"

The lake. He and Columbus were still dreaming of the sparkling water they saw ahead. Was she dishonest to let him go on believing that there would be a wet reward at the end of today's trek? How could she explain a mirage? And how would a trampled mud hole at the Jayhawkers' camp seem in comparison to the lovely oasis they had in their minds? He looked up at her, trusting and hopeful, and she looked back.

"No, Johnny," she said gently. "There's no lake ahead."

CHAPTER 13

T here was no water, just as Doty had said.

Despite herself, Juliet kept hoping for even the smallest puddle until the moment they reached the old lakebed and she felt the packed, white clay underfoot, hard as
stone. It was slightly damp, so James took his shovel from
under the wagon and started to dig a hole. He stopped,
exhausted, after only a few inches and leaned heavily on
the handle.

"Let me try, Reverend." Lewis Manly took the tool from
James's shaking hands and began chipping away at the sides
of the hole, enlarging and deepening it. "It's likely we can
collect some water if we dig deep enough."

After several minutes, he peered into the hollow he had
made. Water was seeping into the bottom. He knelt, dipped
his forefinger into the water, and tasted it. Looking up at the
expectant faces around him, he said simply, "It's brackish.
Terribly salty. It's no good at all."

Juliet felt a lump swell in her throat, but fought it down.
Her body was too dried out to waste moisture on tears. She
turned her back to the wet hole and went to join James, who
had retreated to lean against the wagon in the shade. Kirke

was whimpering behind the canvas, but there was no sound from Bill Robinson. All around them, the cattle were lowing in misery.

She looked at James. He was hunched over, and his eyes looked dull and deep in their sockets. The bones of his shoulders poked up under the fabric of his shirt. It reminded Juliet of the way the cattle's hipbones now jammed up underneath their hides in sharp points. His handsome face was too angular now, giving it a severe, hungry look that Juliet found disconcerting, and his skin was powdered with gray dust.

Even more worrisome was the fact that James still suffered from that peculiar digestive illness. She had checked her remedy book a dozen times and given him regular pinches of goldenseal from her leather pouch, but he continued to lose strength. His heartbeat, when she laid her head on his chest, was fast and weak, as if it were trying to outrun the perils of this hazardous place. Whenever the wagons stopped, he rested too.

"Well, at least the Jayhawkers have found that mud hole," he said quietly, staring out over the poisoned old lakebed. "The children and Robinson should be first on the list for water."

"And you, James. The lack of it is making you sick." She paused and then spoke the words she'd been holding back for days. She kept her voice low. "I'm frightened, James. Frightened for the children. It doesn't seem to me that we

can ever reach California without perishing. Look ahead!"
She pointed across the wide lakebed to the parched mountains that blocked their path. They jutted up in barren heaps
of dry, gray rock and steep, bare cliffs and outcroppings too
rugged to climb.

James gazed up and his eyes followed the sharp ridgeline. "Manly and Rogers will go ahead to scout. They think
there may be a pass to the south. They'll climb up high—
those fellows are real mountain men—and see our way
clear." James looked down at her. "You know it's impossible to go back, don't you, Juliet? We could never make
it now."

"But there's no water ahead, James! The children and
you and I—how can we go much farther?"

"It's true there's no water. But neither the provisions
nor the animals will see us back. It's too far. By now, we're
closer to California than we are to Salt Lake. We've no
other choice but to press on." Every speck of James's boy-
ishness was gone. He looked resigned and weary beyond
words. "There's more bad news. I might as well tell you.
Now that the Jayhawkers have gone ahead, the Mississippi
contingent is talking about splitting off, too. They want to
take a different route, and they think they can move faster
without us."

Juliet said nothing. The Mississippians weren't a large
group, but they were strong young men who understood

hard work. They hunted and helped with the cattle. Without them, the road ahead would be considerably more dangerous.

"They said they'll wait until Rogers and Manly return from scouting and then decide what to do," James went on.

"Oh, James. Can't you persuade them to stay? Splitting up will only make things worse."

"I've tried, Juliet. Believe me, I've tried."

"You must try again." Then she repeated it, louder, so that James would be certain to hear it over the noise of the cattle's constant lowing. "You must try again, James."

The cattle's bawling followed them like a bad dream and left a sick feeling in her middle. No matter how she tried to shut the pitiful sound out of her consciousness, she couldn't ignore it. James seemed to read her mind.

"Patrick and St. John are keeping a careful watch over the animals and finding anything green that grows out here, but the lack of water will kill them." James rubbed a dirty finger across his split lips. "We've got to keep them alive. Not only are they our investment, they might mean our survival, as well. The teamsters know that."

"Have you looked at them yourself?"

"Yes, last night. The smaller ones are dreadfully thin and desperate for water. The big ones are faring a little better, but they're gaunt and parched, too." James lowered himself onto the wagon wheel hub.

"You rest, James. I'll bring you a bit of apple to put in your mouth. It does seem to help with the craving for water. And I must check on Bill Robinson. I'm wondering why he's so quiet. He must be asleep."

She left her husband drooping on the wheel hub and mustered the energy to climb into the wagon. Kirke was sleeping now on a heap of bedding on the floor. His small hand curled under his cheek, and his face was pale. Bill Robinson was on his back on the straw tick. He had removed his flour-sack bandage, and the wound on his forehead swelled up raw and seeping and purple. His eyes were open.

"Mrs. Brier," he greeted her, turning his head slightly. His cheeks were hollow. "Thank you for all your help, but I need to get back to the men."

"Yes. We'll overtake them later today. That will be soon enough."

"They won't wait for me much longer. Once Doty gets back, they'll be itching to be off. No one is going to dawdle in this country. It's too dangerous."

"They'll wait. But you're not ready for miles of walking, you know, and Mr. Doty said your few remaining horses are ready to collapse."

"I feel a little better. My vision is off and my head still aches, but I think I can get around."

"It's a mistake to go before you're ready. It would be best to travel with us for a few more days. That way you could ride in the wagon until you're healed enough for walking."

"I can't do that, Mrs. Brier. The men will be too far ahead to catch by then." Robinson looked away and a deep breath lifted his chest.

Juliet said nothing. She cleaned the wound and covered it again. The young man watched as she worked and then raised his head a few inches off the ticking to look at Kirke.

"And by the way, Mrs. Brier? Your little Kirke here is mighty thirsty. He needs a drink pretty quick in my opinion."

CHAPTER 14

———— ❧ ————

They spotted the Jayhawkers' campfire at last. By the time they straggled into sight of the distant blaze, the stark ridgeline to the west was silhouetted in the last silver light of evening. A few stars began to sparkle in the darkening sky.

Juliet watched where she placed her feet as blackness hid the rocks and sagebrush in her path. Kirke was still in the wagon, and she kept Johnny and Columbus close. She reminded herself that the cattle's pitiful lowing at least indicated that the animals still had some strength, unlike the poor women who dragged along behind her. Sarah Bennett and Mary Wade and Abigail Arcan were silent.

Columbus and Johnny didn't say a word either, not even as the orange campfire flickered into view. Juliet tried to estimate its distance, but she was learning that landmarks, even when they appeared to be nearby, turned out to be long miles ahead. It was another of those cruel tricks of the eye.

When the Jayhawkers' fire was closer, Bill Robinson inched his body from the wagon and stood, bent at the waist, gripping onto the rear wheel until the train began to move again. Juliet tried to persuade him to get back in, but he politely refused. She knew he didn't want to be seen as a sissy, rolling up to his comrades in a wagon like a sick child. Now he was weaving his slow way back to the Jayhawkers, and she was certain that in the morning he would press on with them.

When they finally reached the camp, the night air was chilly enough to make the fire's heat welcome. Juliet threaded her way near, stepping over the dark, sleeping Jayhawkers spread out around it. Their wagons were scattered haphazardly here and there, and off to the side was a dead horse. No aroma of food mingled with the smell of wood smoke, but Mr. Doty brought a tin cup partially filled with water to her. She gave each of the children a long sip and told James to drink the rest. She would wait for the next cupful.

She slept deeply, but was already awake when Lewis Manly and John Rogers trudged into camp at dawn. Rogers, the taller and stockier of the two, limped slightly. Their pants were sweat-stained and encrusted with dust, and both of their faded, threadbare shirts were torn at the elbows. Manly propped his dirty boot on a rock and waited until everyone gathered.

"We walked about twenty miles, I'd guess, to a good vantage point. There's a route around the mountains to the south. The country to the north might have more springs and it may be a bit shorter. It's impossible to tell. To the south, though, we found another small dry lake and a puddle of

water about a day's travel from here. It's enough for us and
the cattle if we're careful. Tastes bad, but it's wet."

"How many days to the settlements do you estimate?"
Mr. Arcan asked. "Are we getting anywhere near?"

Manly looked at him and then glanced around at the
assembled group. The children stared at him with large
eyes. Sarah Bennett twisted her apron string in her fingers.
Manly studied the question and then turned to his companion. "We'll have to do some figuring on the mileage, don't
you think, Rogers?"

"Yep. We'll have to work it out," Rogers agreed
immediately.

"Did you see any game?" Mr. Wade asked. "The hunting is getting worse. Those blasted rabbits are so fast I can't
begin to take aim at them."

"Well, just lizards and hawks and a coyote or two. I'll tell
you what, men. We'll give the womenfolk some peace and
quiet to pack the wagons, and we'll continue this discussion
in the rear."

Juliet's head snapped up. Mr. Manly knew something he
did not want the women and children to hear. She caught his
eye and he looked back at her without dropping his gaze, as
if to confirm that his words would be too much for the likes of
Sarah Bennett. She held a deep respect for this levelheaded
man who knew more about surviving out here than the rest of
them put together, and she needed to hear what he had to say.

She went quickly to the wagon where the children were waiting.

"Boys, sit here on the wagon tongue. I'll be back in a few moments. Stay away from the fire."

"Where are you going, Mother?"

"No questions, Johnny. Just do as I say."

Juliet avoided the other women as she hurried back to where the spare animals were tended. She still limped, but the bruise on her foot was a little better. When she reached the group, she untied the strings of her dusty black sunbonnet and let it slide down her back. Mr. Manly and Mr. Rogers were solemn as the men formed a circle around them. Juliet went closer.

"Men, I'll tell you plainly. We're alarmed at the situation. From that ridgeline, we could see a long way— maybe a hundred miles or more. It's desert, men. After that one sparse spring I mentioned, there's no sign of water or grass anywhere. And beyond that, there are more mountains. Two ranges of them that we could see with the field glass."

"Surely you're wrong, Manly!" James Brier exclaimed. "We must be nearer the settlements than that. And there certainly must be springs along the way!"

"There's nothing, Reverend. Nothing out there but miles of dry desert."

Juliet felt her body go cold. Dear God.

"Do you think there's a chance we could make it back to Salt Lake?" Mr. Arcan asked.

"Less than none," replied Manly. "We've got to move forward. Turning around would be suicide, given the distance."

"If the northern route is shorter and might have water, then that's the way we should go," Ed Doty spoke up for the Jayhawkers.

"We agree," came the unexpected voice of Captain Towne of the Mississippians. He was an easygoing, muscular man with a deep, musical voice that drawled out words as if there were never cause to hurry. Until now, his group of about twenty men from the Deep South had traveled near the back of the train by themselves. Among them were a few farmers, some gold seekers, and three men with the darkest skin Juliet had ever seen. Now, they stood in a tight bunch, their eyes on Mr. Manly and their faces serious. "It sounds like the better route."

"But, men, we're not certain what lies to the north— we're only guessing." Lewis Manly's voice was alarmed. "On the other hand, there's a sure way around the mountains to the south, and at least one source of water. Rogers and I recommend heading south and then turning west."

"We're after the fastest route, Manly, not the slow, take-no-chances way. I believe we'll go north." Asa Haynes, the captain of the Jayhawkers, crossed his arms and looked at Captain Towne as he spoke.

"And leave our women and children in danger again!" Henry Wade's words rang out as if they were blows from a hammer.

"Wade, it would be folly for us to slow ourselves down. You heard Manly."

"You men might be walking into the gates of hell if you go north!"

Doty shrugged. "It's hell out here no matter which route you take, Wade."

"I'm not sure how much longer my family and animals will hold out," J. B. Arcan spoke up. "We've got to find some water quickly. I'm for the southern route. At least we know there's an immediate water source."

Asahel Bennett rubbed his hand over his face. "I'm with you and Manly and Rogers," he said. "I'll trust them no matter what. If they're telling us to go south, I'll do it."

Without warning, James Brier raised himself to his full height. "I'm sorry, men. I just can't agree. I think Doty and the Mississippians are right. There's got to be water somewhere in this country, and from what I can tell, it isn't the way we've been headed."

He glared around the circle of men. "We're in a bad spot here. If we're splitting up—and it sounds as if we are—I'm going north with Doty and the others."

Juliet felt the blood rushing to her head. Had she heard correctly?

"Reverend Brier," Doty looked James in the eye. "We didn't invite you to come with us. You know we men are traveling light and fast. The Mississippians can keep up— they don't have women and children and household goods. But you . . . "

"Just try to stop us, Doty. We're coming with you."

CHAPTER 15

The air had become too thin in this bleak spot. Juliet took several gulps but couldn't fill her lungs. Her heart was racing and she tried again to breathe, wishing the familiar feeling of irritation would rise in her chest to replace the panic that seized her.

Impulsive. That was the only word for James's decision. Worse, he hadn't even flicked his eyes her way to look for her agreement. He knew how vehemently she would insist that trailing after the Jayhawkers and Mississippians was a treacherous and ill-considered choice. How could she acquiesce to this reckless, hasty decision when her whole being shouted that it was a terrible mistake? Anger and fear closed her throat.

She started toward him, but he wandered off from the group, and Juliet knew he was praying. She stopped and lifted her own face to the heavens. The earth began to spin and she took a quick step backward to keep herself from falling.

One thought stood out from the mad jumble in her brain. The children. Columbus and Johnny and Kirke. Already they were dangerously skinny, their dull eyes lined with dark circles. Their small bodies needed water and food more urgently than the rest of them. Their stamina was failing, like her own and James's and everyone else's.

Stunned and moving by rote, she returned to the wagon. While she wrapped the warm stove and loaded it into the wagon, she distractedly answered the boys' questions. In a daze, she checked the mud hole to see if there was enough water to add a few ounces to the canteen, but only the deep empty holes left by the cattle's hooves stared back at her.

The Jayhawkers and the Mississippians would never wait for the Briers' heavier wagon and slower pace. They would hurry ahead, leaving her family to follow their tracks—one vulnerable wagon, a speck on the desert.

And to split from the other women seemed more than she could bear. To say good-bye to the shelter of friendship and warm camaraderie to travel with men who didn't want her along at all. Men who thought it was permissible to drag children into a chilling wasteland where there was no water! She thought of the diminishing flour supply, the failing oxen, and James's alarming weakness. The familiar lump rose in her throat, and this time she couldn't fight it down.

Even the drovers, Patrick and St. John, would follow the Arcans, who had hired them. There would be no one to herd the extra animals—six at last count, since one had broken its picket line and disappeared. She and the children would have to add that chore to their responsibilities.

James came to help her with the packing and she turned away from him. Then, with her body stiff and her mouth tight, she turned back to him.

"James, whatever are you thinking?"

"I know you don't like the idea, Juliet. But the Jayhawkers and the Mississippians are still fairly strong, and the northern route has to be an improvement over where we've been heading. Bennett and Arcan and the others don't have the strength and endurance to go another hundred miles and then cross more mountains. This is our only chance."

"We're splitting from Mr. Manly and Rogers in the bargain! They're the only ones with the skill to survive out here. They're our only seasoned scouts. Are you dreaming, James? We can never keep up with the young men."

"I'm telling you, it's our only chance."

The Jayhawkers threw their things into their wagons and left at a brisk pace before anyone else was packed. Juliet watched Bill Robinson heave himself onto a wobbling horse and ride off with his companions. He lifted his hand to her in thanks as they passed. After a while, even the dust they raised was lost in the distance.

The Mississippians were more polite, but they, too, were gone. Captain Towne spoke briefly with James. "We're leaving, but catch us if you can, Reverend."

The gray clouds that roiled overhead matched Juliet's mood. She welcomed them. They made the sky feel closer and not so horribly infinite. She pulled her old wool shawl over her bony shoulders. Surely God was watching their pitiful progress. Certainly He had a plan for them even if she couldn't imagine what it was. She swallowed.

"I think it's a dreadful mistake, James. A serious and dangerous mistake."

"We haven't time to discuss it now. We've got to leave so we can keep up."

She turned and walked away. She needed a moment, at least, to say good-bye to Sarah and the others. Juliet wondered if Mr. Manly could give her any last-minute advice, a quick course in finding water or hunting game or staying alive out here.

Sarah, Abigail, and Mary were walking toward her. Their faces were pale, and Abigail's hand was clapped over her mouth.

"Asahel told us, Juliet," Sarah said. Her voice trembled. "He said we're splitting up."

"Yes. James wants to join the Jayhawkers and the Mississippians. They're going north."

"Oh, Juliet."

"I know."

She was losing the fight with tears. "I need to go. The Jayhawkers and Mississippians have left without us, and James is waiting."

One by one, they hugged her wordlessly. Sarah was trembling. She gave a quick sob before releasing her. "Thank you, Juliet. And Godspeed."

"Yes." The lump in her throat made it impossible to say more. She looked each of her friends in the eye for a moment before she turned away.

Silently, she walked back to the wagon, her cold hands clenched and her throat aching. From now on, she thought, her hours would drag by without the everyday womanly sharing, the whispered commiserations, even the privacy that her friends' discreetly held full skirts had offered. She gave a quick wave to Mr. Manly and Mr. Rogers, but couldn't approach them or call out her good-bye. Mr. Manly's face told of his distress. James was sitting on the driver's seat, the reins drooping in his hands. The children were waiting, sober and quiet. Johnny clutched George Bennett's toy whistle, a souvenir, she supposed, of their little-boy camaraderie. The small herd of cattle stood off to the side with Columbus. With one last awkward wave at Mr. Bennett and Mr. Wade, Juliet joined Col behind the animals, staring at the wagon tracks that headed north in the dust. They stretched out as if leading to the ends of the earth.

"Come on, Kirke," she heard Johnny say. "Let's go look for Captain Towne and Mr. Doty. Maybe we'll find a drink up ahead."

The wagon started up with a rattle of chains and the low grind of wheels on hard earth. James gave her an apologetic glance as he drove by, but she couldn't look him in the eye. Perhaps this decision would, indeed, turn out to be the best one, but at the moment it seemed rash and heartless. She knew her cheeks were too red and her breath was ragged. Col spoke to the cattle as he had seen the drovers do, and they, too, began to move. She fell in behind them.

Only once, she turned to look behind. Sarah had separated herself from the little cluster of wagons and was standing alone, her pale blue skirt blowing in the cool wind. When she saw Juliet turn, she raised her hand and fluttered her handkerchief. Juliet waved, too. As she watched, Sarah buried her face in her hands and turned back to the wagons.

The last thing Juliet had wanted was to become another hardship in Sarah's life. She shooed the cattle ahead with more intensity than needed.

One thing was clear. The Jayhawkers and the Mississippians were beginning to act as though this trip was each man for himself. She couldn't believe that they would be the source of support and security James imagined. She herself must somehow rally every bit of her physical and mental strength. If she and her family were to have any chance of finishing this journey without perishing, she must be their steady pilot.

Anything less would harm her children.

CHAPTER 16

The day was too quiet. Juliet yearned for the companionable creaking and clanking of the other wagons, the trudging footsteps of her fellow women, and the low conversations among the men. Mostly, she yearned for a visit with Sarah or calm reassurance from Mr. Manly.

To follow the impetuous Jayhawkers was utter folly, but by late afternoon she had resigned herself to the upsetting turn of events and was able to be civil to James in front of the children.

Kirke stopped crying for water and sat silently in the wagon. Johnny and Columbus joined him. The cattle moved at an agonizing pace across the bare dirt, crushing the scraggly, hardy plants that Mr. Manly had called creosote bushes, releasing their strange, strong, peppery odor. Lower to the ground were some lighter shrubby plants called greasewood. Interspersed among them were odd, short trees with tufts of spiky fronds sprouting from their tops. The sky was still overcast and the light breeze brought goose bumps to Juliet's arms. James and the boys wore their heavy shirts.

It was beginning to get dark when the wagon dipped into a dry wash and James spotted a patch of green plants to the west. Juliet knew not to expect a running spring, but she hoped, at least, for a small seep. When they reached it, they found that the Jayhawkers and Mississippians had dug into the damp dirt until brown water seeped in and eventually filled their hole. Juliet gave each of the boys a cupful, then James, and then herself. The boys drank it greedily, without complaint about the mud that swirled in the bottom. The cattle jostled to get near, and all night Juliet could hear their agitated snorts as they pulled on the picket ropes, desperate for more to drink than the unsatisfying seep could give them.

In the morning, Juliet filled the kegs, one slow cupful at a time, before they set off again. The low rise of mountains to the northwest began to take on detail. She thought she might be imagining the slight grade, but the afternoon seemed slower and more labored. James said he would take the rifle and look for game when they got nearer to the foothills. They would skirt the first summit by veering to the east.

At first, she didn't believe her eyes and wondered if the creature that crawled across the sand in front of the wagons was some sort of desert mouse. As she got closer, though, she could see it was a gigantic spider with eight hairy legs and a dark, heavy body. The mere sight of it sent shivers down her back. For the rest of the day, she watched the shaded areas under rocks and scrub vegetation, but she didn't see another. She held her tattered skirts above her ankles as she walked, preferring immodesty to the possibility of one of those horrid things crawling up her petticoats.

"I'd like to sleep in the wagon with the children tonight," she told James at the next rest stop. "I'd never close my eyes all night in the tent. The snakes out here are bad enough, but can you imagine finding one of those hideous spiders in your bedding?"

Late in the morning, they stopped to give the cattle a rest. The animals' sides were heaving after hauling the wagon up a gentle rocky incline, but James was reluctant to abandon the existing wagon tracks in favor of the more level route below. After all, the Jayhawkers had scouts up ahead finding the best trail.

Movement caught Juliet's eye, and she squinted to see ahead. A steep embankment rose at the mouth of a small canyon, and she saw men and wagons. The Mississippians. Her heart leaped. A few moments later, she could see that the men were milling about on the rocks, searching as though they had lost something. A few were clustered about Captain Towne.

James called out to them, and they looked up. Captain Towne held in his hand an odd honey-colored gourd the size of a large apple that glistened like hard candy. It seemed as if human hands must have cultivated it.

"It's some sort of Paiute or Shoshone food," he said. "We found it stored in a crevice in the rocks. We'd best put it back. They'd likely miss it, even if there are others."

"Nonsense!" James reached out and took it. "They won't miss it at all. I say we cut it into pieces and whoever wants a bit to chew on can have it. We're nearly starving, all of us, and this must contain some nourishment."

The captain made no move to stop him, just looked him in the eye.

"We wouldn't want to anger them, Brier."

"Do you think perhaps they've forgotten about it? Maybe it wouldn't hurt to give ourselves a little sustenance." A man named Masterson spoke up.

"It's obviously the result of plenty of cultivation," Towne replied. "They'll miss it, all right. No use being thieves."

"Well, I believe you're outvoted, Towne. Everyone needs the nourishment." James sliced his knife blade into the hard ball and it broke into pieces. He began gnawing at the insides of one. Juliet turned away.

"Maybe you should take a bit for your own good, Juliet," James said. "I think we need to give a piece to the boys, at the very least."

"If the tribes get angry, James . . . "

A whoop came from the gully. A young man with curly black hair and lanky limbs held up a second gourd.

"Time to push on, men," Captain Towne stood up abruptly. "Follow me. We're within a few miles of tonight's camping spot." He turned to Juliet. "There's a nice spring up ahead a few miles, ma'am. We'll reach it near dark. The Jayhawkers are already there."

It was late when the cattle finally hauled the wagons up the last slope. There, indeed, gushing from a crevice in the sculptured rock was a spring of clear water—and the Jayhawkers sleeping under the stars. Juliet felt the lump rise in her throat again, this time from gratitude. They drank, all of them, slowly at first and then again and again. The cattle had their fill before James drove them from camp to forage for the night.

When darkness came, Juliet crept under the bedding in the wagon with the children. James slept with the other men beside the spring. For a while, chilled from the cold air, she stared into the utter blackness. Captain Towne ordered that there would be no fires tonight. He and Mr. Masterson stood guard over the camp in case there was trouble. Juliet shared his anxiety. But outside, she could hear the trickle of blessed water, and she could almost feel the evening's cold drinks coursing through her veins, building her strength and endurance. The kegs were full and the children were refreshed. The cattle were quiet.

She closed her eyes and slept.

CHAPTER 17

S he dreamed that night of Hiram, her brother. He was striding through the sagebrush and rocks with her, carrying Kirke on his shoulders. Johnny and Columbus were in his arms. Hardly burdened by the weight, he took them all to a summit overlooking a body of turquoise water that spread out to the horizon. "There it is, Jule," he said, using his childhood name for her. "The edge of the continent."

She awoke, shaken by the dream's clarity. She thought of Hiram every day as she trudged through the desert. Growing up, the two of them had hunted eggs and pulled weeds together and, side by side, pored over books. Later, when age separated them—Hiram to the fields and Juliet to the kitchen—they wandered the green Midwestern hills after Sunday school, discussing the day's lessons and memorizing the next week's Bible verses. Leaving him behind when she started this journey was one of the hardest things she had ever had to do.

When James rode into her life with his big, outspoken ways and strong-as-steel convictions, she knew that she would marry him. Not only that, she would accompany him to the edge of the continent, if that's where his circuit rider's zeal led him. If he was a bit impulsive and occasionally tactless, she could forgive his faults, as he forgave hers. Out here, even in his illness and fatigue, he worked at spreading the Gospel to their fellow travelers. The bulk of the chores fell to her, but she could manage.

She wondered, though, if James truly understood her—the fierce, protective love she felt for the children, her immense grief at leaving Hiram and the rest of her family, or her extreme trepidation at what might be ahead. Sometimes it seemed as if he couldn't fathom the breadth and depth of her emotions.

She sat up in the wagon and reached for her hairbrush. It was time to start the day. This grinding pace would hardly get them to California by Christmas. How far had they come since they left the original wagon train—was it almost four weeks ago? Without a map, it was impossible to know, but it seemed as though they had been toiling along forever.

She pulled her gray shawl around her shoulders and stepped from the wagon. In the daylight, she could see the messy camp, littered with bedding and blackened pots and worn harnesses. The Jayhawkers stood in quiet bunches drinking from their cups, and they greeted her as she joined them by the fire. James stood warming his hands over the blaze. One of the Jayhawkers, Sheldon Young, sat on a boulder with a tattered diary and a stubby pencil. His chapped fingers were spelling out words. She glanced down to see what he had written.

Nov. 29, 1849 . . . A damned dubious looking country.

Dubious. She looked at Mr. Young in surprise. That one well-chosen word matched exactly her feelings of hopelessness and dismay when she looked out over the vast stretches of desiccated landscape ahead. Who was this young man? From the way he faithfully recorded each day's events in his diary, he seemed to be an educated wordsmith hiding in Jayhawker's clothing. She would make a point to know him better. After all, there weren't many literate people out here. She wondered if he knew Shakespeare or perhaps even a little of Henry Kirke White's poetry.

They spent the next two days skirting the eastern base of the mountains that sheltered the spring. The Jayhawkers and the Mississippians, refreshed by the water, pressed on at a pace that the Briers couldn't hope to equal. The men were still headed north—directly away, Juliet thought in alarm, from their destination at the pueblo of Los Angeles. They needed to veer west, but this everlasting chain of mountains was in the way.

On the morning of the third day, the land began to rise to a high plateau. Here the wagon tracks split. James could

read the signs well enough to tell that the Mississippians'
trail curled toward a gap between the mountains and into a
clay canyon that drained downward to the west. Their tracks
disappeared into its steep, dry depths. The Jayhawkers' trail
continued north.

"We'll try the canyon," James decided. "It looks passable
from here, and surely the Mississippians must have scouted
ahead. If they can get their wagons through, so can we. I
can't fathom why the Jayhawkers are still heading north."

As Juliet rationed the last water for the children, she
hoped there would be a spring or a seep as they descended.
The cattle slowed their pace, bracing themselves as the
wagon pushed them into the gulch, the tremendous weight
forcing itself almost upon them. James attached a stout rope
to the wagon's rear axle, braced himself, and pulled backward to slow the wagon's descent. Juliet held Kirke's hand
and helped Columbus and Johnny keep the extra cattle
back.

"Are you sure we shouldn't take the other route?" she
asked.

"Well, the Mississippians were able to navigate it,"
James replied.

"Our wagon is a little broader and heavier, though."

The cattle picked their way around massive rocks and
through the deepening sand. Juliet kept an eye on the
dark clouds overhead. In a rainstorm, this narrow canyon

would fill with rushing water. She shivered as the breeze picked up.

By evening, the wagon was no longer pushing at the cattle in its eagerness to descend. Now the wheels sank into the soft sand that covered the bottom of the wash. In their poor condition, the cattle strained to pull its weight even a few feet. James hitched up two additional animals, and then two more.

"We'll need to keep going until dark," James said. "We're falling behind."

"Yes," she agreed. "Do you suppose there's water anywhere near?"

"We have to find some tonight or the cattle will give out. If you can guide the wagon, I'll go on down and take a look."

It was dark when James slogged back up the draw. There was no water. Down below, the ravine narrowed and large boulders cropped up in the way. The Mississippians were gone.

The wind snapped the canvas wagon covers and whipped Juliet's shawl from her shoulders. She made sure that the boys found their heavy shirts and she fetched her second shawl from the wagon. They picketed the cattle and then, using the scant fuel Columbus had gathered earlier in the day, she made a small fire in the shelter of a tall boulder. James moved close to the golden blaze and she joined him,

holding her skirts from the flying sparks. She served her
family bits of tart dried apple and old biscuits while James
continued to sit, too tired to set up the tent for the night. The
boys tried to swallow the crumbly pieces, but their mouths
were too dry.

"The best thing to do, boys, is to go to bed. You won't
notice your thirst if you're sleeping."

They escaped the wind by settling themselves in the
cramped wagon. Juliet couldn't doze off. Thirst kept her
awake, and she was chilled, even huddled between James
and the boys. James got up, left the wagon, and then returned
to her side trembling. Under the covers, he reached for her
hand, and she held it while he drifted off to sleep. His fingers felt like bare bones.

This dry place made the Midwest seem like heaven.
Back home, the green weeds she yanked from her garden
would offer the cattle a smorgasbord out here for weeks.
Even the wind there smelled of the nearby damp river bottom and marshy pond and fresh, long grass, not dust and
more dust.

Juliet would give anything for a drink of hot water and
a warm bath in the washtub. She remembered how she had
dreaded Saturday night baths back home—the hauling of
water, the laborious heating of it, and the cleaning of the
wet cabin floor afterward. In winter, when she poured the
wastewater on her frozen garden, it didn't soak in all the way

but sat in puddles that now seemed as miraculous as if it had been liquid gold pooled there on the ground.

A long while later something cold landed on her forehead. Juliet reached up to touch it and found a tiny speck of water. She sat up quickly, not caring that she pulled the covers from around James's neck. She peered into the darkness and saw, in the flickering light from the low fire, snowflakes whirling through the night. Snow! She gave a cry and scrambled from the wagon, pulling the quilts after her and leaving the boys and James awake and stunned.

"It's snowing, James! Help me spread the quilts to catch it!"

CHAPTER 18

Johnny and Kirke crouched beside the fire while Columbus scrounged a few more sticks, and soon a blaze flared
into the night again, illuminating the heavy snowflakes.
After a few minutes, all three children left its warmth and
began scraping the thin layer of snow from the rocks to eat.
An hour later, with water dripping from their chins, they
fell asleep on the ground beside the flames. Juliet covered
them with extra clothing while she and James collected
dirty handfuls of snow from the ground and melted them in
their cups. The cattle were licking wide circles around their
picket stakes.

The snow fell through the night, enough to collect in a
two-inch layer on the spread-out quilts. Juliet set the three
kegs beside the fire and funneled sodden clumps into them,
packing in as much as she could. Her hands were red and
stiff, but she hardly noticed.

As long as she kept moving, she was just chilled, not
seriously cold. James added more fuel to the fire before he
stretched out beside it and fell asleep. Juliet longed to do
the same but was too intent upon catching every bit of snow
she could. She filled the frying pan, the Dutch oven, and the

coffeepot, stopping only once during the night for the cup of hot water she had wished for earlier.

She was still awake at dawn, feeding the fire and making biscuits and brewing coffee. Coffee seemed a miracle. She savored its aroma, its satisfying bitterness, and its lifesaving wetness in her mouth. It stayed warm in her stomach and gave her the strength she needed for the day ahead. She sent her silent thanks heavenward.

When the morning light brightened the sky above the canyon, the children awoke and made a few snowballs but in a lethargic way Juliet found worrisome. Back home, they would have been romping in the first snow of the season, packing the drifts into forts, shouting, and flinging ammunition at each other. Out here, they sat near the fire and talked about the fort they wanted to build, but they made no move to do it.

James hitched six cattle to the wagon again. At first, straining and snorting, they were able to pull its weight short distances, but as the day wore on, Juliet felt her stomach begin to clench. What would happen if they couldn't get through? The worn animals could never haul the wagon back out of this canyon. She soothed herself with the thought that the Mississippians were still ahead. Somehow, they had been able to navigate this treacherous spot.

By late afternoon, the snow was gone. The ravine narrowed and knee-high boulders began to thrust up from the sand like small mountains, leaving no space to weave between them. Juliet knew they were in trouble. The cattle were close to dropping from fatigue.

"We need to unload," James called to her. "Maybe without all the weight inside . . . "

Together they hauled the cumbersome wooden provisions box from the wagon, along with the cook kit, the washtub, the spinning wheel, the straw mattress, James's toolbox, and the trunk of extra clothing. Finally, Juliet paused and looked around. She felt as if her whole life were scattered here in this rocky gully, laid out bare like her most private thoughts. James saw the look on her face.

"We'll reload when we get past this bad spot," he said. "If we can just get over these rocks . . . "

The cattle pulled hard and the wagon inched ahead, tipping first to the right and then to the left as the rigid wheels lifted over entrenched boulders and crashed down again. Finally, the left rear wheel rose over a tilted stone slab and fell with an alarming thud into a deep, narrow crack. James threw down the reins.

For the remainder of the afternoon, the two of them struggled to free the wagon, jamming wedges and levers under the wheel and pulling on ropes to help the cattle. They were like two ants, she thought, worn to brittle fragility, futilely trying to move the massive wagon, which weighed more than half a ton when empty. When they failed, they tried unsuccessfully to separate the trapped wheel from its axle. Finally, James sat down on a rock with his face in his hands, trembling with fatigue. While he rested, Juliet worked her way down the gully to see what was ahead.

It started snowing again as she slipped along. The canyon continued to narrow and fill with more rocks until a heap of boulders forced her to clamber over them. It must have taken the brute strength of every man and beast, she thought, to get the Mississippians' wagons through this terrible place. They would have had to remove the wheels and axles from the wagon boxes, labor the heavy pieces over the bad spots, and reassemble them lower in the canyon. It was the only possible way. A pile of discarded planks, heavy iron tools, and a broken wagon tongue were left among the jumbled boulders, a silent testament to their toil.

She and James would have to abandon the wagon and continue on foot. She recoiled from the terrifying thought. Without the wagon, there would be no shelter from the sun and wind, no shred of privacy, no respite from the grueling travel. The children would have to walk the remaining distance to the settlements, and so would James, for whom even driving had been taxing. He might never make it on foot. They would have to sleep on the cold ground no matter what the weather. To make matters worse, she would have to leave behind the few cherished belongings and the necessities she had chosen for their life in California—every remembrance of home, every bit of comfort.

She turned and began to make her way back to her family. Even from a distance, she could see the wagon stuck in the rocks as if a giant steel trap held fast to its wheel, and she knew it was there to stay.

CHAPTER 19

She sent the boys to hunt for more fuel and then sat for a moment near the fire, watching the snow pile up on the gleaming finish of her spinning wheel, the ornate brass of the trunk, the mattress and bedding. Her shawl was damp and her feet ached with cold. Her wet hair was plastered to her head, and cold drops of water ran down her neck. Impatiently, she brushed away a tear. There was no time to cry. She needed to decide what to take with them—and what she had to leave behind, even if it broke her heart in two. James had gone down the ravine looking for a few frozen spears of grass for the cattle.

She could cut the canvas wagon cover into fourths, and they could use the quarters to bundle up the absolute necessities. The driving cattle were accustomed to the weight of a yoke on their backs, so they might not balk too much if James strapped a pack on them.

They would need one set of extra clothing apiece, in case the ones on their backs disintegrated. One frying pan and the coffeepot. What was left of the provisions, of course. James's gun and bullet pouch and the Bible. The canteens. Her herbs.

Her throat tightened when she thought about leaving behind the few books she had brought along—her remedy book!—and the sketchpad in which she had traced her babies' newborn feet. And the spinning wheel, which seemed to droop under the heavy snow. It was grotesquely out of place here, its smooth oak taking on a dark wetness. It had belonged to her father's family and had spun wool under her mother's slender fingers. How could she leave it behind in this godforsaken place, along with her good dinnerware, the children's toys, and her flower bulbs? Even the tent would be too heavy and bulky to bring.

"Mother, we can't find any sticks." Columbus came up behind her. Juliet wiped her hand across her cheek one more time.

Johnny squinted at her through the swirling snowflakes. "Were you crying, Mother?"

"I'm being foolish about leaving all my favorite things behind here. I believe we're going to have to go on without the wagon."

"Leave the wagon!"

"Yes. We can't get it through this canyon. So from now on, we're going to walk like Lewis and Clark did." She tried to put some lightness into her voice. "Like the mountain men."

"Walk all the way to California?" Columbus's eyebrows shot up.

"Yes, I'm afraid so. And you're right, boys. It's difficult to find twigs under this snow. Climb into the wagon to get warm. We'll spend one more night in it and then start out on foot. And I just thought of something else. We can use the extra boards your father stowed in the wagon bed for fuel, since we won't need them now. I'm going to cook up the last of the beans for supper." Her eyes traveled through the snow to the wagon leaning lopsided on its trapped wheel. Its flimsy cotton covering still smelled of the linseed oil James had rubbed into it to keep out the rain.

"Mother, the cattle are getting cold like us. They're eating snow, but they can't find anything else to eat. I was watching them."

"I know, Col. This trip is even harder for them than it is for us."

"I don't think so, Mother."

"Why is that?"

"Cattle can't think much, can they? So they can't imagine what might happen to us."

"Are you imagining bad things, Col?"

The boy looked at his feet. "Sometimes I wonder what will happen if we can't find any water. Or any food. Or if we never get to the settlements."

"That's for your father and me to worry about, Col. We'll do everything to keep you safe, you and Johnny and Kirke."

"I know, Mother. But . . . what if you can't? Keep us safe, I mean."

"Are you forgetting, Col? God is up there watching over us. If your father and I can't keep you safe, even if we try our best, then God has a plan for us."

"What kind of plan?"

"I don't know. But . . . "

At that moment, James trudged in from below. "I just had to see for myself. There's no way to get the wagon through. None. I'm sorry, Juliet."

"We'll have to press on by foot then. Do you think you can, James?"

"There's no other choice. The cattle won't tolerate a rider at all."

She thought about that. Columbus and Johnny might be able to cover the long miles ahead, but Kirke? She looked down at his short legs and his feet that were not much bigger than a toddler's. His hand clutched her damp, faded calico skirt.

She wondered if she was partly to blame for this agonizing predicament. Perhaps she was simply too compliant to counterbalance James's forceful and impetuous decision-making. In her efforts to be a dutiful wife, she overlooked the fact that quite possibly her own reasoning was superior to his. By following him, had she compromised the children's safety?

She didn't want to think about their chances of survival here. Today in this cold, far-flung gulch, they were lacking every basic necessity: food, water, and now, shelter.

CHAPTER 20

The mattress beneath her was damp and cold and at such an angle that Kirke kept rolling into her in his sleep. The five of them crowded together under all the spare clothing—old pants, petticoats, her second apron—because the quilts were wet and frozen. Juliet stared through the pre-dawn darkness at the sheltering canvas and wondered what it would be like when it was gone.

There were plenty of embers still glowing from last night's fire. The hardwood planks had burned steadily for hours in the December chill. Today James would ignite the wagon to warm the children and the cattle while he and Juliet packed to leave on foot.

On foot. Oh, dear God.

The Paiutes and Shoshones traveled on foot. She had seen their trails winding through the sage. Mr. Manly and Mr. Rogers, now so far away, walked hundreds of miles scouting and exploring. So did the Lewis and Clark expedition. Forty-odd years ago, they tramped across the entire continent, twice. She gathered courage from their journey. Folks back home were still talking about it.

Lewis and Clark had no children, though, nor did Manly and Rogers.

The native people did. She had no inkling how their families survived in this harsh place, but the thought amazed her. Imagine raising children here, where the stark terrain offered no shelter and the search for water and game was an all-consuming task.

James joined her beside the flames she was coaxing from the hot, orange coals.

"Are you going to be all right without the wagon, Juliet?" He asked in a low voice.

She paused for a moment before answering.

"I wish we had made different decisions, James. But I'll be all right. Whither thou goest, I will go, with or without the wagon."

He looked at her gratefully. "It won't be easy, Juliet. There's one good thought I can offer you, at least. We'll be able to travel a little faster without it. If we can keep our strength up, perhaps we can overtake the Mississippians."

"That would help. I'm worried about how far the boys can walk, though. Especially Kirke."

"Yes, I know."

"Johnny is going to give out, too."

"Yes."

"And you, James?"

"I'll manage. Whatever this ailment is, it's not going to get the better of me. As long as we can find water, we'll make our way."

"I wish we could butcher one of the cattle here and smoke the beef while we have wood to burn. We're nearly out of provisions. The beans are gone, and the flour nearly so. There's no telling what's up ahead—certainly no useful game. It doesn't seem possible to shoot those rabbits, they're so fast."

He looked at her steadily. "I'm not ready to do that, Juliet. Those cattle are our only means for making a start in California."

"But you heard Mr. Manly. It's a long, hard trek ahead. A hundred miles is seven or eight days of walking with the children, James. And he said there are two mountain ranges after that."

"I'd rather wait until we've exhausted all of our other supplies."

"At that point, there might not be fuel for a fire. We couldn't smoke the meat."

"Then we'd have to eat it raw."

"Eat it *raw?*" Her stomach lurched.

"I know it sounds barbaric, but it would still give us strength."

"Oh, James. I don't think I could ever manage to eat it raw."

"Let's pack," he said. "We need to get out of this snow."

Later in the morning, James set fire to the wagon. Columbus held Kirke on his lap near the flames, avoiding the thick smoke and occasionally turning around to warm their backs. Juliet paused to contemplate the scene. She swallowed and turned away.

James threw everything he owned except his rifle and bullets, his Bible, and a small bundle of clothing on the fire. Juliet started to do the same with her extra apron and petticoat, but then stopped. What harm would it do to leave the spare clothing and furniture here in the gulch? It soothed her to imagine a native woman wrapping her chilled baby in one of Kirke's extra shirts or taking the mattress back to her shelter.

She pinned her grandmother's sapphire brooch to the front of her dress. It looked ludicrous, of course, glimmering on the torn, stained fabric, just as Abigail Arcan's silk dresses had seemed ridiculous in the wilderness. It was, though, one small reminder of home and family she could keep. She took it off again and pinned it carefully inside her dress pocket. Then she wrapped her books in a flour sack and hid them in a cavity in the gully wall, not sure why she was making the effort but sickened by the thought of burning them. The spinning wheel she left where it was on the sand.

While James strapped the heavy, full water kegs to the back of a balky driving ox, Juliet took her sewing scissors and made the first cut in the wagon cover. The canvas slit easily, and she tried not to think about what she was doing

as she sliced it into fourths. Then she bundled the supplies
and the bedding and bound them with rope. James struggled
to hold the cattle still while Juliet hoisted the burdens onto
their backs and secured the knots. It was mid-afternoon
before they were ready to leave.

She took one last look at the place she knew would be
carved in her memory for life. The bare, clay gully walls
jutted toward the sky where drab clouds scudded by, blown
by the cold wind. Snow fell again and covered her pathetic
belongings, scattered about the ravine like lost chapters of
her life. Ahead, the way was slippery and wet, but James
was certain there would be no snow once they reached the
flats below.

He led the way. Juliet followed, helping Kirke over the
rocks as they clambered down the canyon. She made a point
not to look back.

CHAPTER 21

Later in the afternoon, they came upon the charred remains of the Mississippians' nine wagons spread along a steep section of the lower gully. The wheels, mired in the sand and hung up on boulders, were attached to blackened axles; the wagon beds were piles of burned boards and charcoal. She knelt and felt the ashes. They were cold. Castoff belongings littered the ground: old fry pans, a couple of metal horseshoes, frayed ropes and harnesses, dirty tin plates. Columbus picked up a leather pouch filled with lead bullets and put it in his pocket, and Johnny found a stained gray shirt that he tied around his waist. It hung to his feet, but Juliet said nothing. He would tire of it soon enough.

The canyon walls finally fell away to the north and south, and the gulch dumped its outwash over the slopes below. James was right: There was no snow on the valley floor. Far in the distance, a range of mountains bulged up and beyond that, just as Mr. Manly had said, was yet another range. The farthest one had a long sloping ridge that ended in a gradual snowy peak. Directly in front of them, widening out for perhaps forty or fifty miles, was more desert interspersed with the same odd looking, spiky short trees, scraggly grease-wood, and creosote bush. Juliet shrank from the view.

"Oh, Mother, must we cross all that?" Columbus despaired. "That's too far to walk."

"Well, boys, we'll just do a little bit at a time," Juliet said. "You can pretend you're Lewis and Clark exploring a new land."

"I'm not going that far," Columbus said crossly. "Why can't we just build our new home right here?"

"There's no water here, Col," Johnny told his older brother. The two were close in size now but poles apart in character. "You can't build a cabin where there's no water. Or no hunting."

"I don't see why we came on this trip anyhow. This place is a lot worse than back home."

Juliet put a hand on Col's shoulder. "Come along, Col. Let's guess where we'll be by tonight and see if we can make it that far."

"I think we'll be at those mountains," Johnny said. Juliet was silent. The first range of mountains was easily three or four days away.

"There's a stream down there somewhere, isn't there, Mother?" Col asked. "I guess we'll get to a creek tonight so we can fill the kegs again."

By nightfall, though, they were still clambering over the rocks of the alluvial outwash at the mouth of the canyon.

Juliet peered into the distance for a glimpse of the Mississippians or perhaps even the Jayhawkers, but she saw only a hopeless expanse of land. The men must be out there somewhere, trudging across the valley in their faded clothing, but without the white, billowing wagon tops to flag them, they would be nearly invisible.

They walked until the boys could go no farther and James's face was the color of ashes. It took another hour to stake out the cattle and clear a campsite in the rocks. James retrieved the bedding from the back of their favorite driving ox, Old Red. It was still wet and cold from last night's snow so he spread it over the ground to dry, but he made no fire. Juliet served cold crumbled biscuits for supper while the children sat exhausted. She tried not to think about the spiders and snakes lurking under the rocks. There was no choice but to lie down on the ground beside James and the boys and try to sleep. Goodness knew she was tired enough.

Even so, she stayed awake listening to the night noises and watching the stars turn slowly in the black sky. A coyote yipped in the valley and then another and another until the entire earth seemed to sing their wild song. Then, as if by a signal from some unseen conductor, they stopped. She raised her head to be sure James had his gun beside him and then moved closer to his broad, warm back. There was a stone under her shoulder blade and another under her thigh. She shifted again. James stirred and went back to sleep.

Something rustled nearby. She told herself it was just one of the harmless lizards they saw scurrying in the sand during the daylight, but sat up and pulled her shawl over her head and scrutinized the rocks and greasewood in the starlight. Nothing moved. Eventually she reclined again, pulling her feet up inside her skirts and tightening the blanket around her neck. Snakes, she was fairly certain, didn't come out at night. She wasn't sure about those gigantic spiders. Or the horrible bugs she'd seen with pointed stingers that curled up over their backs.

She forced herself to think of something—anything—else until she drifted into a broken sleep.

As soon as the sky turned from black to silver, James got up. He left camp for a while and then returned to wake the boys. The air no longer held its cold bite. In fact, a warm breeze wafted up from the flats below.

"Let's go," James said. "We're at least two days behind the Mississippians again."

She helped him load the packs and kegs onto the four driving cattle. The big animals bawled and sidled away. Juliet wondered if they would ever be docile enough to carry the boys. Right now, the children would not be safe; even Big Jake, the gentlest of the oxen, was acting up.

She grabbed Kirke's hand and started out on the day's quota of miles. James was ahead, searching for places where the Mississippians might have left a trail of sorts. He walked stooped over, his hand across his abdomen, leading them straight into the desert and toward those unyielding mountains.

CHAPTER 22

It was three long days later when the cattle bolted, making a beeline toward an unseen destination and carrying the precious packs with them. James scrambled after them, but they were gone within minutes—gone with the food, the bedding, and the water kegs.

"They must smell water," James panted as he waited for Juliet and the boys to catch up. "There must be something up ahead. We'll catch them."

He pushed forward and Columbus followed, leaving Juliet with the two younger boys. With Kirke on her hip, she hurried through the greasewood until her knees trembled and Johnny was lagging behind. She turned and waited for him. The glittering afternoon sun was warm, and its white glare was so intense that it was hard to keep her eyes open. The next time she squinted into the west, James and Col were gone.

She didn't know how they could have disappeared so quickly. Logically, there must be a dip in the land, an arroyo or a hollow, but her heart pounded. She strained to see through the shimmer of harsh light and then stood on a rock for a better view. There was nothing but this enormous landscape and the huge dome of azure sky overhead.

When James was out of sight, she knew his absence was necessary, but when she couldn't see one of the children, anxiety overwhelmed her. Now, she had a frantic urge to run ahead and reassure herself that Col was safe. Instead, she scooped Kirke onto one hip and lifted Johnny onto the other. With the weight of both boys pressing her feet into the ground, she strode for another hundred yards until she was breathless.

She slid Johnny to the ground and looked ahead again. The view mocked her, offering only more stony distance, greasewood, and glaring light. What if Col wandered off and James was too preoccupied with the cattle to notice? She pushed away the feeling of panic and hastened ahead.

She had to be careful to follow James's route and not inadvertently veer in a new direction. The trail was evident if she looked carefully. She tried not to think about the fact that the packs and water kegs were gone.

"Johnny, can you hurry up a bit?"

"I'm making my legs go as fast as I can, Mother."

She had heard stories of lone women and children carried off by warriors. Her eyes darted to the boulders scattered on the desert floor before she drew herself up straight and made herself stop. Prayer—not wild imaginings—was what she needed now.

A few moments later, she and the boys came to the edge of a dry river and looked down into the gravelly bed.

James and the cattle were clustered around an open puddle of water. Columbus slumped against a boulder. Juliet gave a tired cry and, holding Kirke and Johnny by the hands, scrambled down the bank to join them.

"Don't drink it," were James's first words to her. "The cattle can manage it, but it's not fit for humans."

"Mother, I tried some, and it tasted terrible, and now my stomach hurts." Columbus was hunched over.

"I don't mind if it tastes bad. I want some!" Johnny tried to wriggle his hand from hers.

She looked at James, and he shrugged his shoulders. "It's not going to kill them. It will just make them sick."

She bent and scooped up a taste. It had an unpleasant, bitter-salty flavor, but her whole body craved it. It would be better to endure a stomachache than to die of thirst. She looked again at James, and he reluctantly nodded his head.

"All right, boys. But only a little."

Later, she sat on the packed dirt with her knees pulled up to her chest to relieve the cramping. Beside her, Kirke squealed in pain. Johnny dozed, but now and then he cried out in his sleep. James was on his fourth trip away from camp. She rubbed Kirke's back and then tried massaging her own stomach, but it didn't help.

It was near nightfall when James returned. He had the bedding, which he spread on the ground for them. When he crawled under the covers next to her shivering, she took his cold hand in her own. With all the hardships out here, all the annoyances and fears, there were times when she nearly forgot how much she loved her husband.

She finally fell asleep and didn't awaken until the sun shone across her face. The boys still slept. James was gone with his gun. Perhaps he would find one of those big leathery lizards to shoot and roast. She could scarcely believe she was hoping for a lizard to eat. What, she wondered, would her gentle family back home think of that?

She rose and spoke to the boys. When they crawled from under the quilts, their faces were pale but their stomach-aches were gone.

"Do we have to climb over those mountains, Mother?" Johnny shaded his eyes from the low morning sun.

"It looks as though we can skirt around them. That would be much easier than trying to go over them."

"Do you think Father will like that idea?"

Juliet nodded. "Yes, I'm sure he agrees. We'll turn south and follow the foothills around that big triangular mountain. After that we should have only one more range to go. Los Angeles might be closer than we think."

CHAPTER 23

They circled the bare rock foothills until the land began to slope upward, making its long, slow way to the distant horizon. It looked as though they were entering a low pass between two ranges of naked mountains. Juliet paced out the distance in her mind, trying to estimate how many weary strides it was to the largest gray boulder up ahead or how many miles until they were opposite the jagged canyon that sliced the harsh wall to the right. Underfoot, multitudes of gray rocks of every size piled up over a coarse gravel bed. The cattle balked at the poor footing, and Kirke and Johnny kept falling on the stones that slid and shifted beneath their weight.

She wished for the wagon, even though getting it over this stony ground would have been a nearly impossible struggle. She knew that its canvas sides had been no real protection against a lightning storm or cold temperatures, but she had felt safe inside, as if the flimsy fabric provided a refuge from the landscape's empty immensity. Once or twice when she was alone, she had actually huddled in the familiar quilts and pulled them over her head like a child hiding. There in the silent darkness, she felt protected and peaceful enough to pray more deeply than the quick, desperate pleas she sent heavenward a hundred times a day.

She burrowed her chapped hands in her apron pockets and began counting her steps to the boulder. In this vast country, distance was tricky. If she estimated that an object was fifty strides away, it would be three times that. A gulch that looked to be a few hours' travel would retreat before her eyes until they finally reached it two lengthy days later.

She stopped for a moment to let the boys catch up. Her fading family was spread out over the landscape like a grim line of soldiers battling the enormity of this place. James, not quite erect, was close behind her. He squinted doubtfully at the horizon. His shaggy beard did not conceal the sharp dips and hollows in his face.

Behind him were the boys, all three together, picking their way over the rocks. Their faces were grimy and their unkempt hair blew into their eyes. Even from where she stood, Juliet could see the pathetic trousers they wore—torn, patched, and torn again—and the cowhide moccasins that, despite her care in making them, were scant protection from the stony ground. Every bit of playfulness had been crushed out of them by this grinding journey. Now, they urged the cattle through the dotted maze of low bushes like somber, miniature adults.

"We'll head toward that low pass and hope for a view of what's ahead," James said. His voice was low and raspy, as if his vocal cords were drying up with the rest of him.

"Do you think we're getting anywhere close, James? It seems as though we've traveled far enough to be somewhat near the settlements by now."

"I don't know, Juliet. There's still another mountain range ahead."

"Kirke is looking peaked, even from here."

"He needs a lift, but I'm too weary to carry him. We could try putting him on Big Jake's back—he's the calmest of the oxen, I think—but I'm afraid the old chap would protest. Then we'd have a hurt child." James rubbed his hand over his face.

"You're right. Big Jake needs a few more days to get accustomed to carrying a load. Maybe I can piggyback Kirke for a while."

"Juliet, you're not much bigger than he is, you know."

She turned to him, her face utterly serious. "I'll carry him to the settlements and back, James, if it will help. I'm determined we're not to be . . . well, *stalled* out here."

Walking all those miles and working around camp—lifting the cast iron Dutch oven, the mounds of bedding, and the children—had made her tough and wiry. Every ounce of her body fat was gone, turned into stringy muscle. Still, the lack of water made her tongue swell until she could hardly swallow, and she trembled from exertion when she carried Kirke. When she stood up suddenly, the desert spun around her as if reminding her of its power and strength.

There were moments when she felt like giving up. Of course, it was unthinkable. Giving up would mean certain slow death for her family here in this desolate, sobering spot. Buzzards would tear at their flesh, and no one would ever know what had become of them. Pressing on wasn't just a possibility. It was the only choice.

She had known hardship before. Scratching a life from the Michigan wilderness taught her about grinding toil and doggedness—and hunger. Plenty of times back home her whole body ached from lifting, digging, and scrubbing. Along with the unending chores, though, there had been feelings of security and accomplishment. Out here, she could put her hard-earned muscles and persistence to good use, but she could not banish the terrible uncertainty and the dreadful possibilities that weighed her down like lead.

She turned again to the horizon. Perhaps they would reach the stark crest by nightfall. She imagined looking out over the valley beyond. She knew not to indulge in hoping for a clear lake or a fresh, cool river. But wasn't it possible that this long, slow climb would bring them out of the desert and into a place that had at least a small pond and a little grass for the cattle?

Perhaps the second range of mountains Mr. Manly saw was the lush, green Sierra Nevada. The thought warmed her like a beam of sunlight. Once they reached the Sierras, this terrible desert would be behind them and they would be near the settlements. There would be water. According to hearsay, the Sierras were replete with cold sparkling creeks, sheltering evergreens, and wild berries. They would summon the tired travelers into their southernmost foothills where Juliet would quench her family's thirst with water straight from the snowfields.

If only they could see the Sierras, she knew they would survive.

CHAPTER 24

Juliet finally acknowledged that it would take another entire day of climbing this long grade to reach the low summit. The children struggled up the rise, slipping and jumping from stone to boulder to rock, while Juliet grappled with the unsure footing herself. She urged the reluctant cattle up the stubborn grade. By nightfall, the horizon appeared as far away as it had at noon.

The ground looked like a dried-up streambed or the bottom of a long-gone lake. After dark, she and James lifted and tossed rocks out of the way to clear a small, uneven place to sleep. By moonlight, Juliet offered the boys half a biscuit. The water was gone, and the bedding was still strapped to Big Jake. James either didn't notice or didn't care. She sat for a moment on a pile of dark rocks listening to the coyotes yip at the round, yellow moon that illuminated the pyramid-shaped mountain they skirted.

She wondered why they didn't see coyotes during the day. Most animals in the desert probably came out at night, she decided, to avoid the hot sun during the summer months. Or perhaps the wild creatures here were simply too swift and stealthy for her family's untrained eyes to spot.

Finally, she went herself to remove the packs. Big Jake stood still as she untied the knots that held the bedding to his back, but shied away as the bundle slid to the ground. He couldn't be trusted to carry the boys yet. She spread a soiled quilt over the dirt for James and the children.

Without the tent, there was nowhere to change into her spare dress or even brush her hair, so she had worn the faded blue calico day and night since they burned the wagon. It was ripped and tattered around the hem and cactus spines were embedded in the threadbare fabric at her ankles. Worse than that, it had a bad odor and a dirty stiffness that she had never before experienced. It frightened her that she was almost too tired to care.

She spread a second quilt over the top of her already sleeping family. The air was chilly, but since the snowstorm, the weather had not been like December at all. Back home, there would have been silver icicles hanging from the eaves and ice on the pond thick enough to cut into blocks and pack in sawdust for summer. Snow would have drifted across the cabin's doorway and blocked the path to the barn. Here, the temperature felt more like March or April. She settled herself between James and Kirke.

James rose at sunup and roused the boys. They stood and then sank groggily onto the nearby stones while Juliet gathered the quilts and took them to Big Jake. He edged away from her and stiffened. She persisted and succeeded in tying the bedding to his back. He looked as though he might protest but listlessly gave himself a shake instead and then resignedly stood still.

Yesterday, Juliet had rationed the last few ounces of water from the keg as if they were gold. She had helped Kirke and Johnny and even Columbus hold the cup to their mouths as she had when they were toddlers in fear they might spill a drop of its precious contents. She finished the last, unsatisfying ounce herself.

Her whole body yearned to drink. If they could not find water soon, she didn't know how she could keep going, and she was sure Kirke would give out again. Johnny and Columbus were seriously dehydrated, too. The salt pork was gone like the bacon, the beans, and nearly all the flour. Even the apples she had dried and packed so carefully were down to a mouthful or two. There was no more tea or cornmeal. Only the coffee remained in good supply, and what good was coffee without water?

This unforgiving country certainly knew how to notch up its treachery. As the day progressed, James clambered up every gully in the foothills to the north searching for even the smallest spring. He returned each time and gave a curt shake of his head. Juliet scanned the arid mountainside for any elusive green patch, but the bare slopes yielded nothing, not even a muddy spot where they could dig down to find a drop or two. The cattle bellowed in misery, but the

boys were unnervingly quiet, except Kirke, who cried spo-
radic thin wails.

She turned to check on the children. They were a hundred yards behind her, stopped on the rocks. Columbus was
trying to hoist Kirke onto his back as he had seen Juliet do.
Kirke locked his arms in a chokehold around Col's neck, but
slipped down until his feet dangled just above the ground.
Col wobbled as he took a step and then pried Kirke's fingers
apart and let him drop.

"You have to jump up better, Kirke," Columbus was telling him. "Here, climb up on this rock and get on my back."

"I can't. My legs won't go."

They tried again, and this time Col fell forward when
Kirke's weight sagged onto him. Juliet saw his arm come down
hard on a rock. She left the cattle and hurried back to them.

"Are you hurt, Col? Your arm?"

Columbus ducked his head to hide his brimming eyes.
He lifted his arm to show her. His skin was abraded and a
long purple bruise started to appear, but there was no serious gash or ominous swelling.

"Thank goodness, it's just bruised, Col. I know it hurts,
though." She touched it gently.

"Mother, if something really bad happens, will we have
to leave one of us behind?" Col held his sore arm.

His boyish fears were still getting the best of him. Here
in this unimaginably difficult place, their lives were so

tenuous and fragile that one small incident could bring on disaster. And Col was old enough to see it. Fatigued and depleted, he invented all sorts of hideous possibilities that he would never think of back home as he skipped his way to school or fished in the creek. The worst of it was that he was completely correct. What would happen if someone did get seriously hurt? What if illness struck or dehydration made them unable to travel? What then?

She replied firmly. "Col, you must banish that thought this moment. There's no possibility that we would leave anyone behind. Especially not one of you children."

CHAPTER 25

Juliet and James reached the top of the long, slow grade together. They stood at last on the overlook and took in the scene below. Juliet felt the blood drain from her face. She released James's arm and sank down on a boulder.

It was not the Sierra Nevada that met her eyes. Instead, there was an enormous barren valley beneath them, dominated by rock and white salt flats and grim distances. Beyond it to the west, a massive wall of stark bare mountains rose abruptly for thousands of feet. She gaped at their dramatic, uncompromising ridgeline. The harsh sight spread north as far as she could see. A deathly silence seemed to echo from the depths of the forbidding valley, prevailing over the ringing in her ears.

Beside her, James sat down abruptly and covered his face with his bony hands.

Was there no respite from this relentless land? No end to its cruel, severe enormity that signaled death for their family? Juliet's heart began to pound. They could stay here and certainly perish. Go back and unquestionably perish. Or they could take on the nearly insurmountable task of crossing this vast, deep valley and the wall of hostile mountains beyond.

Beside her, James murmured. "My God, my God, why hast thou forsaken me?"

She felt a small hand on her shoulder and looked up. Johnny stood beside her, and she took him onto her lap. His tongue was swollen from thirst, so he didn't speak at first but sagged against her arm and laid his head on her shoulder. She could feel his despair as he surveyed the view ahead. She looked behind her and saw Columbus and Kirke a few hundred yards away. The moment she and James had stopped, they had sunk onto the nearest flat spot, stony as it was. The cattle halted immediately, too, and stood with drooping heads and caved-in sides.

For Johnny's sake, Juliet murmured the verses of the Twenty-third Psalm in his ear. Without lifting his head, he listened, and his words were slurred when he said, "Mother? I don't believe the part about the still waters."

"Hush, Johnny." She spoke softly. He was picturing cool springs from which to drink—now—and glistening ponds for swimming. "We just haven't reached them yet."

"Well, it's too far."

"I know it is, Johnny."

James reached over to pat Johnny's knee. He tried to moisten his lips to speak, but his tongue was too dry. He spoke anyway in his newly raspy tone. "Do you see that spot down there where it looks like there's snow on the ground?" He pointed far down into the arid valley to what Juliet knew was a salt flat. "When we get there, I believe Big Jake will be ready to carry you boys without bucking you off. You won't have to walk across that whole valley, John."

"Will we be there today, Father?"

"More likely tomorrow."

"Is there a drink down there?"

"We'll find something. Haven't we always found a spring so far?"

"Yes, Father. But we need one now. Kirke's crying."

"I know, son."

Juliet's heart had stopped pounding, but dread left a sick feeling in her stomach. How could they ever cross the merciless place below? If they found no water today, the children would be in serious danger.

She slid her son to the ground and stood up.

"We've got to press on," she told James. "We can't wait."

James looked at her blankly and then blurted out, "Do you know it's almost Christmas, Juliet?"

She stared at him. Christmas belonged to another world entirely. Back home it had been a simple, spiritual day with a single gift for each child that signified its vital place in the year. Out here, one day was like all the others. The season never seemed to change, and Juliet had long ago lost track of the date.

"Christmas," she repeated, and then after some thought she added, "Yes, I suppose it is."

CHAPTER 26

S he piggybacked Kirke until he could walk by himself
again. Her knees nearly buckled under his weight and
her parched throat felt as though it were cracking. The
ground was still an unrelenting, thick bed of gray stones,
so she placed her feet cautiously to avoid turning her ankle.
Keeping her eyes on the task of walking prevented her from
staring at the alarming scene below, at least.

*Yea, though I walk through the Valley of the Shadow of
Death, I will fear no evil.* Despite the familiar, comforting
words repeating themselves in her head, a terrible chill settled over her.

She stopped and made herself study the dreaded expanse
ahead. Surely, from this vantage point, the Mississippians
must be within sight. She shaded her eyes and squinted
but couldn't see any movement or anything that resembled
their dirt-colored shirts. Far ahead to her left, some whitish
clay hills eroded with sharp gullies tumbled down the larger
slope. The slanting sun made dark shadows in the ravines,
and the hills themselves were so bare of vegetation that they
resembled a child's crude drawing. Badlands, she decided.
An apt name.

If she had the strength, she would name some of these astounding places. The gleaming white salt flat on the valley floor. The peak to the west that jutted up a mile or two, frosted with snow at its summit. This huge basin she entered with such trepidation. The Valley of the Shadow of Death, it could be called, if the name didn't ring out with such an ominous warning for her family.

James was up ahead now, toiling his way between sparse greasewood and creosote bushes. Juliet saw him stop and bend over something large and dark sprawled on the rocks. She squinted again. It looked like a dead animal, but she knew better. They had spotted so little game that James had had the same bullet in his rifle for days.

Columbus and Johnny caught up with her.

"What is Father looking at?" Col asked. His lips were cracked and bleeding and his voice grated like an old man's.

"You boys go ahead and find out." Juliet struggled to form the words with her dry tongue.

The two older boys held Kirke's hands and helped him along. Juliet followed, watching them closely. Of the three of them, Kirke was definitely in the worst shape, stumbling and holding on to his brothers. Dehydration was wreaking havoc on his small body. Col and Johnny were enough bigger that they were faring slightly better.

When she reached James, she saw a rough campfire ring and a spot cleared of rocks for sleeping. James was crouched over the remains of a dead cow. It was then she noticed buzzards circling overhead.

"This is one of the Jayhawkers' animals." James looked up at her. "I can tell by that scarred ear. They must have looped around and found this same route."

"So they're up ahead along with the Mississippians."

"Yes. And look, Juliet. They still have their wagons. See where they've ground out a trail over the rocks? Those iron wheel rims have left scrape marks on the stones."

"How could they possibly get wagons over all these layers of rocks?"

"I don't know. Maybe this poor cow died from the effort. There's a bit of meat left on her bones, though."

"Is it still fresh?"

"It's a couple of days old. The dry air and the sun have begun to preserve it." He sliced off a sliver and put it in his mouth. Juliet's stomach churned. "No, it's not putrid yet."

Suddenly she was so hungry that she nearly asked James to slice off a raw piece for her, too, and the boys. Common sense and her roiling stomach stopped her.

"Col, gather some greasewood sticks, quickly. We'll make a fire and cook a good meal."

"Mother, may I have some meat first?" Col was agitated. "I don't mind if it's not cooked."

"Me, too, Mother. Maybe it got cooked enough by the sun." Johnny started toward the cow.

"Stop, boys. It will take only a minute to heat some for you."

Johnny did as he was told, but Col sidled closer to the dead animal.

"Col, come away from there."

James used his rifle to spark a fire and within minutes was fanning tinder-dry greasewood branches into small flames. Then he crouched over the dead animal, his hands sticky from slicing long thin morsels from the bones. He found a sharp stick, poked it through the meat, and gave it to Juliet.

"This is for the boys. I'll cut more for us."

The aroma of the roasting beef was almost more than she could bear. It took every speck of her self-discipline not to yank it from the fire and stuff it into her own ravenous mouth. Kirke held onto her skirts, pointing at the browning strips and crying. Johnny and Columbus hovered nearby until she felt it had cooked long enough. She quickly divided it for them and pulled their portions into tiny pieces so that it wouldn't lodge in their dry throats.

James handed her a second stick of raw beef and then a third and a fourth. She held them directly in the flames. The heat singed her knuckles, but she hardly noticed. When the meat was charred on the outside, she handed one back to him, gave more to the boys, and finally sat on a rock to devour her own portion. It was tough and stringy, but no one cared.

James sat cross-legged beside the carcass and continued to slice off thin strips. While Juliet chewed, greedily at first and then more slowly, she roasted a supply to carry with them. It wouldn't last long before it spoiled, but it would keep them for a day or two. It would be an unspeakable comfort in this lonely wilderness. Now if only they could find water before dark.

The thought of losing one of her children—or James—made her choke on her last bite. If this extreme and dangerous place exacted such a toll, she knew she would never recover. Hastily she wrapped the meat, gathered her skirts, and stood up. They had to press on, and quickly. Every moment they delayed, Kirke became more dehydrated. They all did.

CHAPTER 27

Tonight's stars were the tiniest pricks of light in an immense black universe. She stared up at them, too tired to sleep. The last stanza of a long-memorized poem ran through her mind like a chant. It was Henry Kirke White again, she remembered, writing about the Christmas star.

> *It was my guide, my light,*
> *my all,*
> *It bade my dark*
> *forebodings cease;*
> *And through the storm and*
> *danger's thrall*
> *It led me to the port of*
> *peace.*

That is what they needed, she thought: a Christmas star to lead them through danger's thrall. But no kind, bright light shone out from the multitudes glittering in this vast sky. These stars were remote and cold—not at all like the friendly, twinkling ones she remembered from home.

She wondered if James had figured out which day was Christmas. Perhaps it had come and gone without their knowing it.

The weeks of travel ran together in her mind, but she tried to reconstruct the route and the days. Finally, she sat up. With her calloused finger, she scratched marks in the sandy patch of ground they had cleared for camp, one for each day since her sad good-bye to Sarah Bennett and the other women. It wasn't until the moon dipped behind the black mountains that she had untangled the days enough to conclude that tomorrow would be December twenty-third or twenty-fourth.

She knew she shouldn't think about home, but tonight she couldn't help herself. She pictured the rough-hewn little house she and James had left behind and the new log church where they had celebrated the Advent season. Suddenly the smell of plum pudding filled the night air, and she drew in a deep breath in disbelief. No, it was simply her imagination playing tricks. The air held the same odd odor of creosote bush mixed with the dusty smell of dry sand and stone. She closed her eyes and pictured the snowy fields where James had taken her sleighing when they were courting. He had put harness bells on the horses—Juliet could hear their merry jingle even now—and they spent whole afternoons dipping breathlessly into hollows and flying across the drifts.

James captivated her from the first day she met him. His irresistible enthusiasm, his unwavering belief in God, his comfortable way with strangers, and his youthful exuberance—squelched now by thirst and fatigue and illness—intrigued her. When he asked her to go on their first sleigh ride, she accepted immediately, to the consternation of her father. He felt that the young circuit rider was rather too brash and impetuous to make a responsible suitor for his daughter.

She rolled over and rested her head on James's shoulder. Her father had been right, she knew. Her husband's hasty decisions and bold confidence often affected them all. Nevertheless, he was as solid as these never-ending mountains. She could never have found another who matched his sense of honor and decency. Conversation between the two of them, under normal circumstances, bubbled up as if from a fountain. He surprised and delighted her with his engaging remarks.

Beside her, Kirke awakened crying for a drink. She hushed him and pulled him closer, but his fretting continued. They had found a little water in the late afternoon, enough for each of them to have about four ounces. It was just enough to keep them from dying, Juliet thought wryly, and it didn't begin to quench their all-consuming thirst or help the poor cattle.

She was still astounded at the ingenious little handmade bowl James had found perched beneath a seeping crack in the hillside. It was nearly full when they came upon it. It wasn't the first sign they had seen of the native peoples, although it may have been the most inventive. The bowl was shaped from what looked like white clay from the badlands to the west. They had divided the water equally, and then Juliet guiltily replaced the bowl and secured it in the crack. Someone's entire existence depended upon the slow drip of that one tiny spring. Juliet hoped that the loss of one day's water wouldn't cause them misery. Perhaps they would think a wild creature had drunk the collected bowlful.

In the morning when she awoke, James was gone. She peered through the early light to the badlands. James had made his way to the top of a bare siltstone mound and was staring down into the valley. He looked insignificant there, perched in the dawn sunlight amid the barren ridges and gullies. At another time, she could have appreciated their beauty, for the low sun radiated a deep orange light across the stark clay knolls and cast long, dark blue shadows in the ravines.

He was searching, she knew, for water. She would hear his report soon enough. In the meantime, she shook out the bedding and rolled it into a compact bundle. She talked softly to Big Jake as she approached, and this time he didn't shy away as she placed the light load on his back. When she reached underneath him for the rope, he flinched and sidestepped but allowed her to tie the knots. Tomorrow, she would use a bigger, heavier load and would begin teaching Kirke how to sit on Big Jake's broad back without fidgeting or letting his dangling feet touch the animal's sides.

While the children slept, she unbraided her long brown hair. Back home she never would have imagined letting it become so dirty and unkempt. She tried to brush it with her slender fingers and let the breeze freshen it, but it was no use. It felt greasy and tangled and matted with dust. With an irritated sigh, she quickly plaited it again, pinned the braid up, and pulled her sunbonnet on.

CHAPTER 28

James returned as sunlight inched across the valley below. Juliet doled out a few shriveled, blackened strips of beef, and they all sat chewing them for a few moments before she hurried them to leave.

"Tonight will be Christmas Eve, everyone," James said wearily. "Let us remember the occasion."

The boys looked up at him but said nothing. Back home, they would be asking if there would be sugar lumps under their pillows or if they could skate on the frozen creek. Juliet would be at the big, black woodstove, hurrying to get the goose started before the church service. She would light an extra kerosene lantern for the breakfast table, and James would say grace in his usual long-winded style. The boys would swing their legs impatiently, waiting for the moment they could bite into the hot cross buns.

Juliet shook her head to clear her thoughts.

"Did you see any sign of water, James?" she asked, not wanting to hear the reply.

He glanced at the children. "I do believe there's water somewhere up ahead," he said carefully.

"How far, Father?" Johnny asked eagerly.

"Well . . . it's hard to tell," James answered, and Juliet knew he had seen nothing. "We'll just keep walking and see how far we get."

She fought a wave of despair as she stumbled along, first holding Kirke's emaciated hand and then carrying him. It wasn't until noon that she began to feel light-headed. She had glanced up to watch a large hawk circling in the sky when the ground spun around her so violently that nausea overcame her. She sat down quickly, still holding Kirke, and closed her eyes until the dizziness subsided. When she opened them, she noticed that James was using his rifle as a cane. He wobbled as he stood watching her. The two older boys had dropped farther behind.

"I'm going to take the cattle and scout ahead, Juliet. Can you manage by yourself?"

"I believe so. Be careful, James, and find us some good water."

"Remember, the animals are searching just as hard as we are."

The thought comforted her. Even if James missed a slight seep or a spring, the cattle would smell it. As frenzied as they were, they were likely to trample any damp spot into an utter mud hole, though. It had happened before, and no one was able to hold them back.

James turned and picked his way over the rocks while she sat and waited for Col and Johnny to catch up. Kirke leaned against her, lethargic and unnaturally still. His eyelids drooped and his skin had a bluish tinge, especially his cracked lips. She shook him gently, and he looked at her dully but didn't speak.

"Kirke!" She shook him again. "Are you all right?"

The boy didn't answer. Juliet stood up and hoisted him onto her back again. To her practiced eye, it looked as though he was nearly slipping into unconsciousness. She glanced back at Johnny and Col. They were resting on boulders, but Johnny raised his hand in a weak salute when she beckoned at them to come along.

Each moment felt like an hour as the sun moved its sluggish, deliberate way across the sky. Every footstep seemed a monumental feat. The only reality was the agonizing distance, the measured pace, and her child deteriorating on her back.

By sundown, Juliet knew that when her vision turned black, she needed to sink to the ground quickly so she didn't fall with Kirke. They didn't need injuries added to this predicament—a head cracked on a boulder, a shattered ankle, a broken arm. After a few moments of rest, she was able to press on. Daylight faded along with her courage. There was no sign of James. The boys lurched and stumbled over the rough ground beside her, failing rapidly, while Kirke slumped on her back, too still and quiet.

"There must be a drink up ahead for us," she said to Col and Johnny for the hundredth time, forcing the words from her split lips. Over the past weeks, she had invented a thousand techniques for urging the boys—and herself— along the trail, but they were not working tonight. Several times, she had to speak sharply to Johnny to get him to continue trudging. He normally was persuaded with a gentle suggestion. She had never needed strong words with him.

Without warning, she felt confused about the direction to take. She looked for the cattle's tracks to show her the way, but she couldn't find them on the stony terrain in the increasing darkness. In a daze, she laid Kirke on a boulder and quickly got down on her hands and knees to look. Hurry. She must hurry. Stones pushed up through her long calico skirt and bruised her legs, but she ignored them as she searched for signs that James and the animals had passed this way. Finally, she found a hoof print in deep gravel. Dizziness overtook her again as she hoisted Kirke to her back, but she kept on, stopping now and then to drop to her knees and look for tracks in the faint, silver starlight.

It must have been close to midnight when she heard a shout up ahead. She tried to call back, but no sound came from her parched throat.

"Can you yell back, Col? That must be your father."

Col shouted, but his voice was weak. Juliet could only hope that James had heard.

They labored on until James's dark figure came into view. He was resting on a boulder, breathing as if he had just run a footrace.

"Oh, James, is there water here? Kirke needs some this moment!" Her voice was frantic and slurred as she laid an unconscious Kirke on her husband's lap.

"No. The cattle stampeded about five miles ahead. They've found water somewhere up there—probably about six miles from here. I turned around and came straight back for you."

Six miles farther. Six miles! Kirke would certainly die before she could carry him that far.

James's eyes searched her stricken face and then Kirke's blue skin.

"I've got a little strength, Juliet, and I know the way. I can take him from here. You sit and rest. When you can, bring Johnny and Columbus." He struggled to his feet with Kirke cradled in his arms. The boy's arms and legs dangled limply.

"Hurry, James. He's not going to last much longer." Her throat constricted from fear and dehydration until she could hardly breathe.

"I'll get him there in time, Juliet, or I'll die trying."

CHAPTER 29

B ack home, she never thought of six miles as a long distance. She had walked twice that far on the leafy, winding trail along the St. Joseph River to nurse her sick cousin Lila. But tonight the stark miles seemed to sprawl out forever. She tried to add up the number of steps in just one mile of dark, stony desert, but couldn't figure the simple sum.

Johnny and Columbus drooped beside her.

"Six miles. That's far, isn't it, Mother?" Johnny's words were indistinct.

"A little far, yes." She wanted to say more, but it was such an effort to talk. She forced her words past the cottony swell of her tongue. The night air hurt her raw dry throat, and she tried to swallow.

"We'll have a drink at the end, though?"

"Yes."

"How will Kirke take a drink if he won't wake up?" Col's eyes were downcast and his voice trembled. He sounded as though his mouth were filled with dry bread.

"Your father will find a way." She wished she felt as certain as she sounded.

She desperately wanted to hurry ahead and help James find the water that could save Kirke's life. But Johnny and Col were stumbling badly and their tongues protruded from between their dry lips. If she tried to hurry them, they wouldn't last the distance. She waited for them to inch their way through the black expanse, stopping every twenty yards or so to rest their wobbling legs.

It was as if she were locked in her old recurring nightmare, the one that made her awaken with a panicked cry. In her dream, she would feel a desperate need to flee from some terrible unseen danger, but her feet would not move. She would be frozen in place, frantic with the urge to run.

She tried silently reciting verses to soothe the frenzied knot in her middle but couldn't remember the familiar lines. Once she tried to carry Johnny when he stumbled and fell, but he was simply too heavy and she was too weak. On hands and knees, she searched out the trail—a hoof print here, an overturned stone there. The night—and the miles—seemed to go on forever.

It was halfway between midnight and dawn, she estimated, when she thought she smelled water. She wondered if her brain was playing tricks again, as it had when she smelled plum pudding, but a little while later she could make out a high, silhouetted bluff and what looked like leafy undergrowth.

"I hear it!" Johnny cried. "I hear water! Where is it, Mother?"

Unexpected golden firelight flickered off the cliff, and without a moment's hesitation, the boys began to stumble toward it. Juliet followed. There was an unusual stillness, and she realized that, for once, the cattle weren't bawling.

She drove her legs toward the firelight. There were few things in life she felt she could never bear, but one of those was the loss of a child. If Kirke had perished for want of water, she knew she would never forgive herself—or James. She lifted her face to the heavens, praying for a miracle.

"Not too much, boys! You'll be sick if you drink too much," James was telling Col and Johnny as she dragged herself closer. But where was Kirke? She looked about frantically. James came to meet her in the darkness.

"I made it, Juliet. I made it in time. I got some water down his throat. He needs more, but for now he's sleeping."

"Oh, thank God, James!" In an instant, her remaining strength drained away, and she grabbed her husband's arm. He led her to Kirke and gently pulled an unfamiliar blanket from the little boy's face. In the flickering firelight, she could see that he was breathing evenly, and although his lips were still dark, some of the color had returned to his face. She knelt and kissed his forehead.

Now that the danger was gone, the full magnitude of the crisis came over her. She buried her face in her hands, too limp to move. James sat down beside her without saying a word.

It was a few minutes before she lifted her head and noticed the Mississippians. Just beyond the fire, they were sprawled under blankets like twelve or fifteen dark boulders. Captain Towne sat cross-legged on the ground, cleaning his rifle. She looked at him across the flames but couldn't speak. Behind him in the blackness, a spring trickled. She could hear it gurgling and murmuring and filling her with peace.

She knew she had to get up and take a drink. The need pressed in on her from every direction, but she couldn't move. She leaned back against a warm boulder and closed her eyes.

"Mrs. Brier! You mustn't fall asleep without taking some water and food. You won't wake up again if you do." Captain Towne stood over her.

"Juliet, sit up." James was beside her with a cupful of water. "Towne's right. You must take a drink."

He helped her to a sitting position and held the cup to her lips. Water dribbled down her chin, and she caught it in her hands before she remembered that there was more almost within her reach. She took the cup and tried to drink a mouthful of the cold water, but with her throat so swollen and sore she had trouble swallowing. James helped her try again.

Mr. Towne took Johnny and Columbus to his blanket and let them slide underneath it beside Kirke. He brought another and handed it to Juliet.

Before she slept, she asked James to refill her cup, and then she awakened Kirke. The little boy drank greedily before lying back and falling asleep again. She tucked the blanket around his neck and gently brushed the hair away from his face.

She slept until the sun was high in the sky. When she opened her eyes, she could see that they were camped at the base of the bluff that had been outlined in the starlight. Lush, tangled vegetation surrounded the spring where it bubbled from the earth and flowed out onto the desert floor until it disappeared into the porous gravel. The water was clear and clean, and there was scuffed, packed dirt at the easiest access points. Old, bleached animal bones littered the ground around blackened fire rings. Juliet felt a surge of alarm. She and her fellow travelers were undoubtedly in Shoshone country by now. She wondered why it hadn't occurred to her last night that the native people would certainly choose to camp here. It was the only habitable spot for miles. Quickly, she scanned the bluff, but only the blue sky above met her eyes.

The boys were still asleep. James was gone, and the Mississippians were milling about cooking, cleaning their fry pans, eating or drinking from their tin cups, swirling the water in their mouths before swallowing it. She rose to greet them.

"Morning, Mrs. Brier," one of the young men welcomed her. "We've boiled up some beef for you."

"Thank you. It's good to see you all."

"You folks were nearly done for last night, Mrs. Brier," said Mr. Towne, handing her a chunk of boiled meat. "You'll need a couple of days to recuperate. I never saw a child so dehydrated as your little Kirke."

"Yes. James barely made it in time."

"All's well that ends well. His coloring is good this morning."

James appeared from the thicket carrying a dripping canteen. He was still walking hunched over, but his voice was stronger.

"Good morning, Juliet. I have a surprise for you."

"What is it, James?

"Are you strong enough to let me show you? It's a short walk."

He took her hand and led her away from the fire to a second spring that bubbled from the hillside. Lush vegetation shielded it from view.

"Touch the water, Juliet. It's your Christmas gift."

"Christmas. Oh, James, it's Christmas Day, isn't it? I completely forgot."

She bent over and put her dusty hands in the water. Instead of the cold chill of groundwater, this spring was warm, as if it had been heated on a stove.

"Warm water . . . oh, James! Warm water!"

CHAPTER 30

The boys were awake when she and James returned to camp. Johnny was drinking again from his cup, and Columbus and Kirke were each chewing on a piece of boiled beef. Mr. Towne handed a chunk to Juliet and one to James as they sank down near the fire, exhausted by their short walk.

Juliet savored the meat as she sat in the cool sunlight with a cup full of water at her side. Kirke came to sit beside her. She gave him the water as she scrutinized his face. If she ignored the grime on his cheeks and around his mouth, he looked better. His eyes were alert today, even if he sat completely still.

One of the Mississippians, a large, dark-skinned man called Little West, lifted the heavy, black coffeepot from the coals and brought it to fill Juliet's cup. She thanked him. The coffee's delicious aroma wafted across her face and its warmth soothed her raw throat.

After a while, she stood and looked around her. Little West's two friends were sleeping in the sun. Two young brothers by the name of Turner were checking the cattle, and Captain Towne had climbed to the bluff overlooking the huge valley, searching for the Jayhawkers, no doubt. The others were absorbed in their camp chores.

Such thick vegetation surrounded the spring that she would be able to bathe in privacy. Back home, the autumn leaves would have blown away long ago, but here they lingered, clinging to the branches as if summer might last forever.

Oh, to rinse the weeks-old grit from her body! She could scrub her dress, too. In this desert air, the thin blue calico would dry quickly.

She found the dusty packs lying on the rocks where James had let them fall last night and pulled her crumpled spare dress from the first one she untied. She had included her gray wool at the last minute, thinking she might get cold enough to need it, but so far, she hadn't had enough privacy to change out of the old calico. She wished for soap, remembering that her handmade bars were gone with the wagon.

She scanned the bluff one last time, checked on James and the children, and then slipped away to the warm spring, parting the bushes with her free hand and clutching her dress with the other. She wished Sarah could be here, not only to stand guard but also to share this rejuvenating Christmas Day discovery.

She undressed quickly and submerged her body in the small, welcoming pool. The water washed over her like a warm breeze. Holding her breath, she submerged her head and scrubbed her long hair with her fingers, letting it stream out behind her with the water's flow. She rubbed her face and then her arms, feeling the dust drift away like a bad dream. It had been so long since she had seen her own small body that she was startled by the way her ribs and elbows and knees poked out at pointed angles and her stomach made a dip between her sharp hipbones. Her legs were skinny and bruised, her skin leathery.

Finally, she floated quietly on her back, watching the leaves and a few little birds flutter against the azure sky and pondering why this spring would bubble up here with warm water, of all things, unless it was a Christmas miracle.

After a time, she pulled herself from the pool and dried herself with her clean long skirts. She tugged the gray dress over her head, smoothing the deep wrinkles with her damp palms, and brushed her hair, 100 strokes, just as she did back home. Carefully, she unfastened her grandmother's sapphire brooch from the pocket of the stiff, stained calico and pinned it inside the pocket of her fresh dress. It would be safe there. Then she began washing the calico and her undergarments. Without soap, they wouldn't come clean, but at least the water would freshen them. Her handmade stockings had long since disintegrated.

When she returned to camp, she found that all three boys had fallen asleep again along with James. The intestinal ailment that plagued her husband was not gone, but at least his eyes weren't so sunken, and his color had improved. She sat near them as she patched the holes in Col's moccasins and then sewed the hole in Johnny's pants where he had fallen on a knee. There were patches on top of patches now, and the hems were shredded beyond repair. Johnny secured the pants around his shrunken waist with a piece of rope.

One of the Mississippians approached Juliet as she worked. His name was Mr. Carr and he wore an old tan overcoat with a ragged collar. His hair had been chopped off in a jagged line across his forehead.

"Don't you think you and the children should stay here, Mrs. Brier? You'd be more comfortable and you'd have plenty of water. Your children could rest and we men could go for help in the settlements."

"Thank you for your thoughts. But every step I take will be toward California."

"It would be risky to stay, too. God only knows how far we are from civilization, and you'd probably have worrisome company here," the man said, glancing at the old fire sites and the scattered bones on the ground. "We just don't know what's ahead, though. . . . It could be dreadful, ma'am."

"Yes. I know," she replied, looking out over the vast valley.

The Mississippians were drying more strips of meat over the fire. Juliet knew they would offer her a little beef to help her family cross the valley floor below, and she would reciprocate with ground coffee. Her mouth watered as the aroma of the roasting meat filled the air. It was best to save it, though, for the long days ahead.

When the boys awoke, she led them to the warm spring.

"Touch the water, boys. Feel the temperature."

"It's warm!" Columbus's forehead crinkled in perplexity. "Why is it warm, Mother?"

"It's our Christmas gift, boys. Why else would there be clean, warm water for us to enjoy out here?"

"May we get wet, Mother?" asked Johnny, already fumbling with his buttons.

"Yes, boys. Scrub yourselves well. We may not have another bath for a long while."

James pushed aside the branches and joined them.

"I think we should leave in the morning with the men," he told her. "Are you able?"

She hesitated for the briefest moment. "Yes. I'd like to stay here forever, but of course we have to carry on."

"The cattle are rejuvenated as much as can be expected. They've grazed well here and had their fill of water. Kirke is better, and I feel a little stronger, too. We'll try to keep up this time."

"Do you think Big Jake is ready to carry the children?"

"I think we can try it."

She wished for another day in this treasured spot, another few hours of respite from the harsh reality, but James was right. They must press on with the Mississippians.

CHAPTER 31

"A ny sign of the Jayhawkers?" James asked when Captain Towne returned from the top of the bluff.

"No. Of course, they'd be mighty hard to spot." Towne sat down and studied the group sprawled around the fire. The daylight was already fading. "We'll leave before dawn, men. We have to keep moving. But, Parson Brier, I've been thinking. It being Christmas night, would you give us a sermon?"

Juliet watched her husband. How frighteningly out of character for him to wait to be asked and then struggle for the energy to preach.

"That seems fitting, doesn't it?" He answered finally. "Give me a few moments to decide upon a topic."

He made no move to stand but sat with his chin propped in his hand for several minutes. Finally, he cleared his throat.

"I believe I'll speak on the importance of education."

Juliet wondered about his choice of topic. Perhaps he was simply trying to take their minds off their dire predicament. Curious, the men gathered closer to the fire, perching on stones or sitting on their blankets. Juliet quieted the boys and sat beside them on the rocks. James lurched to a standing position and wedged his leg against a boulder for balance. He looked better, she thought. His hair and beard were no longer matted and dirty, and, although he supported himself with his rifle, he was upright and his eyes were clear. She had scrubbed his threadbare shirt and trousers.

"Early education is a building block to a strong foundation," he began, looking at Columbus and Johnny. It was almost outlandish to hear his cultured voice expound upon a subject that seemed as remote as the moon out here where the pressing emergencies of survival weighed them down.

She sat up straighter. What was that noise behind her in the blackness? A large creature stumbling over the stones? All three of the children turned and looked. James's eyes followed their gaze, but he didn't stop speaking and his voice rose in volume.

"It is essential to study well to discipline the mind," he was saying, when out of the darkness a man's figure appeared. Juliet stifled a scream. From the corner of her eye, she saw Captain Towne reach for his gun. Little West and the Turner brothers scrambled to their feet. Kirke dove for Juliet's lap.

The dark figure stopped and held up his hands. "Whoa, there, friends. Would you shoot an old comrade?" Juliet knew the voice. She squinted harder into the blackness and recognized the ragged figure of Lewis Manly.

"Manly!" James called in relief.

"My God, Manly, we thought you were a Shoshone."
Captain Towne greeted him.

Juliet snatched her cup and rose to dip it in the spring
for him, but he was already flat on the ground with his face
in the cool water. A few minutes later, he joined the men at
the fire and ravenously bit into the charred beef strip James
handed him.

"Anyone else with you? Where's Rogers?" Towne
asked.

"No, I'm alone. Scouting for water."

"Are the Bennetts and Arcans and Wades all right?"
Juliet asked.

"They're two days back and out of water. They're terribly
dried out. Those poor children are desperate. Rogers stayed
with them."

"Everyone is still . . . alive?"

"Yes, ma'am. I'll fill my canteens and go back for them
after I nap for an hour or two." A bushy brown beard covered his face, but his cheekbones cast sharp shadows in the
firelight. His eyes were bloodshot and his shirt hung loosely
from his angular shoulders. He excused himself and went to
the spring for another drink.

Juliet followed.

"Is Sarah Bennett faring all right, Mr. Manly?"

"Well, she's distraught, of course. I've found her weeping several times. But she and the other women are holding

up as well as can be expected. It's the children I'm most worried about. Little Martha. And Charley."

"Yes. We almost lost our Kirke to thirst until we found this spring."

"The little ones have the hardest time. I need to hurry back with these canteens. I'm too tuckered out to leave now, though. I'll have to nap."

"You'll be able to make it back all right?"

"Well, I've made a promise, Mrs. Brier. Rogers and I gave our word to see those families through to the settlements. That's what we have to do."

A remarkable man, she thought. How much easier it would be for him to abandon the families and strike out for civilization alone. How much safer for himself. Yet he was committed to seeing these acquaintances safely to Los Angeles, even if it meant putting himself in danger.

"Thank you for watching over them. It's good of you, Mr. Manly. Give my fondest regards to them all, especially Sarah."

"I will, ma'am."

Juliet went to find the ground coffee. She would send some of her precious supply back to her friends. It didn't weigh much and it would give the families a heartening lift. She bound a few ounces into crumpled flour sacking and went to give it to Mr. Manly, but he was already asleep beside the fire. She placed the packet on top of his canteens.

In the morning, Juliet awoke just as the gray morning light began to brighten the sky. She lay beside James for a moment, watching the last stars fade. It was time to get up and load the packs. She lifted her head to see if Mr. Manly had left and then rubbed her dry eyes. Where was everyone?

In the dim light, she could see that Manly was gone. So were the Mississippians.

CHAPTER 32

Juliet worked quickly, cinching the packs onto the animals and filling the kegs before James tottered to his feet to help. Her hair was coming unfastened, and she shoved it into her sunbonnet so she could see to heft the last dripping keg onto Old Red.

"Hurry up and drink as much as you can hold, Kirke. You, too, Johnny and Col. Then we'll let the cattle have their fill."

The Mississippians had a few hours' head start, she estimated. Her fingers fumbled with the ropes as she tied the coffeepot to the packs. Why hadn't they awakened her? There was only one explanation. They simply didn't want to be encumbered with her and the children. Her hollow cheeks flushed.

James drove the cattle ahead. Juliet gave one last glance at the pleasant, welcoming place that had sheltered them for Christmas, and then she and the children began their slow march into the desert again.

They descended into what looked like a dry streambed between two high sandy bluffs, but suddenly the sparkle of water caught Juliet's eye and a slow, shallow creek fanned out in front of them. She caught her breath. Water again! She tasted it and recoiled.

Nevertheless, it felt good to remove her shoes and wade barefoot down its shallow bed. It was less tiring than trudging through the deep gravel and sand on either side. She and the children made haste downstream, watching some tiny bluish fish skitter into the shallows when they approached. It was a wonder anything could live in water so salty that it left white deposits along the banks.

Juliet tried to see ahead, but the creek bed was down in a hollow. Pools of deeper water blocked the way. Little lizards sunned themselves and darted under low plants as the children splashed near. On another day, in another age, the boys would have stalked those lizards by the hour, plotting ways to catch them, building ingenious homemade traps, and running after them with boundless energy. Now they barely noticed the small, quick creatures.

As they skirted the pools of brine and came up over the rise, Juliet could once again see into the distance. James and the cattle were plainly in sight, but the Mississippians weren't. Miles ahead—maybe twenty or so, if she had learned anything about the deceiving distances out here—a cloud of gray smoke hung over the desert.

"Col," she said to her oldest son. "Look ahead near those low whitish hills. What do you see?"

"It looks like smoke, Mother. Or maybe dust."

"Can you see any flames or people?"

"No. Just smoke."

A fire meant human life, and, oh, if it were the Jayhawkers! If not, though, she and James could be leading the children into a Shoshone camp. There was far too much smoke
to be mere campfires. Perhaps it was some sort of ceremo-
nial fire.

Up ahead, James stopped the animals and retrieved his
field glass from one of the packs. Juliet paused for a moment
and rubbed her small feet while she waited for the children
to catch up. Her skin felt stiff and irritated where the briny
water had dried. She put her broken-down shoes back on.

"Mother, you said we could ride Big Jake today," Columbus said as he came closer. His feet were already dragging.

"When we stop for a midday rest," she promised. "For
now, let's hurry and catch Father. Maybe he can see what's
making all that smoke."

A few moments later, James held the field glass out to
her.

"They're too far away to tell for certain, but I think I can
see some animals," James told her. "Take a look."

She held the lens to her eye and peered into the wavering distance. The land ahead was littered again with rocks
and stones and scattered greasewood to slow them down.
She thought she could make out a few dark figures through
the smoke.

"Do you suppose it's the Jayhawkers, James? I don't see any wagons."

"Me neither. I can't imagine it's a Shoshone camp, though. Why would there be so much smoke?"

"We've got to get closer."

"But not too close." James took the field glass and looked again.

"I think we should let Columbus try riding Big Jake. If Col can manage it, then we'll know it's fairly safe for Kirke."

"Big Jake is as ready as he'll ever be. Let's try it here where there's soft sand in case he misbehaves."

The big ox stood while James lifted Columbus onto his back. He sidestepped once and then resignedly lowered his head and, at James's command began plodding ahead. Juliet gripped the tether.

"Don't touch his sides with your heels, Col. And don't fidget."

By afternoon, Kirke and Johnny were riding. The ox picked his way through the stones, flicking his tail now and then but keeping a steady pace. A cool breeze brought the distinct smell of wood smoke. James looked again through the field glass.

"It's the Jayhawkers, I'm certain of it. Look, Juliet. I think I can see a wagon there on the right."

She stared through the long slender glass, scanning the scene. Near the smoke, there was a long dark shape that could certainly be a wagon. She saw a few stocky animals in the haze and smaller figures that could only be men.

"I think you're right. How long will it take us to reach them?"

"If we keep going until dark tonight and start early in the morning, we should be there by tomorrow evening. Let's hope they stay there that long."

They walked for another hour before the desert's colors took on the muted shades of evening and the mountains on either side of the broad valley began to look like dark paper cutouts against the lighter sky. Underfoot, the layers of rocks turned gray and then black. Finally, James stopped, and they began clearing a place to sleep. If they could overtake the Jayhawkers—and undoubtedly the Mississippians, too—they would once again find safety in numbers.

Perhaps this time, with the children riding, they could keep up with the men's faster pace.

CHAPTER 33

They arose before dawn and set off as the sunrise turned the sky a deep, brilliant gold. The color reverberated from every rock until it seemed as if the whole earth glowed with its warm light. Juliet led the way, holding fast to Big Jake's rope and herding the other cattle with Columbus, while James limped off by himself into the greasewood and caught up a little while later.

"They're burning their wagons," James told her as he looked through the field glass at mid-morning. "That means . . . " He glanced at the boys.

Juliet knew what it meant. The Jayhawkers' scouts had failed to find a wagon route over the harsh wall of mountains to the west. She drew in a long, quiet breath while her eyes scanned the line of rugged foothills rising like a stony fortress beneath the higher cliffs and outcroppings. Thus far, the capable Jayhawkers had overcome every grueling obstacle in their way, breaking trail through impossible canyons, streambeds, and passes to bring the wagons through. The route ahead must be more dreadful than anything they had yet encountered.

By noon, the Briers could see the camp clearly. It was nestled at the base of gentle, ash-colored sand dunes—the first they had seen—that rose and fell against the blue sky.

Compared to the stony ground underfoot, they looked inviting, even if utterly dry. A handful of men lay on the sand amid the carcasses of several cattle while others milled about. Off to the side, the wagons were burning, sending clouds of gray smoke into the air. The long, narrow wagon boxes were reduced to jumbles of charred boards piled high with blackened wheels and axles.

Juliet doled out a few ounces of water—already they were on the last keg again—and the last bits of dried apple as they traversed the remaining distance. By the time the sun was halfway to the western horizon, the aroma of roasting beef wafted on the air.

"Mother, do you think the Jayhawkers will give us something to eat?" Johnny asked.

"I hope so. They must be drying a supply of beef to carry with them over the mountains."

As the family topped a small rise, Juliet could see the Mississippians sprawled on the sand with the Jayhawkers. She did a quick count of both groups. Yes, it seemed as though they were roughly all there, more than thirty Jayhawkers and about half as many Mississippians. She looked illogically for the Bennetts or Arcans or Wades, but of course they were stalled far behind. She turned and used the field glass to search the barren landscape behind her, although she knew there was probably no hope of glimpsing her friends.

"Ho, there!"

Old William Isham broke away from the Jayhawkers and came to greet them. He was thinner than ever and his white beard reached to his chest.

"Greetings!" James gripped Isham's bony hand in his own. Juliet smiled, glad to see that the older man had made it this far. He must be at least fifty years old. His snowy hair fell over his eyes, and there were deep lines in his face that Juliet hadn't noticed before. His clothing gave off a dirty odor.

"Reverend and Mrs. Brier." Mr. Isham's voice was hoarse, but cordial. "We're happy to see you again. And the boys are here, all three of them."

Juliet knew he was thinking that it was a miracle the children had survived the desert this far. She helped them down from Big Jake's back, and Mr. Isham handed them each a blackened chunk of beef.

The extra cattle shied away from the scent of the bloody carcasses that littered the campsite, but Juliet finally was able to untie the ropes and let the dusty packs fall to the sand. Sand! Tonight they would have a soft bed with no stones to disturb their sleep. She removed her shoes and savored the cool softness between her toes as she spread a quilt for the boys. She was glad it was December and not summertime, or this sand might have been as hot as a stovetop. A cluster of green plants signaled a spring, but everyone avoided its brackish water.

The children wanted to nap. Juliet made certain they were asleep before she wandered among the men, greeting them by name and asking after their health.

"We've done all right, Mrs. Brier." It was Bill Robinson who spoke for his comrades. "We've made it this far. The lump on my head is better, although it's still a little tender." Under his dirty skin, the gash on his forehead had healed into a long red scar. His tan shirt had a rip down the front and it hung too loosely on his shoulders. "I had a hard go of it the first few days after we left you folks, but I'm a little better now."

"Doty, though, has a gut ailment," Robinson went on. "Maybe you can see to him, Mrs. Brier. He hasn't been himself for days. There's been no mischief." He smiled weakly. "And we still have a long way to go."

"I will," she answered. "Perhaps he has the same ailment my James has. James hasn't been able to shake it off, and it's sapping his strength. Look how thin he is."

"I noticed that he's lost a lot of weight, Mrs. Brier. But we're all skinnier out here without game or water. And now we'll be on foot, the way you folks have been. With the wagons gone and all the horses dead . . . "

"Is there no route for the wagons over the mountains?"

"None," Robinson said flatly. "Richards and Young scouted ahead. They said it would be hard enough to get pack animals over. We decided to kill our cattle so we'll have some jerky, at least, and they won't slow us down. We're going to try to move fast. We've got to get out of this cursed valley before we all perish."

CHAPTER 34

She continued through camp, swallowing bits of the tough beef strip Bill Robinson fetched her straight from the fire and greeting the worn-out men. Some she knew from earlier camps, but others she was barely acquainted with: dark-haired William Rood with his ever-present rifle; Sheldon Young, who reclined on the sand with his battered journal held to his chest; and tough, short Luther Richards. Asa Haynes, the Jayhawkers' soft-spoken captain, was tiredly roasting strips of beef. Of them all, Richards looked in the best condition. He seemed wiry, not just skinny, and he moved about camp with a subdued vigor the others lacked. He was about thirty, Juliet guessed, and his vigilant eyes were always squinting, as if he were scrutinizing everything he saw.

She found Ed Doty curled up on the sand, his knees drawn to his gaunt chest. Gray circles underlined his closed eyes. His long, black eyelashes rested starkly on his protruding cheekbones as though they had been drawn there with a fine ink pen. His cap-lock rifle was at his side.

She knelt and shook his arm.

"Mr. Doty. Wake up."

His eyes opened large in his smudged face.

"Mrs. Brier! Where did you come from?"

"We've just come into camp. We've been on foot for a long way now."

"Is your family all right?"

"Yes, they're all here with me."

"That's a relief."

"I've heard that you're struggling with an ailment. What's wrong?"

"Oh, some bad internal cramping and such. I've lost a lot of weight because of it."

"Reverend Brier has the same trouble. I've been giving him herbs for it. Would you like to try some?"

"Yes. Please." The young man's eyes closed again.

"You should have some water, too."

"It's in short supply, and there isn't a good spring here to replenish it." Doty ran his hand over his forehead. "Mrs. Brier?"

"What is it?"

"We Jayhawkers and Mississippians are going to start out again in the morning. If we can turn west and cross these dunes before noon, we'll be ready to tackle those wretched mountains. I never thought this would be such a bad route. Maybe you folks can stay with us this time."

"I hope so."

"I'd feel mighty bad if anything happened to your children, Mrs. Brier."

"Yes. We've been fortunate to make it this far. God must be watching over them, Mr. Doty. Over us all."

"Well, forgive me, ma'am, but He's taking His time offering help."

"Maybe we're just not recognizing help when we see it." She smiled wryly. "Before I get your herbs, is anyone else sick?"

"No, ma'am. But you might look at John Colton's ankle. He hurt it bad a few days ago. It's swollen and sore, and he's mighty sober about it."

"I will. And I'll make you a good cup of hot coffee if you've water in your canteen."

"Thank you, Mrs. Brier. There's still a bit in the bottom."

She emptied the water from his tin canteen into the coffeepot. Doty didn't look good. It wasn't like him to be lying around letting others do the work.

She unknotted the frayed ropes on the packs and took out her dwindling herb kit and her package of coffee. When Doty's water was hot, she added coffee, poured the steaming beverage into his cup, and delivered it to him with a dose of goldenseal.

There was a little flour left. She wondered if she should make it into biscuits. They would keep without molding in this arid place, and she didn't know when she would have another opportunity. It frightened her to use up the flour, though. As long as she had a handful left, it was a meager protection against starvation.

If they could reach the ridgeline of the unforgiving mountains ahead, she was certain they would finally see the Sierra Nevada, though. There would be plenty of game there. Taking a deep breath, she sat on the ground and poured the last powdery lump of flour into her spread-out apron, shaking out the bag carefully. She scooped it into her hands and added a little water from her canteen. Perhaps using up the flour was not as drastic as she imagined.

When the biscuits were on the coals, she rubbed her hands to remove the last of the flour. Sticky bits of dough fell onto her apron, discolored from the dirt embedded in her palms. She popped them into her mouth, savoring the raw taste of them as she never thought possible.

Then she pulled her blue calico dress from the packs and clutched it close for a moment before she began tearing the long skirt into strips to tie the children onto Big Jake. Without a harness, Kirke could fall off and be trampled before she even noticed.

She had made this dress only last spring, but it seemed a century ago. She remembered sewing the pieces with her neat, even stitches and whipping the hem on a sunny afternoon back home. Outside the cabin's open door, the boys had played beside the creek. She had been committing verse to memory as she worked, Shakespeare or Henry Kirke White or perhaps a Bible chapter. James—where had James been? Out riding the circuit, no doubt.

A cool breeze rippled the sand beside her. She felt as small as one of those tiny grains, picked up by the wind and set down in an unknown place, at the mercy of the great elements. Looking west at the great wall of mountains, she took in the terrifying grandeur of this place. There was a stark beauty in the earth-toned colors, the shifting light, and the long blue shadows marking the canyons.

But she could think only of the steep, terrible incline and the nearly impenetrable wall before them.

CHAPTER 35

Crossing the pale, ash-colored dunes was like slogging through deep, heavy snow. Juliet's legs ached
as she hauled herself along, her slender bare feet sinking
into the sand. The dunes rose and fell in exhausting hills
and hollows interspersed with low-lying greasewood, tall
plants that clustered like corn shocks, and the delicate
trails made by lizards scuttling from bush to sheltering
bush.

She followed the deep, meandering footprints of the
men and led Big Jake by a rope. Kirke and Johnny swayed
from side to side on his back, but the blue calico harness
held them securely in place. Behind Juliet, James drove his
dwindling herd of animals. Another ox had wandered off last
night when its picket came loose from the sand, and the animal couldn't be found in the morning. There was no time to
search if they wanted to keep up with the men, but James's
herd was down to five.

Big Jake's bones showed through his dusty hide, and his
sides caved in, yet he was still strong enough to lumber his
way over these slippery dunes with the two boys on his back.
The animal was a gift from heaven, no matter what Ed Doty

said. Juliet gave the poor creature every gulp of water she could spare.

It was mid-morning when the wind began, softly at first, but then gusting and whipping sand into Juliet's eyes and across her bare forehead. It blasted up under her skirts, where the grit stung her bare ankles. She tugged her shawl tighter around her neck. The boys scrubbed their eyes with their fists, and Big Jake began to snort. Juliet retied her faded black sunbonnet, but the wind snatched its protective brim and flattened it against her head. The air drove through her clothing.

James led the way into a sheltered hollow. Juliet helped Kirke and Johnny from the ox and wrapped the saddle blanket around them and Columbus. They scrunched down with their eyes shut. James huddled with the cattle.

"I say we stay here for a while," he said through clenched teeth.

Juliet rubbed her gritty forehead.

"We'll fall behind again if we do. This is miserable, though."

"We'll catch the others tonight. It's not hard to follow their trail."

"I suppose you're right. Maybe if we just wait out of the wind for a little while . . . " She dug three beef strips from her apron pocket and handed them to the children.

"I'm hoping there will be a spring in the foothills."

"Mother, the sand feels like it's biting my face," Johnny said as he picked grit off his meat.

"Me, too. And I'm so thirsty," Columbus added. He rubbed his eyes again. "There was only a little water in the bottom of the cup at breakfast."

"That's all we had, son. There isn't any more."

Juliet pulled her shawl close again and faced the chilly wind. She fought her way to the top of the dune and looked west. The sand hills ended in less than a mile, and the rocky flats began again. The men were there, walking in spread-out bunches toward the foothills. No wagons. No cattle. Nothing but the small dark knapsacks on their backs. She stared at the retreating men while the wind pressed her skirts against her legs.

At her feet, a dry husk of a bush crackled, startling her. It sounded like a rattlesnake. Her nerves were jarred by the wind and her uneasy speculation about where they would find water. How much faster these agonizing miles would pass if someone like Sarah or Abigail or Mary were here to smile encouragingly at her through cracked lips. Someone to trudge beside her, squeeze her hand now and then in understanding, or make an ordinary, everyday comment to divert her attention. James was a companion, to be sure, but his voice and his spirit had dried up out here and he was as distracted as she was about the dangers, the distance, and the terrible lack of water. He loved her—she never doubted that—but it was an effort for him even to blink an eye by now. Limited as he was by his own problems, he could barely help sustain her. All too often in camp, she found him lying on his back staring at the sky or gazing into the fire. Given his condition, Juliet marveled that he was still so patient with the boys.

The wind let up for a moment, and Juliet slid back down the dune to her family. With less than a mile more of stinging sand to go, they had best not tarry any longer. She hoisted Kirke and Johnny onto Big Jake while Columbus held the rope. James got slowly to his feet.

Johnny held one sleeve in front of his own face and one in front of his little brother's.

"Stop it, Johnny," Kirke said crossly. "I can't see."

"I'm keeping the sand out of your face," his brother replied. Kirke grabbed his arm and tried to push it aside until Juliet spoke sharply to them. "No quarreling, boys."

She squinted into the biting wind and pulled on Big Jake's frayed rope. The sooner they were out of this exhausting sand, the better.

CHAPTER 36

They left the sand dunes and crossed the rock-strewn flats that butted up to the foothills. The wind pushed against them and dried any last moisture from their mouths. Juliet's tongue felt like a piece of thick leather, and swallowing was difficult. She tried to breathe through her nose, but it, too, was cracked and painful. Desperately, she scanned the immense foothills for any patch of vegetation that wasn't the usual resinous creosote bush or dried-out greasewood.

Nothing.

James overtook her when she stopped to rest.

"I'm going to look for a spring, Juliet. There has to be something in these foothills. Keep following the men."

If they could clamber over the forbidding terrain that rose in front of them, they would reach the summit by mid-afternoon, Juliet thought. Then, remembering that her calculations were often far short, she amended her estimate. Sometime before nightfall, she would stand on the ridge-line and look out over the land ahead. This time, she would surely see the gently forested Sierra Nevada. In contrast with the mountains just ahead, which were a jumble of bare boulders and rocky cliffs as uninviting as a stone prison, the lush Sierras would offer a panoramic hint of the promised California valleys.

The thought gave her strength.

She was used to the sharp, broken rocks underfoot, but as they ascended the grade, the stones became boulders interspersed with taller bunches of scrub and a silvery plant with pale, holly-shaped leaves. She scrambled her way through, leading a reluctant Big Jake around the biggest obstacles. Far ahead, the Jayhawkers and Mississippians clustered in a large group, but as she watched, they split in two. A few resumed their trek straight west toward the rough pass that opened above them. The larger group turned south and began climbing into a steep, rocky side canyon. The wind blew cold and strong. She suspected it always blew here, sweeping up from the west and whistling through the high pass. On either side, dark peaks jutted into the blue sky.

"Mother, my back side hurts." Kirke's voice was weak.

"Move around until you're comfortable, but be careful to keep your heels away from Big Jake's flanks," Juliet answered.

They stopped every hundred yards as the grade got steeper. She tried to swallow, but her tongue got in the way and blocked her airway. For a moment, she panicked and drew in huge gulps of cool air until her heart stopped pounding. Fatigue bore down on her.

The day crept by as they continued to climb, following the men who headed for the pass instead of turning off to pursue the larger group up the canyon. Kirke fell asleep, and Johnny wrapped his arms around him to keep him from sliding off Big Jake's back, but by mid-afternoon, Johnny, too, had closed his eyes. His freckled face rested on Kirke's slumped shoulder. Juliet checked the harness. It did its job.

"I'm so thirsty, Mother," Columbus mumbled as he stumbled along beside her. "I hate this place."

She knew she should give him a lecture about using the word *hate*. At home, she and James considered the word profanity and never allowed it. Instead, she simply nodded her head and didn't answer.

It was late afternoon when the pass began to widen. Boulders the size of wagons were strewn down the mountainsides above them. The sky was pale and empty. James rejoined them, answering her silent, questioning look with a brusque shake of his head. He leaned on his gun and sluggishly herded the cattle through the maze of thick greasewood and rocks.

By evening, they still hadn't reached the summit, but Juliet could see it clearly now. Just a little farther and they could gaze over the top at the pleasant view that had encouraged her all day.

James reached it first. Juliet thought he would shout out his relief upon seeing the Sierras, the signal to this horrendous journey's end. Instead, he stood there as if numb. She stepped up beside him and looked out over the scene. Then she scrubbed her hands over her face and looked again.

Below her stretched another desolate valley, as vast and deadly as the one they had just left behind. It spread out, flat and harsh and severe, until another wall of barren rock mountains jutted up in appalling starkness. She turned her back on the sight and a cry escaped her cracked lips. Columbus began to howl. James lifted his face to heaven and swallowed.

Juliet looked again, as if the horrible sight might magically have disappeared while her back was turned, but there it was in all its dreadful reality. In the fading light, she could see a whitish pool of water halfway across the huge basin. Snow-like sediment surrounded it. Salt.

She reached for James's hand to steady herself. He grasped her fingers, but his arm was shaking. He turned to look at her with complete desolation and tried to speak, but no sound came from his throat.

Behind her, Johnny and Kirke awakened. She went to them, untied the harness, and silently pulled Kirke down. He tried to stand, but his knees buckled, and Juliet knew that dehydration was taking its toll again. When she turned to get Johnny, he searched her face and asked, "What's wrong, Mother?"

She felt like screaming at the heavens and then falling on her knees and sobbing aloud. Instead, she dredged up enough strength to look into his eyes and answer, "Nothing we can't overcome, Johnny. Nothing we can't overcome."

CHAPTER 37

Fierce wind whipped over the ridge, so they descended a few hundred yards to escape its cold blast and camp for the night. Juliet hoped to find the men settled among the boulders with a blazing fire. But they were gone.

While she unloaded the pack animals, James disappeared into the boulders. When he returned, he said, "I need the field glass, Juliet. I think I can see a patch of snow up there." He pointed to the peak above them in the fading daylight.

"Oh, James!" She dug in the packs until her fingers found the instrument, wrapped carefully in an old flour sack.

He trained the glass on the mountainside and then handed it back to her. "Yes, it's snow. A good-sized patch."

"Do you have the strength, James? Should I go instead?"

"You take care of the children. What can I carry it in?"

She thought for a moment. James would have barely enough stamina to climb that high. The canteens would be heavy and might impede the use of his hands. She knew there must be a better answer, but her brain was slow and confused. "Pack it into your old brown shirt," she suggested finally. "That way you can carry it down on your back."

He left then, his extra shirt tied around his waist. Juliet watched him struggle up the slope and over the boulders and then disappear. It was getting dark. She turned to the children. Kirke was cold as well as dehydrated. Col had found him a sheltered spot behind a mass of boulders, and she settled all three of them there with the quilt, gently brushing the hair out of their eyes. She crumbled half a biscuit for them to share. They could never swallow a whole mouthful without saliva, but perhaps crumbs would go down. She gave a piece to Col first, so he could try it. If he could swallow it, perhaps Johnny could, too. She wasn't sure about Kirke.

The cattle were bawling. The pitiful sound echoed off the mountainsides, a fitting and dissonant mourning. Despair settled over Juliet like a suffocating weight, and she sat down on the ground out of the children's sight and put her face in her hands.

She was certain of it now. They were lost. None of the rash and impetuous Jayhawkers or the unassuming Mississippians—not even her husband—knew where they were. This reckless shortcut had led them into the jaws of death. For all they knew, they were traveling in confused, desperate circles, getting farther from California, farther from safety. And there was nothing she could do.

Nothing, except find the will and the strength go on. The courage to lead her family out of this unthinkable place. She felt a fierce protectiveness for the children, a determination palpable in her chest. It was up to her to keep them safe.

Juliet stood and found a sheltered place in the lee of a boulder and made a fire. The dry greasewood twigs, fanned by the wind, caught quickly. She held her cold hands over the blaze and tried not to think of tomorrow.

The provisions were gone—the beans, bacon, and now, even the flour. The smoked beef from the Jayhawkers' wagon-burning camp was running low. There was enough for only three or four days more—time, Juliet had thought earlier, to reach the Sierra Nevada. Now, the only choice would be to butcher another cow. Thank heavens they had one to slaughter, although Juliet wasn't sure James would have the strength.

The image of the vast valley below with its dried-up salt flats and desolate miles pushed its way into her mind. She wondered if she could summon the spiritual depth to rise above this brutal landscape and get her family across it.

There was the sound of sliding rocks on the mountainside. She stared into the darkness, but could see nothing.

"James?" She called out. There was no answer.

Finally, she saw him. He was laboring down the slope and clambering over the rocks, stooped forward with a dark shape on his back. The old shirt. Packed with snow. Quickly, she fetched the coffeepot.

James staggered into the firelight and collapsed onto a boulder. Juliet rubbed his shoulder quickly before she untied the knotted shirt and carefully slid the blessed load of snow to the ground. Her hands trembled as she formed a little snowball for each of the boys and James to eat. She put a handful in her own mouth. Then she packed as much of the granular, icy mass as she could into the coffeepot to melt. The rest she lugged away from the fire for the cattle.

James sat for a long time staring into the flames while the coffeepot steamed. Finally, he said, "I'll have to go up in the morning and get another load. There's only enough here for the cattle to have a few mouthfuls each."

"Just rest, James. For now, just rest."

"We've got to fill the kegs, too. And the canteens."

"Yes."

The children were sitting silently under the quilt. Juliet poured Kirke a cup of water and helped him hold it to his lips. He grabbed it with both hands and swallowed the liquid eagerly. She refilled the cup for Johnny and then Col, and gave them each a sliver of beef for their supper. When she handed a shredded piece to James, he hesitated before he took it.

"Is this the last of it?"

"Almost."

He shifted his haggard body.

"We still have the biscuits, though," she added. She would leave them tied up in their flour sack for tomorrow. Perhaps she could face counting them in the morning.

CHAPTER 38

❦

It took two days to descend the harsh, 3,000-foot drop into the valley. There the flats widened out before them for perhaps thirty miles until the next bank of mountains rose like a blockade.

"The north end looks impassable," James said dully, staring at the upper end of the basin cut off by a high, bare escarpment. "We'll have to go south."

"I don't see a source of water in either direction," Juliet answered. Only one of the kegs lashed to Old Red's back was still full of melted snow.

"Will you look at this?" James pointed to two distinct trails of footprints leading away in different directions. They showed clearly in the dust. "This boot print belongs to that Mississippian named Masterson. I noticed that notch in his heel back at the wagon camp."

Masterson's tracks were among those cutting straight across the valley floor. He and the Mississippians—at least most of them—were heading toward the massive rock mountains fencing its western edge. A few wobbling prints split off and led south; whoever had made them was undoubtedly looking for a spring and an easier way to cross—just as James was.

They stopped there as the sun set and the sky in the west turned deep purple. A few small clouds hung low over the mountains, framed in brilliant gold. It was then that Juliet remembered it was New Year's Eve, the herald of a new year. 1850. Back home, she would have been making promises to herself, resolving to keep the cabin tidier or plant a larger garden come spring or accompany James on his circuit more often. Tonight she had but one goal: to reach the settlements at Los Angeles before her family succumbed to starvation, lack of water, or pure exhaustion in these cruel valleys.

In the morning, they pressed on, leaving the Mississippians' trail behind and instead turning south with the hope of finding water. Juliet wondered if they would encounter the group again or if this was the parting of their ways.

Even on the flats, each mile crept by as though reluctant to fall behind them, and every hour seemed an eternity. James lagged to the rear with the cattle. For the past two days, Juliet's goldenseal had done nothing to hold his dysentery at bay. He staggered on, leaning heavily on his rifle, until Juliet and the children had to stop and wait for him.

She led her family to the gigantic salty mud flat she had seen from the mountain pass. It was cracked and as hard-packed as an old wagon road. Farther out on the valley floor, she could see the sheen of water.

"Col, do you have enough strength to walk out there and scoop up a cup of that water?" she asked. Of them all, Columbus was holding up the best. "Don't drink it."

Col nodded while Juliet scrutinized the desert. She could see for miles in all directions, and there was no apparent danger, yet she still felt anxiety grip her chest as Col got farther and farther away. He looked so small in the distance. At last, she watched him bend over with the cup, turn around, and start back.

"It's brine," James said after tasting it. "Poisonous."

They made their way along the hard mud, finally free of the sharp rocks and stiff creosote bushes. There was no vegetation here at all, not a blade of grass or even the smallest sprig of sage for the cattle. Back home, she could never have imagined a landscape like this. She squinted in the glare as she poured a few ounces of water from the last keg to ration among them.

They made a dry camp that night—and the next—rising early each morning to begin the unrelenting, monotonous march again.

"The animals are getting too weak to carry anything but the blankets," James told her on the second day. "We'll have to leave some of their load behind. Not the coffeepot and the rifle, of course, but . . . "

"Oh, certainly not the kegs, James!"

"We must, Juliet. The cattle are on the verge of collapse. We won't find enough water out here to fill them anyhow. And we still have the canteens."

She knew he was right about the cattle. Slowly, she loaded the bedding onto Old Red, leaving the empty kegs in the dirt. Whenever she glanced back that day, she could see them sitting on the desert floor like cast-off little men defeated by distance.

The next afternoon Big Jake lifted his dusty, copper-colored head, sniffed the breeze, and stepped up his sluggish pace toward a cluster of bare mesquite. Judging by the trails that led to the thicket, it was a well-established Shoshone camp. Juliet marveled again that anyone could live an entire lifetime out here. How many of those skittering little lizards would it take to make a meal—if one could catch them in the first place? James said he'd seen a large buff-colored animal with curled horns off in the distance, but otherwise this desert's cleverly camouflaged game seemed utterly elusive. Elusive, hard to spot, and harder still to shoot. The occasional hare or rodent that caught James's attention darted away so quickly that he didn't even have time to raise his gun. There were big, dark hawks that rode the air currents high overhead, and insects. She wondered if one could eat insects.

As they drew near the thicket, she could see the Jay-hawkers camped: Doty, Young, Rood, Colton, Haynes, and the others, along with a couple of stray Mississippians. She took a deep, relieved breath and said a silent a prayer of thanksgiving. The Jayhawkers must have continued their way up the desolate side canyon and come over the ridge to find this same valley and welcome spring awaiting them. They looked like dull-eyed skeletons hunched on the dirt in holey boots and threadbare clothing. Some were sprawled on the ground under dirty blankets, asleep. She said her weary hellos as she looked around. A few of the men answered in subdued voices.

"Greetings, Reverend and Mrs. Brier."

She led the children straight to the spring, where fresh water emerged from the ground surrounded by tangles of bare mesquite stalks and branches. The shrub's bean pods and old leaves littered the ground, and the dirt was packed hard underfoot. Not waiting for a cup, the children scooped water into their mouths with their hands. Juliet, too, drank quickly.

When she returned to the Jayhawkers, Ed Doty was speaking, his voice flat with fatigue.

"We'll need to stand guard tonight. Who will take the first shift?"

His men sat with eyes downcast. Finally old Mr. Isham spoke up.

"If none of you youngsters can do it, I can."

Doty scrutinized the younger men and shifted uncomfortably. Father Isham, as they called him, had trouble standing now, and during the day he lagged behind. His lined, white-bearded face reflected the journey's toil.

Juliet looked at James, but he was lying on his back staring at the sky. He didn't seem to be listening. William Rood spoke up.

"Me and Young, we can take the midnight shift."

"Good," Doty said. "If it ain't too dark, Young can write in his little leather book." The corners of Doty's mouth turned up in the barest of smiles. "Now. Isham's got the early shift, and Rood and Young come on at midnight. Who's next?"

Luther Richards raised his eyes. "Me. And Colton says he'll take the early shift so Isham can rest."

"It's settled, then." Doty lay back on the ground before he had even stopped speaking.

Juliet yearned for respite, but Old Red must be unloaded, and the children needed food. James needed his herbal concoction, and, if the mud in the spring had settled from the cattle's frenzied trampling, the empty canteens were waiting.

CHAPTER 39

They stopped for a day while William Rood and Luther Richards searched for a pass through the mountains or at least another spring. James reclined in the mesquite as Juliet brought him water and then let him sleep. She paused to look around the camp.

Hunger was taking its huge toll on the despairing group, but despondency was the greater enemy that dogged them now. By every calculation, they should have been at the settlements long ago, yet here they were, plodding through this endless valley, with no hope of sustenance and no end in sight.

If she thought about it too much, the bleak prospects and overwhelming fatigue threatened to snuff out her own determination, so she occupied herself with small, useful chores. As she cut cowhide to make another sole for Col's moccasin, she realized that what the Jayhawkers needed was someone to encourage them to march out of here in a mind-over-matter kind of way. She worked her needle through the tough hide. No one was strong enough to do that—unless she did it herself.

Captain Haynes and Ed Doty continued to take charge, but in a worn-to-the-bone, accomplish-the-tasks kind of way. What was necessary now was mental encouragement, a shred of hope and comfort, and spiritual fortitude. Did she have the strength to devote herself to the task? She took a deep breath. These men needed her with rare desperation. She would try, if it was the last thing she did on earth.

Deftly knotting the rawhide strip, she stood and waited a moment for the ground to steady itself. She would check on James first and then Mr. Doty and give them each another dose of goldenseal. Then she would see about young John Colton. At eighteen, he was the youngest of the Jayhawkers. The boy had a new apprehension on his youthful face despite his steady demeanor. He sat rubbing his sore ankle. He tried hard to act like one of the men, but he was young enough to be soothed by comforting, motherly words.

"Juliet," James spoke as she knelt down beside him. "Captain Haynes tells me his men are out of food. In fact, he was so weak from hunger two days ago that Doty and Stephens had to use the last of their provisions to make a soup for him. He says it saved his life. As much as I've railed against butchering our animals, we're going to have to kill at least two if the men aren't to starve."

"I know. Mr. Young says they're out of everything except the barest amount of flour."

"That will put the herd at three, plus the four pack animals. Hardly enough for a strong start in California."

"Yes. I know. But we'll manage somehow."

"The cattle are going to fail soon anyway. And we need the sustenance ourselves."

She drifted from James to Doty to Colton while the morning sun climbed in the sky and warmed the January air. Old Mr. Isham, still a gentleman despite his poor condition, thanked her when she brought him strong coffee. His chest rose and fell feebly as he lay in the pale sunlight.

James struggled to his feet and went a few hundred yards south of camp to select the two weakest animals for butchering.

Later that afternoon, Bill Robinson rubbed his scarred forehead as he roasted a strip of beef over flaming mesquite and watched it shrivel and brown. When it was ready, he handed it to Juliet.

"Ma'am, would you like this? I just can't stomach it."

"You need it, Mr. Robinson."

"I know. I just don't think I can, Mrs. Brier. My stomach is so poor. I've had a presentiment that I'm not going to reach Los Angeles with the rest of you."

"Nonsense. Let's . . . " A sound from Doty interrupted her. He leaned over and grabbed a bleached animal bone from the ground beside him.

"This is a horse bone!" he said, lurching to his feet and seizing another. "Men! These are horse bones! Do you know what that means?"

He handed them to Sheldon Young, who examined them quickly. "Why'd we never notice this last night? They're from horses, all right."

"Horses. Driven from the settlements. It looks like they were butchered here by the Shoshone for food." Doty's face was animated.

"Maybe the settlements aren't too far then!" John Colton's boyish eyes brightened.

"You're absolutely correct, Colton. Men, that's a good sign if ever I saw one."

Juliet's heart lifted. Maybe there was reason to hope after all. She wondered, though, how far the Shoshone would drive horses. Distances on horseback didn't compare to distances on foot.

Afternoon shadows fell across the camp as Juliet patched the ragged holes in Mr. Young's shirt and dried beef strips over the fire. Young wore his gray wool blanket over his shoulders while she worked. Now and then, she glanced at the children still dabbling in the spring. The Jayhawkers chewed bits of leathery beef and napped while they waited for Rood and Richards to return from scouting. Mr. Isham rested on his blanket. Juliet filled his canteen with fresh water and brought him meat from the fire, but both remained at his side, untouched.

"Mr. Isham. You need to eat."

He stared blankly at her for a moment before he spoke.

"I will, Mrs. Brier. Give me a few moments."

Doty broke in. "Here come Richards and Rood."

It was another hour before the dusty figures trudged into camp. Rood's chiseled face was gray with fatigue and dirt. As they got closer, Juliet could see that his pants had new rips at the knees. Mr. Richards's toes stuck out a hole in his boot. They went directly to the spring. Juliet took them each a ribbon of of beef.

"Thank you kindly, ma'am," Rood looked up at her as he knelt by the watering hole. "Much obliged."

They joined the others at the fire.

"There's another spring about eight miles ahead. It's nothing great, but it'll do. As for a pass over those miserable mountains, we're not so sure."

"What do you suggest, Rood?" Doty asked.

"There's a belt of buttes cutting across this valley south of here. We didn't climb them—we were too used up for that. But I reckon that from their top, we'll be able to see a route to the south. I don't know exactly where it will take us, though." Rood leaned on his rifle, then laid it carefully on the ground and sat down beside it. He ran his fingers through his stringy hair and stretched his legs in front of him.

"Nobody knows exactly where we're going, Rood. We'd best admit it, plain out." Captain Haynes looked around the group. "At least we know there's another spring ahead."

"We'd better bake up that last bit of flour while we're here. There's no fuel for a fire up ahead," Rood said. "I'll wager that if we're careful, there's enough for each of us to have a biscuit to carry with us."

Juliet spoke up.

"I'll bake biscuits for us all if I might have an extra one for the children. One is all I ask."

Haynes thought for a moment. Finally he said slowly, "All right. For the children." Juliet mixed the dough carefully and formed enough undersized biscuits so that everyone could have one. Colton swallowed as he watched over her shoulder. Haynes fished in his pocket and pulled out a five-dollar gold piece. He held it out to the group.

"I'll give this gold piece to anyone who will sell me his biscuit." The coin gleamed in his calloused palm. Back home, it would buy 250 pounds of flour.

"Are you mad, Haynes? Gold won't do us much good if we're dead from starvation!" Doty snapped.

"Sorry, Haynes," Young said in his mellower tone. "It's a matter of life and death."

Haynes's hand shook as he stuffed the gold piece back in his pocket. "I have the best 160 acres in Knox County, 100 stock hogs, and 2,000 bushels of corn in the crib, and here I cannot get an extra biscuit for love or money."

An awkward silence hung over them as Juliet finished her baking and handed a single hot biscuit to each person.

She wrapped the children's extra one carefully. In the morning, she and James would follow the Jayhawkers south to the next spring. After that, it was anyone's guess.

CHAPTER 40

At dawn, the Jayhawkers hoisted their knapsacks and straggled out of camp as Juliet loaded the pack animals.

"See you tonight, Mrs. Brier," Mr. Doty said over his shoulder. "Try to keep up."

Hurriedly, she secured the ropes and then lifted Kirke and Johnny onto Big Jake. She led the way with James trailing behind, driving the remaining cattle. His rifle lay abandoned beside the watering hole, and instead, he leaned on two mesquite walking sticks cut from the cluster at the spring. It was then that Juliet knew how utterly exhausted her husband was. Leaving his rifle was almost akin to leaving his Bible. She briefly considered carrying the firearm herself but knew it was too heavy to add to her burdens. They would just have to depend on the others if they needed a gun.

After a few minutes, they overtook Mr. Isham, already far behind the younger men. Juliet walked beside him for a while and slipped him a sliver of beef from her apron pocket. He gave a bare nod of thanks, but didn't speak. His feet dragged as if his worn-out boots were filled with rocks, and his white hair and beard stood out like a faltering beacon in the brown desert.

"We'll watch for you up ahead," she promised. "Just be slow and steady. You'll make it."

"Good, then," he replied finally.

They camped that night at the spring Rood and Richards had found. It wasn't much more than a hole in the ground dampened by a slow seep, but there was enough brush for the cattle to browse a few mouthfuls. By the time Juliet's family caught up, the men had dug a pit and collected what little water oozed into their cups. Richards and Colton were scouting.

When Mr. Isham stumbled out of the darkness and collapsed onto the ground beside the fire, Juliet hurried to give him water. He stretched out beside the hot coals and fell asleep before she could fetch a piece of beef, but she set it aside for him to eat in the morning.

Richards and Colton were back when Juliet awoke. As the camp began to stir, they reported on the route ahead.

"We got to the top of those buttes, and from there we could see a lake. It's big and it looks deeper than that salty shallow thing behind us," Luther Richards said. "I think it might be drinkable. But these mountains keep going. They're just like a wall."

Juliet turned away to hide her face from the children. She tried to think about the lake ahead with good water to refresh them, but all she could hear in her mind were Richards's last words: just like a wall.

She was still coaxing muddy water from the seep when the Jayhawkers left camp to face the day's chore of reaching the buttes. Mr. Isham limped along with them but fell behind in the first hundred yards.

"We'll see if our ox can carry you," she told the older man when they overtook him. "Johnny should be able to walk a bit, even if Kirke can't."

"I doubt your animal can manage so much weight," Isham answered, but with James's help, he hoisted his tall frame onto Big Jake's back. The animal took a few unsteady steps and then stopped. Juliet pulled on his rope, and James shoved from behind, but the animal wouldn't budge. James swatted him across the rump to no avail. They tried again.

"It won't work." Isham slid down.

Juliet hesitated. It haunted her to leave the old man behind. Still, she saw no other alternative that wouldn't put the children in more danger. After a few moments she said softly, "We'll see you at camp tonight. Keep on as you did yesterday. We'll watch for you."

The water in the canteens was gone before the day was half over. Juliet felt herself droop, but she and the children were able to overtake the men, with James lagging a bit behind. The Jayhawkers traveled in silence, weaker than she had seen them yet. They made slow work of climbing the buttes, stopping every few hundred yards to collapse on the rocks until Haynes or Doty hollered at them to get moving. James caught up when they stopped.

It took all day to reach the butte top. Doty turned to look back.

"I'll wager we've come only four or five miles today. At this rate, we'll never get out of here."

Juliet barely heard his words. Holding tight to Big Jake's tether, she looked out over the wide, arid expanse ahead. There was the lake, far in the wavering distance. She would have to take the scouts' word that it looked drinkable. To her, it appeared to be sitting in a whitish basin, although she couldn't be sure. Even when she propped the field glass against a boulder, she wasn't able to keep the instrument still, but the shoreline seemed to have the dreaded white tinge that indicated brine.

"We're out of water, all of us," Doty said, fiddling with his empty canteen. "It's going to be a mighty dry camp tonight."

"You're right. But the men can't go much farther. We'd best stop until morning," Captain Haynes said.

Until now, no one had been left behind because of illness or frailty. Tonight, every time Juliet thought of Mr. Isham stumbling along back there alone, the bleakness of their situation felt like the heaviness of an impending storm, and she struggled to rise above it.

Already her tongue was dry and her lips were cracked. Kirke had his sunken-eyed look, and Johnny wasn't much better. Columbus tripped more frequently than he should have, and James kept plodding along, head down, eyes on the ground, bent at the waist, leaning heavily on his two walking sticks.

They made a dry camp. No one could swallow the beef strips without water or saliva. Juliet attempted to get a piece down her throat, but it made her choke and she spat it out. She waited and watched for Mr. Isham, and finally, near midnight, he lurched into the camp and fell to the ground. This time, there was no water to give him.

In the morning, they descended the bluff. Once again, Isham dropped far behind. When they finally reached the valley floor, the lake seemed to have retreated. It shimmered in the wavering light. If Juliet hadn't seen it from the bluff, she would have thought it was another mirage. She forced one foot in front of the other. Mindless phrases repeated themselves in her mind. Big Jake stumbled.

"You'd best get down for a while, boys." She patted the animal's neck.

Johnny slid off the ox's back. "How far is it to the lake?"

"Not too much farther," she told him as she pulled Kirke down and settled him on her hip. "Kirke, stop crying. I know you're thirsty. We'll get a drink as soon as we find one."

When he cried, there were no tears.

It took the entire day to reach the lake. They hauled themselves through the poor, sparse sage and creosote that pushed up from the soil, and neared the smooth, white flat as evening fell. Juliet knew from the smell and the crumbling minerals where the water pooled that it was undrinkable. Nevertheless, Doty and Richards shuffled their way over the encrusted surface attempting to reach the water, until they broke through to the briny muck underneath. Covered with mud to their knees, they returned, despondent and gloomy.

The group sat on the cold ground as night fell around them. No one spoke or built a fire. The children fell asleep instantly.

"We're going to die out here." John Colton's young voice quavered in the darkness.

"Or turn into pillars of salt, like in the Good Book," Sheldon Young added.

Everyone else was silent.

Finally, Juliet roused herself. The men's faces swam before her in the starlight.

"We've got to keep our spirits up, men. If we don't, Mr. Colton is right. We'll die right here." The men stared at her, stunned by her blunt words. She made the effort to get to her feet.

"We'll sleep as best we can. In the morning, we'll move closer to the mountains and the strongest of you can fan out and search for a spring. There has to be something in the foothills." Her head ached, and dizziness brought a wave of nausea, but she stayed on her feet. Doty and Haynes gave one brief nod apiece.

"The only way we'll make it out of here alive is to stay strong and not let ourselves give up."

No one answered. Their haggard faces looked up at her. She forced herself to go on.

"Mr. Isham is still back there somewhere. One of us will have to go and see about him if he doesn't come into camp." She stopped. Her heart was pounding and a painful thumping in her head echoed its beat. She could tell her lips were bleeding, but she forced herself to speak again.

"And say your prayers, gentlemen. Say your most fervent prayers."

CHAPTER 41

I have to go back for Isham," James told her in the morning.

"I don't see how you can, James. You're so weak. Let one of the younger men go."

"If he's dying, he needs a preacher. There's no one else who can help him," James said. He lifted his two walking sticks, but handed her his empty canteen. "You might as well pack this with the bedding today."

"We'll try to have some water waiting for you tonight."

The Jayhawkers were like old men this morning, bent and slow and silent. They strung themselves out, each man for himself over the salt-laden soil, following Doty's lead through the intermittent sage and heading for the foothills a few miles away.

Juliet gathered the children and started out behind the men. Someone—she thought it was Robinson—fell hard, but picked himself up and stumbled along again. Columbus walked just ahead of her. His shaggy, matted hair hung nearly to his shoulders and hid the filthy neckline of his ragged shirt. Beneath his torn tan pants, his feet were stuck into the moccasins she had sewn for him. The rawhide had hardened and curled up around his feet in an odd way, but at least it protected him from thorns and gashes. His vitality was gone, dried up with the miles.

They went on toward the foothills, stopping, starting, and stopping again. After a while, Juliet helped Kirke down and let Johnny ride on Big Jake's back. The animal's head drooped low, but he plodded ahead. Kirke's knees buckled, so she lifted him to her hip. After a few feet, she put him down again.

"Johnny, I'm sorry. Kirke will have to ride."

The Jayhawkers were collapsed on the weather-beaten boulders when she and the children reached the foothills at midday. Doty was asleep. Sinking down on the rocks herself, she overcame a wave of nausea as she scanned the hostile country behind them for any sign of James and Mr. Isham. There was nothing.

"Mr. Richards, are you strong enough to scout for a spring?" she asked, her parched throat on fire. "How about you, Mr. Colton? Mr. Haynes? If six or eight of you can fan out, you'll find something, I'm certain."

"I can go," Colton said. "Robinson? Want to search?"

"I dunno," Robinson said weakly. "I can try. I'll take the next canyon to the south."

"Rood and I'll go north." Richards stood up unsteadily. "We'll meet back here, men. If any of you find a spring, fire your gun if you've got one."

Doty opened his eyes. "I'll go, too."

"You take that gully south of Robinson's canyon, then."

The sun crept across the sky while Juliet waited with the children. Kirke stopped crying, and she knew he was on the verge of unconsciousness. She held him in her lap, talking to him in a low voice and trying not to cry. Johnny and Col lay at her feet, too dehydrated to move. There was no sign of James.

Juliet felt as if her own strength had seeped away until she was as drained as this desperate desert. Even opening the packet of herbs in her apron pocket was an effort, but she left Kirke with Johnny and Col for a few moments to look after the men, murmuring encouragement or offering them a bit of beef to suck on. She forced a chip of meat into her own mouth, but it felt like a stick without moisture to soften it.

Robinson was the first to return. The discouraged shake of his head told them he had found nothing. In the early afternoon, Juliet saw James dragging himself toward them, alone. She forced herself to walk out to meet him.

"He's dead, Juliet. Isham's dead. The poor soul crawled as far as I could see on his hands and knees trying to reach the lake. But he died there on the flats."

"Oh, James."

"I didn't get there in time. I covered him with some sand and dust, at least, and said a few words of prayer, but I was too late."

"Come rest, James. Sit by the boys."

"How's Kirke?"

"Not good at all. We've got the scouts out searching for a spring."

Doty came back next, weak and discouraged. "There's not a drop of water anywhere to the south. I'm afraid we're going to perish, Mrs. Brier."

"Nonsense." Juliet spoke with a thick tongue. "God wouldn't bring us this far and then let us perish. The others will find something."

But when Colton and then Rood stumbled back into camp and crumpled to the ground, gloom pressed in on her from every side. The group sat in silence. That left Richards. Just one more chance.

Juliet scrutinized Kirke again and bent to stroke his cheek. His face was bluish gray. Johnny's was taking on the telltale hue, too. Col had dark circles under his eyes and the tip of his tongue protruded from between his lips. James sat beside them with his eyes closed and his lips moving almost imperceptibly.

Then came a gunshot from the north.

Juliet struggled to her feet. "That's Richards! Come on, everyone! He's found some water!"

CHAPTER 42

"I t's fresh and sweet. The best water we've found in some time," Luther Richards told them when he met them.

"How much farther?" someone asked.

"About five more miles."

Five miles. Juliet's heart nearly stopped.

"I filled my canteens," Richards continued, his bloodshot eyes sweeping over them all. His voice was raspy. "There's enough water for each of you to have a couple of ounces before you go any farther. Especially the little boys."

Richards poured a dribble for Kirke first, and Juliet held the cup to her son's blue lips. She managed to get the water into his mouth and watched him swallow. The older boys drank theirs in one gulp. Juliet savored hers in her mouth before letting it dribble down her throat. She gave Kirke the remaining ounce.

"Let's go." Richards took command. "Robinson. Wake up."

Walking across the salt flats, they headed northwest behind Richards. The seat of his pants was wearing through in holes. Juliet looked away. Richards led the way up the bare foothills, and the Jayhawkers spread out in a lagging, wobbling line behind him. Juliet led Big Jake. The ox faltered and bawled under Kirke's weight.

Today, despite the glare, she was grateful for the pale sun that washed this country in its white light. Its small warmth felt good after shivering under the blankets all night while the moon crossed the January sky with infinite slowness.

The Jayhawkers stopped to rest. James was trembling with exertion, and Robinson lay down on the rocks.

"Let's go, men." It was Richards. "We've made a good start, but we can't rest too long. We've got a ways to go."

"Mr. Robinson, walk along with me, will you?" Juliet offered.

The young man looked at her.

"I'm plum worn out, Mrs. Brier. I don't think I'm going to make it."

"You've no choice. Come on now."

Robinson stared at her as if to protest, but slowly brought himself to his feet. They trudged toward the mouth of a narrow canyon. Suddenly, taking Juliet by surprise, Big Jake lifted his head, sniffed the air, and lurched ahead with new energy. Kirke's harness held him in place, but Juliet almost lost her hold on the rope as the ox pitched forward.

"Johnny, Columbus, grip the harness and walk beside Big Jake. He'll pull you along."

"We're nearly there, men," Richards called out. "Just another mile or so. You're doing fine."

They found the water where it left the canyon, turned from a trickle to a damp spot, and then disappeared entirely into the sandy dirt. By the time Juliet came up, the cattle had stopped bawling and were drinking from the small flow of water. The men were upstream, face down in the cool, wet rivulet.

"Not too much, men," Richards warned them.

Juliet pulled Kirke from Big Jake's back as the frenzied animal joined the others in the trampled mud. Johnny and Col flopped on their stomachs and drank immediately. She dipped her dirty hands into the clear water and scooped a few quick swallows into her mouth. Then she turned to help Kirke, letting the water dribble over his tongue and down his throat.

"Johnny and Col. That's enough for now."

She held another cupped handful to Kirke's mouth while offering her prayer of thanks.

"Providence Springs," she said aloud. "I name this place Providence Springs."

She looked around. They were near the mouth of the narrow canyon, but the water came from farther up. Now that their thirst was somewhat quenched, they would find a camping spot, perhaps back in the protected canyon, and lay over a day to recuperate. A whole day with clear, sweet water and a chance to rest. The men would kill an ox for meat. They would build a fire, and she could bask in its welcome glow. Then they could sleep. By the following day, they would be restored enough to find a pass and cross the mountains.

She looked around to see how James was faring. He was lying on his stomach beside the little stream, already asleep on his folded arms. He was close enough to reach out and scoop more water into his mouth when he awoke. Bill Robinson was on his back beside James, looking up at the sky. His face was wet.

Upstream, she could see the rest of the Jayhawkers sprawled out like heaps of withered crops. Doty scooped water over his head and let it run down his neck. Colton rubbed his hands in the small flow. A few of the others, like James, were already napping.

She drank another mouthful. Blessed water. Gathering the children around her, she held them close as she waited for it to course through her veins and bring back her stamina.

CHAPTER 43

Refreshed, they started up the narrow, vertical canyon, following the trickling stream closer to its source. Juliet rejoiced in this beautiful slit in the mountains, this hidden treasure that renewed them. The gurgling water made her heart quicken in relief, and the vegetation—so different here from the stiff, dry creosote and greasewood of the valleys, pleased her. She didn't recognize the undergrowth along the route, but there were long slender reeds and a beautiful plant with dusky leaves. Other green vegetation grew in protected depressions, and through it all, the determined stream trickled with its melodious sound. How she loved the music of running water!

The streambed grew rough, and tangled undergrowth choked the way, but the men pushed on, determined to see if this route could lead them over the mountains. In only a mile, the canyon ended in a circle of high rocks. The air smelled of dampness and native plants—willows, flourishing sagebrush, reeds, and even a hardy, bare cottonwood. Birds flitted about, calling to each other. The word oasis came to Juliet's mind, and she understood its meaning as she never had before.

Several springs bubbled up in this oblong bowl. The largest was in the center, and it was here the party stopped for another drink. It seemed as though they could never get enough water; their parched bodies would take days to replenish. There were animal tracks that Juliet didn't recognize and what she supposed was a Shoshone trail leading diagonally up and over the rim.

"Fill your canteens again, men. We'll have to retreat and search for another route." Captain Haynes's tongue no longer got in the way of his quiet Midwestern pronunciation. "There's no place to camp here."

They descended the brushy trail to the canyon's mouth and set up camp where the water disappeared into the parched ground. Juliet slid the packs from the cattle and built a fire while the men chose the weakest ox to butcher. Doty collected its blood, which Juliet cooked along with the lean strips of tough meat. Then she joyfully filled the coffeepot to the brim with clear water and added enough ground coffee to make the hot drink strong and bracing.

"Pour me a cup of that, would you kindly, Mrs. Brier?" Doty rinsed his bloody hands in the stream.

"It's almost ready. Fetch your cup, and by then it will have brewed."

"It smells like home."

They passed the evening and the next day alternately resting, drinking, eating, and finally, talking.

"It looks to me as though there might be a pass up that gulch immediately to the south of us." James pointed around the ridge of rock beside them.

"Or we could follow the mountains south to the end of this valley and see if there's a good way through down there," suggested Doty.

"We've got to be close to the settlements, don't you think?" Robinson asked. "Or are we lost?"

"We're not lost, son. It's just farther than we ever imagined," James answered, but Juliet could hear hesitation in his usually assured tone. "Certainly the Sierras are close."

"When we find them, we'll need to skirt around their southern end to reach the settlements," Doty said.

"*If* we find them," Robinson said.

Sheldon Young spoke up. "These valleys are killing us, one by one."

For a moment, no on replied.

"What I wouldn't give for a good map," James said. "This uncertainty is torture."

"A map, yes." Young Colton spoke up. "But if I could have one wish, I'd ask for a big chunk of my mother's cornbread, dripping with butter."

"Not me. I'd take a whole apple pie," Doty said. "I feel like I could eat two or three right now. I even dreamed about one last night."

"How about some fried potatoes with onion?" Robinson suggested.

"Men! You're tormenting us." Richards bent over and poured steaming coffee into his scratched cup. "We'd best be grateful for what we've got."

"Mr. Colton, your moccasin needs a new piece of rawhide in the toe to cover that big hole," Juliet changed the subject. "Anyone else? Mr. Richards, how are your boots holding up?"

"That patch you put in earlier is doing fine, ma'am."

Kirke curled up on her knee. He had reverted to sucking his thumb lately when his mouth wasn't too dry. He put it in his mouth now. Juliet said nothing. He was too old for such behavior, but the child had to comfort himself somehow. She worried that the boys would suffer lasting effects from this journey. Being near death from thirst couldn't be good for a growing child. Neither could a diet of tough beef and strong coffee.

Columbus came up beside Johnny with a brimming cup of water. Juliet expected him to sit down and drink it, but instead he dribbled it over his brother's head.

"Col! You asked for it!" Johnny grabbed his own half-full cup and tossed it on his brother's shirt.

They would have to leave this place in the morning, Juliet knew, but for this moment, they were safe. She could enjoy her children's mischief since it signaled their partial rejuvenation. James was sick—she wondered if he weighed even 100 pounds now—but he could still travel.

She had surprised herself with her own stamina. Back home, she never would have thought she could continue under such terrible duress. She wouldn't have dreamed that she could become the subtle backbone of this expedition or rise above her own desperate needs to see to the others. It startled her that she could carry on with the grinding chores of survival when James was unable to do so and conquer petty irritation in favor of the larger good. If they made it through to Los Angeles, she would be a different person. This wretched country would see to that.

CHAPTER 44

As the white saline flats to the south lifted to the mountains, curious rock spires jutted from the ground like jagged teeth guarding the canyon's mouth. Juliet studied the dark, pillarlike formations as she boiled ox bones in the coffeepot for what nourishment they contained. In her old life, she would have considered the spires a harsh but beautiful oddity. Today, knowing what probably was beyond them—no water, no visible game, a grueling climb over the desiccated mountains—they seemed like the ominous gates of hell.

Captain Haynes sat nearby scraping the hair from the ox's hide and cutting the tough, leathery mass into pieces small enough to boil. Given the situation, it wouldn't do to waste even the most undesirable part of the slaughtered animal.

Haynes didn't want to spend another day waiting for scouts, so the men began to pack up, reluctantly preparing to ascend the canyon to the south without knowing where it led. Juliet hurried to finish her cooking and fill her family's canteens, wishing again for the empty kegs they had left behind.

One by one, they left, following Doty and Haynes. James and Robinson fell back in the first half hour but continued at a slow, steady pace. Juliet halted the animals now and then and waited for the two to catch up. The Jayhawkers didn't wait, but Juliet could often see the last of them disappearing behind boulders or sharp turns.

She was glad Kirke was up off the ground today because these foothills were filled with rattlesnakes. Already, she had seen several of them hiding under rocks or curled up in the open trying to absorb the sun's slight warmth. It helped that there was very little vegetation here. Although it made the terrain seem harsher, the rattlesnakes were easier to spot, camouflaged as they were with the surrounding beige clay and dust. She held Big Jake's rope in one hand, lifted her skirts with the other, and told Johnny and Kirke to walk beside her.

She was getting better at spotting the desert reptiles and rodents, the birds and other wild animals out here. Not that it did any good, for the men could never raise their guns and shoot quickly enough. But when she took her eyes off James and the children—and when the Jayhawkers up ahead didn't scare off whatever creatures might be near—she began to notice a few hidden ground squirrels, quail, jack rabbits, and occasional deer-like animals that could run faster than a horse. At night, she was sometimes awakened by rodents that scurried across her legs, and she could hear the long, mournful hoot of owls.

It was when she turned to look back for James that she saw Bill Robinson fall. The rock he stepped on rolled from under his foot and his worn-out boot slipped hard into a deep crevice. Even from her distance, Juliet heard a terrible scraping and the sound of ripping cloth. Robinson yelped in pain. James bent over him, murmuring something. The Jayhawkers stopped and looked back. Juliet handed Big Jake's rope to Columbus and hurried to Robinson's side.

His face was gray, all but the red scar across his forehead. Juliet knelt beside him.

"Are you all right, Mr. Robinson?"

His trousers were ripped from ankle to knee and there was a long jagged laceration across his kneecap and around the side of his leg. It was deep. Blood ran down his leg into his boot. Already, purple bruises were rising and the knee was swelling. He looked at her, his jaw set, and didn't answer.

"Well, it's a mean gash," she said, purposely trying to understate the injury. "We'll clean it and wrap it up and then we'll see if you can walk on it. If so, we'll know that it's nothing more than cut and bruised."

"What if it's broken?" Robinson asked.

"We'll not borrow trouble. It may look worse than it is."

"But honestly, Mrs. Brier. Have you ever thought about what would happen if one of us couldn't travel?" Robinson asked. "Would the whole group sit here and perish, or would they leave the weak one behind? I know the answer. I'm not stupid. If my knee is broken, I'll be left behind."

"We're not leaving you, Mr. Robinson. You can depend on that."

"That's right, son," James spoke up.

"What if leaving me means saving the rest of you?"

"Bill, look at me." Juliet used his first name for emphasis. She reserved first names for the men in her family. "We're not leaving you."

The Jayhawkers wandered back down the slope to assess the situation.

"We'll need to stop and camp here for the night," Juliet told the men. "We've got to clean and bind this knee and see if he can walk on it."

"Robinson, I'm sorry, mate, but I want to press on," Ed Doty stated flatly. "Every minute we waste out here means we're that much closer to disaster."

Without warning, James drew himself to his full, imposing height. For the first time in weeks, his dark eyes snapped under his glowering eyebrows.

"Doty, you hold up a minute." His voice rang out with startling force. "Listen to me, because I'm going to tell you what we're going to do. We're going to stop right here and look after Robinson. All of us."

Doty opened his mouth and then closed it again. The others put down their bedrolls and rifles and settled onto the rocky ground without a word.

She took her time washing the wound with a few ounces of water from the canteens. She wished she could flood his leg but didn't dare use so much water. There was no telling where the next spring might be. Then she used flour sacking to bind his knee. Robinson sat hunched over, his dirty hair falling into his eyes as he watched her work. He clenched his hands in his lap.

When she was done, she asked him to stand. He couldn't straighten his leg but was able to put some weight on it. He raised his eyes long enough to look at Doty.

"Doty, I know this is slowing you all down. I reckon it's all right if you want to go on without me. I can catch up later."

"Nonsense," Juliet said briskly. "We're standing by you—all of us. You'll be able to travel tomorrow."

"Do you think so?"

"I'll make a poultice for it and we'll let it rest overnight. Tomorrow it will be much less painful." Good thing Robinson was a suggestible young man.

She was right. In the morning, Robinson was able to hobble around the camp. She didn't know how far he could walk, but for now, he could probably keep up with James.

Blood poisoning would be the only danger.

That, and the ruthless distance ahead.

CHAPTER 45

As they climbed the canyon toward the pass, the temperature dropped and the wind rose until Juliet stopped and retrieved the boys' heavy shirts and her second shawl. Bill Robinson and James overtook them, limping around the gigantic boulders that spilled from the volcanic peak above. Robinson was doing his best to keep up, and she gave him a tired smile.

The ox-hoof broth she had doled out for breakfast was barely any sustenance at all, and its paltry nourishment had faded long ago. With a group this large, and the animals so near death, even a big ox yielded only enough to eat for a day. She made it last a second day by boiling the hide and hooves, and by squeezing the contents from the entrails and then cooking them, but they were a repulsive substitute for food. At an animal every two days, they wouldn't have food much longer, even if they ended up butchering poor, faithful Old Red or Big Jake.

Her spirits drooped, and she forced herself to think of something positive. She and James would have a simple cabin this first year, with a vegetable garden in back. She would plant lettuce as soon as the soil was ready—leafy, succulent lettuce—and juicy strawberries. She would nourish her family with food as never before and attend to the boys' schooling, long neglected on the trail.

The sun was directly overhead when the Jayhawkers approached the top of the pass. She could see them just ahead, eager to reach the rise and look out over the vista to the west. One by one, they came to the overlook and stopped abruptly.

Then Doty threw his cap to the ground, and Rood shouted something that sounded like an oath. Colton squeezed his temples as if a headache was coming on and scrubbed his eyes with his fists. A few of the others sank onto the boulders. Haynes and Young stood together, pointing and gesturing.

Juliet hurried to the viewpoint, pulling a plodding Big Jake behind her. She barely heard Captain Haynes clear his throat and say, "Hold on, men. Before you get too discouraged . . . "

Below lay another wide forbidding valley, with a barren dry lake to the north and miles of the same greasewood and sage to the south. Another solid wall of mountains made a snowy, jagged line across the sky to the west. Juliet's heart seemed to stop. They must be traveling in circles, stumbling around in an endless loop. Desert, mountains, desert. More mountains. The compass showed them heading southwest, but the country ahead looked indistinguishable from that behind them. Indistinguishable and just as foreboding.

Columbus caught up with her and a disbelieving look crossed his face.

"Is that California, Mother?"

"I don't know, Col."

"Where are the grassy meadows?" The boy asked, his chin beginning to tremble.

"Well, we still have a bit farther to go, I suppose." Juliet sat down.

"A *lot* farther." Columbus's voice was glum.

"Damn this country anyhow!" cried Doty. "Does it never end?"

Richards ran his hand over his eyes. "I thought for certain we'd see the Sierras this time."

Haynes rubbed his forehead while he scrutinized the snowcapped mountains across the valley. Then he turned to face the group.

"Hold on a minute, men. I think those are the Sierras."

There was a stunned silence.

"The Sierras? Come to your senses, Haynes. You've heard about the Sierras. They're supposed to have forests and rivers and good grass. Those bare rocky things can't be them," Doty said.

"Still, I think they might be. Lewis Manly said the trees and such would logically be on the western slopes. This is the eastern side."

"What makes you think they're the Sierras, though, Haynes?" Luther Richards squinted at the older man. "You're not one for wishful thinking."

"Well, look at the way they slope down to the south, as if they're petering out." Haynes turned and pointed. "And look up north. See that snowy peak in the distance? That could be the landmark the Shoshone tell of. From here, it looks as though it has some altitude."

The men were silent. Then Sheldon Young spoke up. "I think you might be right, Haynes. They're a dubious looking range from this angle, though."

"Even if they are the Sierras, we've got some serious distance to cover yet." Doty leaned heavily on his rifle.

"At least this time we might not have to cross the mountains." Colton sounded hopeful. "If Haynes is right, we could skirt them to the south."

Juliet rubbed her neck, mentally revising everything she had heard about the Sierra Nevada. She realized now that watching for lush green forests and clear running brooks was impossibly naive. Of course this enormous, unforgiving desert wouldn't halt itself at their foothills at some miraculous green line.

James and Robinson had begun to hobble up the slope toward them. Robinson used one of James's walking sticks to help support his weight. She studied the two of them pulling their feeble bodies to the ridge. James's face was nearly as gray as Robinson's. They took a few steps, then rested, and then took a few more.

Behind her, Kirke began to cry. She went to him, pulled him down from Big Jake, and held him for a moment. He buried his face in her neck, and she stood for a moment on the hard-packed crest, clutching him close.

The Sierra Nevada. As dry and bleak as the rest of this grim landscape. She swallowed the lump in her throat and wearily slid Kirke to the ground. There was only one productive response to this discovery, and it wasn't despair. She squared her shoulders and called down to her husband.

"Good news, James! The Sierras are in sight!"

CHAPTER 46

In the morning, Asa Haynes found Juliet bending over the packs tightening the frayed ropes.

"Mrs. Brier, I came to tell you something."

She glanced up at him. She liked Captain Haynes and his soft-spoken manner.

"A few of my Jayhawkers were talking last night. They say it's each man for himself now. They want to hurry ahead as best they can and not be held back by Robinson. I tried to talk them out of it, but they're determined." He paused and then added, "I feel obliged to go with them."

"That would split us up again," Juliet said tiredly.

Haynes dropped his gaze.

"Yes. I'm sorry. We'll scout ahead for you, though. All you'll have to do is follow." Haynes scuffed his rawhide moccasin in the dirt. "Maybe you'll be able to overtake us again."

Nearby, Doty tightened his bootlace and stood as if to join them. Then he sat down hard on his boulder again.

"I desperately want to go along, Haynes. But I'm just too far gone."

"It's all right, Doty. The rest of the men need you. You'd best stay with them. If we get to the settlements first, we'll send help. Horses, maybe, and a doctor for Robinson."

"A big pot of chicken and dumplings, Haynes. And an apple pie." Doty gave a ghost of a smile.

Luther Richards came over to Juliet.

"I know you have to stay with your husband, ma'am, but I wish you could come with us. You've been a godsend with your kindness and help. I want to say thank you."

"You're welcome, Mr. Richards. Travel safely. I hope we'll see you again in the settlements."

Then they were gone. Juliet looked around at the small group of Jayhawkers that remained. Richards had been their best scout, and Haynes had a thoughtful, sensible way about him that made this bad situation better. Now it was up to Doty, Young, Rood, Colton, Robinson, James—and her. She loaded the animals.

"Haynes marked the trail well," Colton reported as the remaining group started down the pass. "We'll be able to see them once they're out on the flats."

She watched the sun move across the sky. This pass was more gradual than the last one, so she knew they would reach the desert floor today. Descending the slopes was more difficult than slogging their way up, though. The footing was always treacherous, and Juliet's skirts prevented her from seeing where to place her feet. Sometimes she was able to hold them aside with one hand while she picked her way through the rocks, but in the worst places, she needed both hands to grasp boulders and prevent herself from sliding. She wished she could wear pants like James and the boys.

Being the only woman in a party of men had its difficulties, but lately she had never found it necessary to wander discreetly from camp and find a boulder large enough to hide behind. Her body used every drop of liquid she put into it. The children, too, had almost completely stopped urinating.

The sun was setting when they came onto the flats and saw a Shoshone trail leading across the desert. They would camp here. Juliet told Columbus and Johnny to look for sticks for a fire. She shook her canteen and poured the last water into the coffeepot. By the time darkness had settled over the desert, the coffee was ready. She turned away from the disgusting dinner of ox hide and sat shivering in the cold air, looking at the black outline of the Sierra Nevada, darker even than the night sky. It stretched south as far as she could see. She cradled her allotted ounces of hot coffee to her skinny chest.

Thousands of stars shone steadily overhead. They covered the sky in numbers too large to imagine, but they didn't flicker and sparkle as they had in Michigan. James said it was because there wasn't as much smoke in the desert air. Unbidden, the words of Henry Kirke White drifted through Juliet's mind.

> *God help thee, Traveller, on thy journey far;*
> *The wind is bitter keen,—the snow o'erlays*
> *The hidden pits, and dangerous hollow ways,*

And darkness will involve thee.
No kind star
To-night will guide thee, Traveller . . .

She stared again into the heavens. No kind star. How she wished there were just one kindly, beaming light leading them straight to the settlements.

Tomorrow, they would follow the trail straight out onto the flats behind Asa Haynes's party of Jayhawkers. The Shoshone knew all the water sources, and their trails led to the best ones. Juliet took comfort in the thought. Although the march across the valley floor would be dry—and any water out there would certainly be briny—perhaps they could count on another spring in the far foothills. If nothing else, there was snow on top of the Sierras if anyone was strong enough to make the arduous climb.

James came up behind her.

"Are you all right, Juliet?"

"Yes. Just resting."

"Robinson managed to keep walking today, although he was slow and in pain. I think you should look at his knee, though. He says it hurts like the devil."

"Yes. I'll put another poultice on it tonight."

"His water is gone."

"I'll give him coffee. How are you faring, James?"

"I'm worn out, Juliet. Worn out."

"How much farther can it be?"

"I thought we were almost there weeks ago. I'm not so certain now."

"Are you certain we're not lost?"

"Yes. Doty and Young and I all agree. The compass can't be wrong. Young—he's quite a scholar—has studied the stars enough to know we're on the right track. The distance just turned out to be much farther than we thought."

"Do you think the children will suffer permanent damage?"

"Children are tougher than we think. Columbus and John will be all right if we reach the settlements soon. Kirke might need some time to regain his strength."

"At least Kirke is too young to remember this trip. I'm glad of that."

"Yes."

"The beef hide is almost gone."

"I know. There's no choice but to kill another ox."

"I'm not sure I can stomach another piece of that hide. It nearly makes me retch." Juliet rose. "But I'll get you a piece, James."

The remaining Jayhawkers were dark lumps hunched around the fire, and Juliet was struck by how much smaller the group had become. She found Bill Robinson with his back turned to the flames, rubbing his knee, and she gave him the last drink from the coffeepot.

CHAPTER 47

In the morning light, Juliet examined Bill Robinson's wound. She didn't like the way his leg felt warm or the way reddish streaks radiated from the injury, but she cleaned the bruised gash again, applied another poultice, and wound the strip of flour sacking around it.

She lost track of the hours as they plodded across the dry valley floor, skirted the edge of another shallow brine lake, and finally used James's field glass to spot a patch of bare willows and cottonwoods far ahead. The group straggled over the bleak landscape, a line of skeletons with the single-minded thought of water. Deadening fatigue pressed down on her, but rest stops were a dangerous misuse of time.

Although the sun's warmth felt good, the glare bouncing off the salt-whitened soil was torturous. She shaded her eyes with her hand until her arm ached, but nothing could subdue the blinding brightness. Her head began to pound as she squinted. At least she had a sunbonnet to help. The men and the children were worse off.

"If that's a spring, Doty, we'd better approach carefully." Sheldon Young scanned the vegetation ahead. "It looks like the Shoshone use this place."

"I know. You and Colton take your rifles and make sure no one's there. Haynes and his men are probably already gone."

They waited long minutes before Young raised his rifle in the distance—the signal to proceed.

The scene at the spring repeated itself. Once again, they blocked the frantic cattle from trampling the drinking hole, drank greedily, and collected enough water to fill the canteens and then the coffeepot. Juliet carried water out to James and Mr. Robinson when they finally drew near. Then she washed her arms and face, and let the children dip their feet. Later, the Jayhawkers butchered the weakest ox, and she began preparing every part of it for food.

The men were napping when Juliet looked up and saw two figures in the distance approaching camp.

"James. Wake up. Get your field glass." She shook her husband's shoulder.

"It's buried in the packs somewhere."

"There's someone coming."

James sat up quickly. "What?"

"Two people. Coming this way."

"Get Young. He's got his field glass in his pocket."

She spoke louder than she meant to in waking Mr. Young. He stood quickly, shaking off sleep.

"Where? Two, you say?"

"Yes. Right out there." She pointed toward the center of the valley.

"I see them." Young held the instrument to his eye. "Damned glare makes everything waver. It doesn't look like Shoshones, though. The hair's too light in color."

"Should I wake the others?"

"It wouldn't hurt." Young continued to stare through the lens. "They're coming at a steady pace."

Doty stood and grabbed his rifle. Colton did the same.

"I swear it looks like Manly and Rogers."

"Let me take a look, Young," James said. He peered through the glass and nodded. "You're right. I believe the one on the left is Manly."

Minutes later, Lewis Manly and John Rogers fell into camp. They grabbed the full tin cups Juliet handed them, while the Jayhawkers clustered around, waiting for them to speak.

"Where are the rest of your men?" Manly asked as he dropped onto the nearest boulder.

"Gone ahead," Doty said shortly. "We're traveling slower. Brier's sick and Robinson's injured. Where are your people?"

"Stalled," Manly said, with a despairing shake of his shaggy head. "Unable to go farther. They're two valleys back. We're going to the settlements for help."

"Are the women all right?" Juliet asked. "And the children?" Sarah and her children! Abigail Arcan and her little Charley. Mary Wade and her four young ones.

"They're not doing well, ma'am," Manly replied. He untied his moccasin and pulled it off. "They just can't make it any farther. They're parched and half-starved and dreadfully weary. The children are all still alive, but Asahel Bennett fears they'll die if they don't have relief soon. We settled them beside a small spring with their wagons, and they're waiting for us to come back with provisions. The trouble is, it's a lot farther to the settlements than we thought. Rogers and I have been trying to hurry, but it's slow going."

"It's going to take longer than we thought. Much longer," Rogers added. He, too, lowered himself to a boulder. His elbows stuck through the holes in his brown sleeves at sharp angles.

"How much food do they have?"

"A couple of skinny oxen and whatever game they can find. Mrs. Arcan has a little flour left, and Mrs. Bennett and Mrs. Wade both have a few beans. Not much. It won't last long, especially with all those children."

Manly rubbed his foot. "We can't stay. We have to hurry on as best we can. We'll fill our canteens and get moving again. Now that we've got water, we'll make some more miles today."

"Captain Haynes and his men are a day or two ahead of us."

"We'll watch for them."

"Does your foot hurt, Mr. Manly?" Juliet asked.

"It's sore, but my moccasins are holding out. Mrs. Bennett made them strong. She and Mrs. Arcan made our knapsacks, too."

"I'll give you a bit of padding for your foot and some of our beef to help you on your way."

"Thank you, Mrs. Brier. Thank you kindly."

Doty was staring at them.

"You mean that if you reach safety, you'll actually turn around and come back?"

"We have to, Doty. They'll die if we don't. Plain and simple. They can't make it out."

"Who's there?"

"The Arcans and Bennetts. The Wades were talking about heading south toward the lower end of that first long valley—the one we've all been calling Death Valley. But the Bennetts and Arcans, at least, are stranded."

"How do you propose to get provisions back to them?" James asked. "You know how rugged it is."

"We'll have to buy horses or mules. Arcan gave us gold for that and for supplies. We'll do the best we can."

While she listened, Juliet wrapped a package of meat and coffee.

"Do you still have your field glass, Manly?" James asked. "You could take one of ours if you don't."

"Mine's in my bedroll. You can bet I take good care of it," Manly replied. Juliet handed him a piece of flour sacking to pad his foot and he put it in the toe of his moccasin. She gave him the food packet.

"You'll be in our prayers, Mr. Manly. You, too, Mr. Rogers."

"Thank you, Mrs. Brier. We'll be off now."

CHAPTER 48

In the morning, the group began the slow trek southward along the arid flanks of the Sierra Nevada. Big Jake grunted under Kirke's slight weight but shambled along while Columbus held his rope. Juliet patted the poor animal's neck, and a puff of dust rose into the air. As usual, Robinson limped heavily, and James pushed himself on with the aid of his two walking sticks. Robinson had found a stout stick of his own.

It was another dry camp that night, so Juliet made coffee from the precious water in the canteens. She saved a bit for morning and enough to make another poultice for Robinson's knee and then sat by the fire trying to calculate the date. January 20, 1850, she decided without certainty.

In the first morning light, Juliet looked around her. Finally, they were nearing the southern tip of the Sierra Nevada. The mountains had dwindled to low mounds and the route led past a rounded hill capped with black rock and then down into a narrow wash lined with pinkish walls. There were the same desert trees with frond-like spiky leaves and spiny trunks, and a rounded, fragrant, silver-gray bush that grew amid the creosote.

She wandered to the fire to stir up last night's coals. She could see James's chest rising and falling under the blankets. Kirke and Johnny slept beside him. Where was Columbus? She looked again. He wasn't there.

Quickly, she scanned the hills and the scrub nearby, but didn't see him. Most of the Jayhawkers were still asleep, and she hesitated to call out for him and rouse the entire camp. Col knew he was never to leave the group. She walked a few hundred steps up the wash and then a short distance down. Her heart beat faster. Where could he be?

"Columbus!" she called, not caring now that she was awakening everyone. "James, I can't find Columbus!"

James sat up, dazed and groggy. "Columbus? He's right here under the blankets."

"No, he's not. Look for yourself. I've searched all around the camp. He's not here."

Perhaps he fell, she was thinking. Fell and knocked his head on one of these thousands of pink boulders.

"Col!" she called again, and this time Doty got to his feet and pulled his holey boots on. Colton stirred and sat up.

"What's wrong, Mrs. Brier?" He asked, his young face drawn in concern.

"It's Columbus. I can't find him. He was here, sleeping with us, and now he's gone." She was nearly crying now in panic.

James labored to his feet and limped off to the north searching behind bushes and in dips and hollows calling out for his son. Col was too old to wander off as Kirke might have done. He wouldn't hide for so long, even if he needed to urinate, which was unlikely given the scarcity of drinking water.

John Colton overtook her as she continued down the wash. The walls were steeper and more canyon-like here, and the pink hills gave way to sharp red cliffs that jutted up diagonally and dropped their debris onto rock piles at their base. Still favoring his sore ankle, Colton limped gamely over the rough ground.

"I'll go farther down and look, ma'am. I overheard Col and Johnny playing last night. They were pretending that there was a spring ahead near the lower mouth of this canyon. I imagine he's just pretending he's scouting or finding us all a good drink. I'll hurry on and have a look."

"Oh, thank you, Mr. Colton. I'll send Mr. Doty and Mr. Young to search the top of these cliffs. James is going north."

"Robinson's going to stay in camp to watch your other two boys, Mrs. Brier. Little Kirke, he's not to be trusted around those hot coals. Just like my little brother at home."

She hurried back to camp, looking left and right, and stumbling over rocks in her path. Doty and Young were already on the upper ledges of the cliffs, calling out Columbus's name.

The familiar swirling dizziness began to close in and she leaned over to restore the blood to her head as she tried frantically to think. Where would he be?

He loved to mimic the men around him. It was a matter of concern to Juliet, since some of these rough-hewn Jayhawkers had left their manners in the Midwest. More than once, Col tried out a curse word he had overheard. When he had the energy, he carried a stick over his shoulder like a rifle, and around camp, he took on the Jayhawkers' slouched posture.

"Johnny. Wake up!"

Johnny opened his eyes and looked at her face. He sat up immediately.

"What's wrong, Mother. You look . . . "

"Johnny, tell me what you and Col were pretending last night. Remember, you were sitting by the fire and Col was scratching something in the dirt with a stick. What was he saying?"

"We were playing that we went scouting and we found a spring for everyone."

"Come show me in the dirt. Where the spring was, that is. Quickly."

Johnny scrambled out of the covers.

"What's the matter? Where's Col?"

"He's gone, Johnny. I think he might be looking for that spring."

"But it was pretend."

"I know, son. Maybe he thought it might be real, though. Maybe he's gone to find it."

She led Johnny to the fire. Footprints obliterated the scratch marks, but a few still showed.

"Draw it again, just like you had it last night."

Johnny took a twig in his hand.

"Well, we were right here. And this is the canyon we're going into." He etched crude lines in the pink dust. "Down here is where he drew the spring. It was a long ways away, but we were scouts. We pretended we had horses to ride."

"Good. We'll go down the canyon then. Mr. Colton has already started looking there."

"May I go, too, Mother?"

"No, son. You stay here with Kirke and Mr. Robinson."

"But I want to find Col!" His voice quavered. "What if he's lost?"

"You stay here and take care of Kirke. Mind that he doesn't go near the coals. All the men are out searching. We'll find Columbus."

Johnny gulped. "Yes, Mother."

"I'm going now, Johnny. I'll be back."

"All right. And Mother, there was a big rock right by the spring in Col's canyon. A big, big one."

She hurried down the canyon again. The morning sun was creeping over its rim and reflecting off the red walls. Juliet's eyes searched the base of the cliffs for any place an eight-year-old child might find appealing—a cave, or a small seep of water, or a place where this colorful rock glowed in the sun like smoldering embers. There were signs of the Shoshone everywhere, including a trail down the center of the canyon and dead fire pits, and even a few stick drawings etched on the cliffs. The native people's trails and cleverness at finding water had saved her family more than once, so she had a grateful feeling toward them. It was the stories one heard, though, that scared her. She wondered what would happen if a child were found wandering alone.

"Col! Answer me!"

She heard a sound behind her and spun around, but it was only Mr. Rood stumbling along, searching in cracks and crevices. He waved to her and then came her direction.

"I'm going down the canyon, Mrs. Brier. How long has he been missing?"

"I don't know. He was gone when I got up about an hour ago."

"So he could have a good head start. He won't have much energy, though."

"No, but Col surprises me sometimes with his determination."

"Just like his mother." Mr. Rood smiled slightly as he hurried ahead. "We'll find him, ma'am."

She pressed on, looking left and right and calling as she went with her voice getting shriller and shriller. Perhaps she was heading the wrong direction. Perhaps Col wasn't looking for water at all but had awakened, dazed from exhaustion and thirst, and simply strayed away. Maybe he collapsed somewhere among these boulders. His clothes were so covered with desert dirt that they would blend perfectly with the soil and rocks.

She stopped to listen. If someone had found him, there would be a joyful shouting from camp or the sound of a signal rifle. The only sounds she heard now were the men's voices calling out Columbus's name and the call of a bird in the brush. A rabbit darted to safety. Her throat hurt from the lump that wouldn't go away and her heart pounded. She leaned over, sick with anxiety. Again, she repeated a frantic, silent prayer and hurried down the canyon, as frightened as she had ever been.

CHAPTER 49

A rifle shot exploded and echoed back and forth between the canyon walls. Oh, thank heavens! Still, the meaning of a gunshot was never certain. It could mean Col was safe— or it could be a signal calling for help if he was injured, or worse.

She stopped, confused for a moment. Had the shot come from up the canyon or down? The echo made it hard to tell. It might have been Rood's rifle, so that would mean it came from the south. She continued down the trail, dodging rocks and bushes as she hurried. A second shot rang out, closer now.

Then she saw them in the distance, Mr. Colton and Mr. Rood and Columbus, making their way toward her. Her knees buckled and she nearly fell, but she kept on, sobbing quietly while she murmured her thanks. Col trudged up the canyon flanked by the two gaunt men as if nothing had happened. He was not limping or covered in blood. Gradually, her heartbeat subsided and her breath came more evenly.

Columbus stopped when he saw her. Apprehension settled on his freckled face as she approached. He had her scratched canteen in his hands. Beside him, Colton stopped, too. Rood rubbed his sooty rifle barrel on his stained shirt.

"Col, where have you been?" She hurried to him and hugged him until he squirmed. "We were frantic with worry."

"I thought I found a spring, Mother. I even dreamed about where it was. I was going to fill your canteen for you."

"I know, Col. We're all so thirsty. It would have been a good find. But you were in danger. You must never leave camp again."

"I couldn't help it, though. I had to go look. It was almost a river in my dream. There were sweet berries there, too, thousands of them."

They started back to camp and met the other men coming toward them, strung out across the red-rock canyon as if to leave no inch unsearched. When they saw the boy, they turned and quietly went back to camp, all but James, who waited. His dark eyebrows frowned low across his forehead.

"Where have you been, son?"

Columbus stopped and looked at the ground. His moccasins curled up around his toes, and he kicked sandy dirt over a stone.

"I thought I found a spring, Father."

"So you wandered off to go exploring."

"Yes, sir. I'm sorry. But I was going to fill Mother's canteen."

"We'll have to punish you, son. You know that, don't you? For now, we have to hurry and pack. We're getting a late start."

Back at the fire again, Juliet sank to the ground, drained of strength. Her whole body still trembled and her muscles were weak, but no one noticed. Johnny greeted his brother with a hug around the shoulders.

"Where were you, Col?"

"I was out scouting for water. I almost found some, too."

"Where, Col? We need some."

"Well, I didn't find some, but I almost did."

"Oh. Was it by the big rock?"

"I found the big rock and some tall cliffs. That's where Mr. Colton and Mr. Rood joined up with me. But I hadn't found the spring yet. They said we had to go find Mother."

"Let's go, men." Doty swung his bedroll onto his back and grabbed his rifle. "Brier, you and Robinson can catch us tonight. You still need to pack up."

"All right, Doty, if you can't wait a second."

Juliet got to her feet. How could she possibly walk the whole day, feeling as she did? She scooped up the blankets but wadded them into a jumble instead of neatly rolling them, and cinched them onto Old Red with corners hanging down and lumps pushing up from under the ropes. James looked at her, but handed her the coffeepot to tie on top of the mess.

Robinson was still sitting by the fire with his leg stretched out in front of him. His pants were ripped nearly to the thigh and the dressing on his puffy knee was stained. He closed his eyes and lifted his face to the sun. His tattered bedroll was still rumpled on the ground behind him.

"Columbus, pack up Mr. Robinson's bedroll for him, please. We'll let the cattle carry it again today."

Her fingers still shook as she knelt beside Robinson and unwound yesterday's soiled bandage. The wound wasn't healing as it should. More red streaks radiated from the gash. He needed water and several days of rest. She left the injury open to the air while she took the herbs from her apron pocket and mixed a quick poultice. When she was finished dressing the wound, she and Columbus helped Robinson to his feet. He swayed, but stayed upright. James handed him his stick, and the two of them started slowly down the trail.

Juliet loaded Kirke onto the ox and fell in behind. Her legs still felt as though they might not hold her, but she knew it would be only a matter of minutes before James and Mr. Robinson would need to stop. She could rest with them.

CHAPTER 50

The days that followed stacked up like bricks in Juliet's mind—hard, unyielding, and monotonous. The red canyon receded as the landscape opened onto a broad, dry valley, and, after that, a desert so vast that its far end disappeared into the brown distance. She shrank from the sight, but the exacting compass pointed the way straight across it. She saw the needle's unflinching direction herself as James held the instrument in his shaking hand.

Just when they were weakest, Juliet thought, this gigantic, waterless wasteland appeared in front of them as if it were a daunting new enemy in a long war. All these weeks, she had urged herself onward with visions of the lovely Sierra Nevada forestlands, but there were no sparkling streams or sheltering evergreens there, just as there seemed to be no end to these harsh deserts. Who could have known that God bundled His sand and dry stones, His packed dirt and desolate flats, His unwanted spiders and lizards and scraggly plants, and tossed them all down in this immense part of the world?

The men were silent ghosts, reeling their way across the desert. Juliet's body felt as if it were made of glass—fragile, brittle, and ready to collapse at the slightest touch. Images flitted in and out of her mind: Johnny almost too weak to walk, her sore toes poking from the ends of her disintegrating shoes, half cups of blood from the last butchered ox to drink. No fire at night.

In camp, the Jayhawkers slouched on the ground each morning long past dawn. They watched Juliet with vacant eyes as her fumbling fingers untied the flour sack holding dried-out pieces of beef. One by one, they reached for it with hands that looked as if the life had drained from them, leaving nothing but leathery skin and bones.

"We're almost there, men. I'm certain of it," she said. No one answered. Finally, Mr. Doty said, "Yep."

James tried to heave his gaunt body from the ground but fell back again. Juliet grasped his hands and pulled him up. He steadied himself on her shoulder, swaying and bent at the waist. His clothes hung in dirty shreds from his emaciated shoulders.

"I can't walk, Juliet." His voice was barely audible.

"James. You must. You can lean on me."

She loaded the pack animals and dressed Mr. Robinson's wound while the others struggled to their feet. Mr. Doty laced his crumbling boots as his eyes roamed the pathetic camp. The men's faces were blank, and their hair hung down in lank, matted strings. Colton limped. Robinson's eyes were too big and dark.

"Young, can you scout for water?" Doty asked.

"I'll try. I'm nearly done in, though."

"The little boys are going to need some this morning."

"I know. Robinson, too. And Brier."

Young stood and caught his balance. "Colton, can you come with me?"

"I guess so."

Juliet watched them trudge away as she gathered enough strength to lift Kirke onto Big Jake. James wobbled over to the animal.

"I'll steady myself by holding onto Kirke's harness," he said. "I can't lean on you, Juliet. You're too worn out yourself."

"This is a test of our resolve, James."

"And our bodily strength. If I don't make it, Juliet . . . "

"James! Of course you'll make it." Her voice was alarmed. James, who used to exude energy and enthusiasm and liveliness. Juliet cringed to hear him now. She took his hand and softened her tone. "Please don't say that, James. It frightens me."

"I don't mean to frighten you. It's just that this infirmity and this everlasting, brutal desert are getting the best of me."

"When we get to the settlements there will be a doctor."

He looked at her without answering.

She released his hand reluctantly, pushing away the unbearable thought that this journey might claim her James's life, and they started out, skirting the scrubby creosote bush and picking their way around rocks. The sun warmed the air until it was nearly pleasant. She tried to swallow, but her tongue was too dry; it was beginning to block her airway again. She took a deep breath to clear her head and steadied herself as she placed one foot in front of the other to begin the day's long trek. Behind her and ahead of her, the desert stretched on forever.

CHAPTER 51

Night had come again when Sheldon Young and John Colton stumbled back to camp with the news that the nearest spring was another half day's march ahead. Their canteens were filled with enough muddy water for everyone to have a couple ounces. In the moonlight, Juliet could imagine that her portion was clear and clean, even though she could feel the grit in her mouth and smell the bad odor of old vegetation.

The Jayhawkers sagged on the ground, barely bothering to crawl under their blankets, although the January night was cold and there was no fire. Their despondency pushed its way into Juliet's cloudy mind. If the men lost their will to finish this journey, if they just gave up . . . James sat among them with his head in his hands, his swollen tongue still. Her husband, for whom the spoken word was key to life itself, was as quiet as the next man.

She forced herself to spread the quilts for her family and another for Mr. Robinson. As she straightened up, it felt as though the world tilted, and she nearly fell. She would sleep now, alongside her family. In the morning, perhaps, she could manage a few of the chores.

And then, the sun glaring on her face awakened her. She lay still. Her mouth felt as if it were packed with gritty sand that scratched her burning throat and filled up her airway. She had no sensation on her tongue, which poked out between her lips even when she tried to draw it in. Her eyes stung, and she had to summon the energy to raise her hand to rub them. She whispered her morning prayers.

Holding onto a rock for balance, she sat and then stood slowly. Most of the men were awake, but they continued to lie silently on the cold ground. One thought came clear. If the party was to reach the safety of today's spring, she was going to have to push them there. She would have to dredge up strength enough to drive them all.

"Men." Her voice didn't work, so she tried again. "Men! The sun is up. We've got to move out."

The bodies on the ground stirred, and she spoke again, not caring that her words sounded thick and slurred. "It's not far to the spring. We can make it by afternoon."

Young pushed himself onto his elbow. Doty followed and then Colton. Robinson didn't move.

"We're going to make it, men." She stopped, exhausted, and then pulled the blanket from over the children. The children. Why did she ever acquiesce to bringing them out here? Their scrawny, undernourished bodies huddled together in ragged clothes layered with dirt and grime. Juliet rubbed her neck as she stood staring at them numbly. Johnny and

Columbus opened their eyes, and Kirke shifted. She braced herself and grasped their hands, one by one, and pulled them to their feet.

Later, as the group straggled out of camp with bedrolls and knapsacks tied haphazardly to their backs, Juliet looked around the campsite. Another rifle had been discarded on the desert floor.

Mr. Doty let the group go ahead and waited for her to finish tying Kirke and Johnny to Big Jake.

"Thank you, Mrs. Brier." His voice grated, and his words were indistinct.

"We can't let despair set in." She looked past his long lashes, encrusted with dust and debris, and into his haggard eyes. "Determination is what we need now, Mr. Doty."

He looked back at her for a long moment.

"Yes."

"Will you help me get Mr. Robinson to his feet?"

"Yes." He lowered his voice. "He's not going to make it much farther."

"I know. I'm afraid his blood is poisoned."

When they got him upright, he draped his arm over Doty's shoulder to support himself as they started walking. Juliet stayed beside them, pulling on Big Jake's rope and encouraging Columbus and Johnny to keep up.

This morning, instead of wishing for other women to share this journey, as she usually did, she was grateful that no one else had to endure it. By now, she had perfected a way of focusing her mind on others to keep from dwelling on her own misery. As she wobbled along, she made herself concentrate on Sarah Bennett and the others who were stalled in the desert waiting for Mr. Manly and Mr. Rogers to return with provisions. Juliet could almost see Sarah stranded there, miserable and scared, in her tattered old dress and flyaway hair, dwarfed against the brown wall of bare rock mountains and the immeasurable flat desert. She would be crying, but her tears would have dried up from thirst.

And what about Asahel? She wondered if Sarah's good, conscientious husband was sick or injured. Why else would he stop traveling and put all his hopes into the remote chance of a rescue? The Arcans, too. Abigail was expecting a child and she had to look after her little Charley. The hunger and thirst would be too much for her.

Manly and Rogers said the two families were camped beside a spring of sorts, so there would be a little water— and a couple of weak oxen, whose sparse, stringy meat would have the disagreeable flavor of the greasewood they'd had to scrounge. The most difficult part—the thing that would make Sarah's stomach clench—would be the waiting and not knowing. Everyone thought the settlements were much closer than they were, so when Manly and Rogers didn't return in a reasonable number of days, Sarah would be ill from worry that her family and friends had been abandoned.

At least Sarah and Abigail had each other. That was slim comfort, considering the agonies they must be suffering. Mr. Manly said he thought the Wades had left the others and attempted to bolt out of that desperate valley by taking a southern route. Poor Mary could be trapped somewhere in this exacting wilderness, too, alone with her husband and her four trusting young ones.

Mr. Manly was devoted and principled, Juliet thought, and Mr. Rogers showed the same qualities. Yet she found herself wondering how anyone could stumble from this mammoth wasteland alive and then willingly turn around, exhausted, footsore and crazed from thirst, and traverse it a second time—and then a third bringing the families to safety. No one in his right mind would do that, promise or no promise.

And yet . . . she herself would, wouldn't she? Perhaps Mr. Manly and Mr. Rogers, too, considered a promise sacred.

CHAPTER 52

———

Y ou've got to help me, Mrs. Brier." Robinson's voice was only a whisper as he reeled along beside her.

The terrible hissing in Juliet's ears and the swirling blackness that threatened unconsciousness were her constant companions now. Despite the last dismal spring, where a few willows and a poor seeping dampness broke the merciless aridity, her strength was nearly gone. She tried to think, but it was as if a curtain had been drawn inside her head. Blankness stifled her mind and jumbled the miles and slogging footsteps, the thirst and hunger. She couldn't remember how many days it had been since their last good drink.

"Take my hand, Bill," she responded slowly. In his worst moments, Robinson responded to her use of his first name. He reached out, but his knees buckled and he fell. Juliet bent over to banish the reddish darkness that swept over her. The Jayhawkers were up ahead, usually within sight but too far away to hear any feeble shouts for help. If Robinson couldn't walk any farther, she and James would be hard-pressed to get him to tonight's camp.

She pulled Big Jake to the man's side. The poor ox was parched and ready to drop, but he kept lumbering along with Kirke and sometimes Johnny on his back and James clutching onto his harness. Now, using the animal for support, Robinson was able to stagger to his feet. He put his arm over the ox's back. Wordlessly, they started up.

The desert swam in a fluid motion, tipping and swirling as the sun moved higher in the sky and then seemed to stop overhead. The afternoon ground on as they trailed the Jayhawkers. Juliet saw someone's discarded bedroll behind the tangled greasewood and then another rifle. Farther along was a second abandoned bedroll.

A few times, when he remembered, James pulled the compass from his pocket. In contrast with the earlier deserts—those wide, deep valleys between mountain ranges— it was difficult to orient themselves in this one. There were no bordering mountains, and no end was in sight. Instead, this desert unfolded before them, as infinite as the sky. Perhaps the infuriating compass was broken, insisting as it did that they were still inching southwest.

They overtook the Jayhawkers at dark. Again, there was no fire, no food, and no water. Juliet counted the sleeping bodies. One was missing. She looked again. It was Ed Doty, probably out scouting for water. She willed herself to think. Everyone's judgment was clouding. Sending a scout out alone was evidence of that. Her own thinking was hazy, she knew; she must make a better effort.

She awakened, chilled, at the first hint of an icy dawn to find Mr. Doty stretched out on the bare ground nearby. He stirred when she summoned the energy to sit up.

"I found a little puddle up ahead," he told her. "Just frozen mud, but it's not far."

Together they roused the camp and pushed them on to the spring. Just as Doty had described, it was a muddy puddle, almost outlandishly out of place in its desiccated surroundings. Its edges were frozen into a thin layer of brown ice. Juliet joined the others in breaking off small pieces, careful not to let them melt in her fingers and waste even a drop of its precious moisture. She helped Kirke and Johnny and Mr. Robinson put chips on their tongues, but James and Col were able to gather their own.

Mr. Robinson was shaking violently. Angry red streaks shot outward from his wound. Juliet pulled off his cap to let the air cool his head. He looked at her but didn't speak. His eyes were glazed and bloodshot. She took a piece of ice, rubbed it on his hot forehead, and tried to think of what more she could do.

When the ice was gone, she scooped as much water as she could into the bottom of the coffeepot. It crossed her mind that back home these travelers would sooner have died than drink this mucky sediment. Here, it seemed like a gift from heaven, a life-saving miracle. Mud or not, they would swallow it with thanksgiving—and with a primitive, animal-like desperation.

"How much farther is it, Father?" Col asked. "After this spring, I mean?"

"We don't know, son." James's voice was only a raspy whisper.

"Are there more mountains?"

"I don't know."

"Will there be more springs after this one?"

"No one knows, son. There must be more springs out here. We just have to find them."

Juliet looked at Col and tried to think of some words that might comfort him. But nothing came to mind.

And then, the next day, the landscape began to change, almost imperceptibly at first. Foothills edged into view, and the scruffy creosote bushes grew closer together. They were thicker and more abundant compared to the sparse specimens they had encountered before, and their peculiar peppery odor was stronger. She could finally see low mountains ahead. She wondered if this could be the last mountain range Mr. Manly thought existed. What name had he given it? San Gabriel. The sight of their hazy ridgelines both pulled her forward and made her falter. Could the children possibly climb another range of mountains? Could any of them? Yet if this pile of ridges and gullies was the last obstacle in their way . . .

The mountains drew closer and then seemed to retreat in the shimmering, cool sun. She had given up trying to estimate the miles. It was easier just to keep her mind plodding along with her feet. They passed a small, crooked rock cairn, and she considered briefly who could have placed it there.

It didn't matter. All that mattered was placing one foot in front of the other and making sure her family and Mr. Robinson were dragging along behind her.

CHAPTER 53

The creosote bushes were taller than the children here. They crowded together on the hilly flanks that now rose before them. Juliet wondered if whacking through a dense, scratchy jungle of brush could be the obstacle that stalled them for good. With Mr. Robinson and James both in such feeble condition, her family had already straggled too far behind. James crept along with his walking sticks, and Robinson pulled himself forward with Big Jake's help.

The evening sky faded from orange to gold to gray and finally black as they tried to overtake the bedraggled Jayhawkers. Bright stars shone steadily, then swirled like a sparkling whirlpool, then steadied themselves again. Juliet took a deep breath. Was that smoke she smelled? She looked ahead. In the distance, a small orange flame flickered. One of the men was strong enough to build a fire. That meant there was water. After a while, she could see their dark shapes lying near the flames. Sparks flew into the cold night air and disappeared.

Then Mr. Doty was beside her holding a dripping tin cup. She reached out, and he helped lift it to her lips.

"Is there more?"

"Yes, Mrs. Brier. Plenty more."

She took a few sips and then pulled Kirke down from Big Jake and held the cup to the little boy's mouth.

"Col, Johnny, go find the spring and drink slowly."

Robinson had fallen to his knees again. Doty saw him collapse and hurried unsteadily to fetch a beat-up coffeepot filled with water. He set it beside Robinson with another cup.

"Are you all right, old comrade?"

Robinson couldn't answer. Juliet helped him drink the first sips. After a few minutes, he could lift the cup to his own mouth, and he began drinking long, eager draughts.

"Slowly, Bill. Slowly." Juliet watched the young man. "Don't drink too much at once."

Suddenly, there was a snort and a long bawl, and then the panicked pounding of hooves as Big Jake, Old Red, and the remaining two pack animals bolted into the darkness. Juliet hurried the children to the campfire.

"A bear," Mr. Rood was saying. "I thought I saw the old fellow earlier. He's a big one, straight from these mount . . . "

"Say, that's a good sign!" Colton interrupted. "Bears like greener territory than deserts."

"Maybe you could get a shot at him, Doty. Bear meat would taste mighty good right now," Young said.

"We'll have to wait until morning," Doty answered. "Chances are he'll be long gone, though."

"We'll need daylight to find Briers's oxen, too," Colton said. "It's too black out here now. Let's hope they don't go far."

Kirke's eyes were big, and he sat close to Columbus by the fire.

"Where's Father?" Columbus asked. "I can't see him."

"He's coming," Juliet answered. "He'll be along in a few moments. You boys stay here while I see to Mr. Robinson. He needs his knee bandaged again."

She made her way to where she had left the young man sprawled beside the old coffeepot. The pot was empty, and Robinson was sitting up clutching his head in his hands. He looked up at her blankly as she approached.

"My head hurts an awful lot."

"Did it start aching just now?

"Yes, after I drank the water."

"You drank *all* that water in the coffeepot, Bill?"

"I think so. I can't quite remember."

Juliet stopped short.

"You can't *remember*?"

"I don't believe so."

Fear stabbed her. She knelt beside him and looked carefully into his glassy eyes. He stared back in a vacant, confused way and pressed his hands to his temples. She pulled the last piece of dried beef from her apron pocket.

"Bill, eat this meat and then sleep for a while. I'll wash and dress your knee while you rest."

Juliet worked to clean the gravel and dirt from his seeping wound while the young man leaned back and shut his eyes. As she finished, she glanced into the darkness and saw James laboring up the slope. She grabbed her cup, filled it, and went to meet him. He steadied himself with a hand on her shoulder while he dribbled it down his dry throat.

"Thank you, Juliet," he said hoarsely when he could speak. She marveled that his habitual courteousness was so ingrained that he thanked her even when he was ready to collapse. Out here, after these suffocating hardships used up all patience and composure, one's true character came through. Even the children showed their most fundamental qualities. Columbus carried on with the tenacity so evident in his personality. Johnny waited for the journey's end with patience rare in one so young, and Kirke, weak as he was, still offered his tender, childish affection.

"Come rest by the fire, James. I've saved a place for you. And . . . the cattle have bolted. We'll have to find them in the morning."

CHAPTER 54

In the morning, Bill Robinson was dead.

Juliet knelt beside him to check his leg before she realized that his young eyes were staring at nothing at all, and he wasn't breathing. She shook his shoulder, hoping for movement, and then shook it harder and called out his name, but he didn't respond. She tried again, praying silently. Then her throat closed, and she bent double and buried her face in the shredded folds of her old gray dress. Her chest ached as dry sobs escaped her, and she drew in breath after ragged breath.

She stayed by his side until the sun came up, as if to offer him one more hour of comfort. Then she went and awakened James and Mr. Young and Mr. Doty. Soberly, they struggled to their feet, gathered around Robinson, and stood for a few moments with their heads bowed. After a whispered discussion, they wrapped him in his tattered brown blanket and carried him from camp. The hard earth resisted their tired efforts to hollow out a shallow grave, so they found an overhanging rock and placed his body underneath, covering it with stones and brush.

Juliet stood aside and watched. The old familiar lump blocked her throat. In a few minutes, Mr. Colton and Mr.

Rood crawled from their bedding and came to stand beside her. Colton took a deep, quavering breath and bent to fiddle with his moccasin. Mr. Young got out his stubby pencil and wrote a few terse words in his journal. He cleared his throat, then, and looking at the ground, began to sing. Dumbfounded, Juliet listened to his hoarse baritone and Henry Kirke White's lovely hymn she knew so well.

> *And thou wilt turn our wandering feet,*
> *And thou wilt bless our way;*
> *Till worlds shall fade, and faith shall greet*
> *The dawn of lasting day.*

At least she could take comfort in the thought that Bill Robinson had seen the dawn of lasting day.

James gave a short prayer, fumbling for words and speaking in a faint, slow voice. When he was finished, the men turned away and straggled out to search for the oxen.

"Don't blame yourself for Robinson's death, Mrs. Brier," Mr. Doty said quietly as he led the way. "We'd have lost him a long way back if it hadn't been for you."

She couldn't stomach any coffee. After the children awoke, she drew them close as she told them about Mr. Robinson. Johnny scrubbed his eyes with his fists and his lower lip quivered. Col kicked a few pebbles into the fire, and Kirke climbed onto her lap and put his thumb in his mouth. Juliet held him for a while, silently praying, and then busied herself patching Kirke's moccasin with a strip of fabric from the threadbare edge of her skirt. Any scraps of ox hide must be saved for food.

Two hours later, the men returned with Big Jake and the other three cattle, and the group began trudging toward a canyon that opened like a solitary slice in the mountains. Anguish over the morning's events haunted Juliet as they entered the steep-sided gorge and fought through bushy scrub oak that snatched at their clothing and scratched their arms and faces. She parted the bushes as her family descended into a streambed where it was damp underfoot and Big Jake's hooves sank into the sand. There were unfamiliar animal tracks, including the big rounded paw prints of the bear. She shuddered at their size.

The day dragged on. They overtook the Jayhawkers after nightfall when the men halted on a sloping bare spot. Surprisingly, a little water flowed in the streambed where there had been none during the day. James murmured something about an underground river, but Juliet wasted little thought on when or why it ventured above ground. There was enough water for tonight's camp, and that was all that mattered. She filled the coffeepot to the brim, but was too weak to lift it from the stream. She poured half out and tried again. This time Mr. Colton helped her lug the sloshing pot to the fire that Rood had started. Her soup would consist of hot water, three pieces of scraped ox hide, and a pinch of rosemary from her herb packet to make it taste less foul. As she worked, Juliet looked over the dismal gathering. The men were walking skeletons, exhausted beyond all recognition. Hopelessness and gloom settled over camp as if vultures were circling overhead.

By noon the next day, Juliet could see that the wide canyon they traversed crossed a low divide in the distance. Mr. Doty and Mr. Colton were staring at its gentle rise, and Doty was pointing.

"Look, Col," she said to her oldest son. "See that divide up ahead? That's where we'll go. Then we'll see what's on the other side."

"I don't care to see, Mother. There's always another big valley and more mountains."

She started up again, watching where she placed her feet. He was right, of course. Every time they had crested a ridge, they had seen nothing but wild, deep valleys and mountains that rose like stockades between them and their deliverance. If that happened this time, Juliet knew the men would sink onto the hard, dry ground and surrender. They would yield to this vast unforgiving country and concede defeat, handing over their very lives in forfeit. She begged God for the fortitude to keep encouraging them on their way.

She lifted her chin. They could wander in this enormous wilderness for a lifetime and never come across the minute speck that was the tiny pueblo of Los Angeles. But they had to keep trying.

CHAPTER 55

The canyon wound through the mountains where the damp riverbed cut a path. Tufts of new grass began to appear, and Juliet waited patiently when Big Jake stopped to snatch at them. The poor animal deserved their tender gratitude, and the short stops gave James a chance to catch up. The Jayhawkers hauled themselves toward the divide at a snail's pace. There was no worry today that they would get too far ahead.

Snow on the ground took them by surprise, and they gratefully packed snowballs to eat as they walked. Soon the children had water running down their chins and arms that made dark, wet spots on their heavy shirts—a glorious sight that Juliet did not fail to appreciate.

They had seen snow on the mountaintops, of course, but did not expect it here in this protected canyon. At first, it lay in shaded areas, but as they went higher, it blanketed the ground. Juliet looked in dismay at her worn-out shoes, barely held together by her repeated patches and determined stitching. Stained and leaky with holes in the soles, they were scant protection against this cold snow.

She passed Colton and Rood, who had stopped to cinch their moccasins tighter.

"Might as well go barefoot," Colton said, poking his dirty finger into a hole in one thin sole. "How are yours, Rood?"

"Better than Young's, I guess. His are just chunks of rawhide curled up around his feet."

"I wish my boots hadn't fallen apart."

"Me, too."

Juliet looked back at James. His were holding up, thanks to her attention. But his emaciated legs were bare to the calves where his pants had ripped and frayed and finally disintegrated. Juliet guessed he must have lost nearly half his body weight—seventy or eighty pounds—since Salt Lake. His arms hanging from his shredded sleeves were like sticks. Beneath his abrupt cheekbones, his cheeks were deep caverns that disappeared into his dark, unkempt beard.

She was too depleted to be mortified by the state of her own clothes. Her dirty, long gray dress had caught and ripped so many times that it now hung only to her knees, and her skinny legs were in plain sight. There were holes in both elbows and smaller tears where shiny black buttons had once been. Back home in Michigan, her attire would have been disgraceful. Out here, it seemed a trifle compared with the fight for their lives.

By mid-afternoon, they slogged through old snow to the top of the divide. Juliet steeled herself for the view, but this time there was no long vista, just more of the same canyon winding downhill between the mountains. The drifts were deeper here, but the snow had a crust that allowed her to walk gingerly on the surface. The poor men sank nearly to their knees. Wild animals left meandering holes.

The canyon descended and widened, and suddenly a small muddy stream appeared. Running water! They stopped at its banks for a long drink, and then camped, exhausted, hoping to feel stronger in the morning.

When Juliet awoke, Doty was standing near the water with his eyes fixed on a brushy patch upstream where a large shadow moved. He leaned over for his ever-present rifle and brought it slowly to his shoulder. Juliet froze as he struggled with the weight of the gun, but he shakily took aim and fired.

"Got her! A wild horse, of all things!" Doty said. "Provisions, men."

"Our first game in weeks! My God, Doty! You've done it!" Rood slapped his friend on the back. "We'll have a good hot meal and some meat to carry along."

It took two long days to navigate the thick brush that choked the canyon. The stream became a muddy river. Juliet repeated her silent thanks for its heartening presence, but it was too much effort to wash her hands or face. All that seemed important was putting the miles behind them, one weary step at a time. Searching for water no longer consumed their time and strength, but now it was snow that plagued them. They spent the long, cold nights huddled on its icy surface, packed together for warmth, trying to sleep. In the gray morning light, they arose, exhausted and chilled to the bone.

On the third day, the men snaked out behind her, floundering deep into the snow while Juliet tiptoed atop the hard crust to an overlook.

Then, suddenly, she was crying with joy and relief, breathlessly singing out her prayer of thanksgiving, and calling to the men to hurry. Below her was a stunning panorama of green rolling hills, peaceful meadows, and a thousand sleek grazing cattle. Overhead, wild geese called.

Could she be dreaming?

She looked again. The gentle hills rose and fell to a distant blue river that wound through a pleasant, sunny valley. Everything about this verdant landscape contrasted with the brown, dry deserts behind them. Even now, in the dead of winter, the snow was gone, and trees and undergrowth thrived, and there were lovely meadows like those she had expected in the Sierra Nevada. The fragrance of new grass scented the balmy air. The civilization she had dreamed about for so long was right here—a rancher's cattle grazing so serenely they looked as though they were the foreground of an alluring painting.

"We've made it!" Her voice was jubilant. "Hurry! Come look!"

Doty's head snapped up in disbelief. He and the first of the men quickened their feeble pace to the hilltop.

"Finally!" It was all Rood could say when they looked out over the scene.

"Cattle! Someone's cattle," Doty said in awe. "That means there's a ranch!"

"That means there's a *meal!*" Colton added.

"Civilization . . . " Sheldon Young said the word as if he were savoring it on his tongue. "Civilization, folks."

And then they were all there: James, the rest of the men, and the children. James, wheezing and panting, stared at the scene below, then rubbed his hand over his eyes and stared again.

"That's California, isn't it, Mother?" Columbus's voice sounded as it had back home when he was excited.

"Yes, Col. We've made it." She slid Johnny and Kirke from Big Jake's back. Impulsively, she threw her arm around the old ox's neck and hugged him.

"Are those the valleys where flowers grow in winter?" Johnny asked. "And there's food to eat all the time?"

"Yes." Juliet smiled and lifted her face to heaven.

"What are we waiting for?" Doty asked. He shouldered his rifle. "Let's get down there and make a fire. I'll shoot a nice fat calf."

"We'll have us a feast!" Colton grinned.

They moved down the slope toward a pretty meadow partly shaded by wide branching oaks. A rushing mountain creek bordered it on one side. Imagine crystal clear water gurgling past, dancing and sparkling in the warm sunshine! Her throat tightened with emotion. After drinking from mud holes, briny puddles, and moldy seeps for so long, this glittering, melodic creek was an incredible gift. She followed the men through the soft grass—grass that would nourish and restore the faithful oxen—that sprang from the rich, dark soil, and kept her eyes on the welcoming land below.

CHAPTER 56

D elicious fat sizzled on the roaring fire. Juliet devoured a long strip of the exquisite calf meat. It was tender and dripping with juice—a wondrous change from the dry, stringy, creosote-flavored beef on which they had been surviving. Some of the men had eaten theirs raw, not able to wait for it to cook. Beside them were full cups of clear, fresh water.

Juliet leaned back against a fallen log and savored the blessed nourishment and the utter relief of knowing that nearby was the help they sought.

"No more starvation, Juliet. We are here at last!" James said as he sank down on the log with a pink chunk of beef in his hands. The children were silent, ravenously swallowing their meat.

A sound and sudden movement from Doty startled her. He grabbed his rifle and stood up, staring intently through the trees at the meadow's far edge. Rood and Colton scrambled to their feet. Juliet heard it now. The sound of galloping horses coming closer.

"Children. Quickly. Behind this log." All at once, her whole body was shaking with a terrible realization. In the West, rustling cattle was a crime punishable by death. Any rancher would be furious about losing a prime calf, perhaps angry enough to shoot. She ducked behind the log with the children as the Jayhawkers clustered in front of the fire.

Six horsemen burst from the trees in a flash of bright colors, black hair, sleek horses, and leather saddles. They shouted to each other in a language Juliet did not understand. Galloping across the meadow, they pulled up short when they saw the calf's carcass lying bloody in the sun. A shadow crossed the lead rider's dark face, and he spoke rapidly to the others before he whirled his horse to approach the Jayhawkers, who stood with rifles ready.

Juliet could see him clearly now. He had deep lines in his face, a large hat that shaded his dark eyes, and a bright yellow shirt worn open at the neck and partly covered by a vivid, multicolored vest. A black silk kerchief was knotted around his neck. He dismounted easily, one hand holding the braided leather reins and the other hovering near the handle of a knife secured in a casing on his leg. His horse, a spirited black, gleamed and pranced in the sunlight. The other riders wore brilliant shirts under dark capes, fringed leather chaps, and similar broad-brimmed hats with narrow chinstraps. They held their lathered horses still, their eyes darting from one Jayhawker to the next.

The man—a Spanish rancher, Juliet thought in amazement, and the owner of this dead calf—stood frozen in place as he took in the emaciated group before him, and the angry

frown faded from his face. His black eyes swept over the skeletal figures dressed in threadbare shirts, the shredded remains
of holey pants, and hard, baked rawhide curled around their
calloused feet. He spotted James, holding himself upright
with the help of two walking sticks, Doty with his hollow eyes
and caved-in cheeks, and the others with their filthy, tangled
hair and bony limbs. Another sweeping glance noted Rood's
bloody hands, the sticks of tender beef still roasting on the
fire, and the battered old coffeepot steaming on the coals.

Slowly, Juliet stood up from behind the log, and he
looked her way, spotting the children.

"Dios Mio!" he said finally. For a moment longer, he
stood motionless and silent, as if there were no other words
for the scene in front of him. Then he quickly turned to his
cowboys, said something swiftly, and handed his reins to the
nearest rider.

He went straight to the downtrodden men with his hands
outstretched, speaking rapidly in his melodic language and
gesturing down the slope beyond the meadow. Rood and
Doty set their guns down. James, more from old habit than
clear thought, lurched forward and extended his right hand
as if to shake. The rancher enveloped his dirty, stick-thin
fingers in his own strong, brown hand.

Then a voice from the Jayhawkers said, "Padre." Juliet
wasn't sure who spoke the word, but the effect on the rancher
was profound. He stared at James.

"Padre?"

The cowboys began to talk rapidly. Padre. What did it mean? Juliet searched her sluggish brain for the word. Padre. Patriarch. Father. A man of God.

"Pobre Padre!" The rancher whirled and began issuing orders to his men.

Juliet heard the word *rancho* and her heart lifted. Ranch.

Without hesitation, the cowboys dismounted and helped hoist the travelers onto their horses. Johnny and Kirke rode with Juliet on a curious-looking leather saddle with wood stirrups, and the men lifted Col onto another in front of James. The Jayhawkers doubled up on the remaining horses. Without another glance at the slain calf, the rancher led the way on foot, gesturing for the others to follow.

The meadow curved downhill and over a sunny ridge, and then spread out along the burbling creek. Cattle raised their heads and watched them pass. Juliet saw a doe disappear into the trees, and an unfamiliar bird called from a thicket. Overhead, a few puffy white clouds floated by in the moist air. The horse moved gracefully beneath her. She held Kirke and Johnny close as they rode through the warm sunshine, through the wondrously green and beautiful California foothills to the rancho, putting the desert behind them forever.

CHAPTER 57

The buildings sat on a peaceful knoll overlooking the pastoral scene. Juliet had never seen a sight more welcome than that cluster of small, clay structures, built in a charming architectural style she had never encountered, and the thousands of cattle that grazed upon the surrounding miles of sweet pastureland. The stories about California were true, if this lovely place was an example. The air was balmy—not thin and parched as it had been in the desert—and the warm breeze smelled of new grass. Near the ranch house, a vegetable garden grew and Juliet spotted a cluster of flowers near its edge. If her calculations were correct, it was February 4.

A woman left the low buildings and came toward them. She wore a blousy, white shirt and a long, yellow skirt that came to her ankles as she made her way gracefully down the hill. Her black hair was swept into a smooth braid that was twisted up and secured on her head. It was adorned with something red over one ear. Juliet pulled back slightly on the reins and tugged her shredded skirt lower on her dirty, bruised legs.

When the woman was near enough to hear, the rancher called to her in urgent Spanish and gestured to the group behind him. Her black eyes opened wide as she saw the ragged travelers. For a few seconds she stood still, taking in the scene: the ghostly people riding the horses, the emaciated oxen. Tears filled her eyes when she spotted Juliet and the children. Then she turned to the rancher—her husband, Juliet guessed—and spoke in rapid Spanish, gesturing to the ranch house. He nodded.

A few minutes later, they reached the adobe buildings. Juliet's legs collapsed as she slid from the saddle, and she stayed on her knees for a moment, hanging onto the smooth, oak stirrup until the world stopped tilting. Then the beautiful woman was at her side, grasping her hands and helping her to her feet. She looked into Juliet's eyes and spoke quickly in her soft, lyrical voice. Juliet gazed back at this kind stranger. It was not important to understand her words. Her warmth and her intentions were clear without them.

The interior of the rancho had a clay floor and a long table down the center of a large room. An arched doorway led to an enclosed courtyard where several children played. The *señora* led Juliet and the others to wooden benches around the table and gestured for them to sit. She issued a few pleasant commands to three barefoot girls in coarse dresses who were chattering around the outdoor oven. In a few moments, the air was filled with the fragrance of wood smoke and something baking.

One of the girls placed a tray of corn cakes on the table. The Jayhawkers and the children gaped before they helped themselves to the warm, crumbly chunks. When the tray was empty, the children picked up even the smallest crumbs and licked their fingers. The señora appeared then with small, clay cups filled with a steaming beverage. Juliet thanked her with a smile and said another silent prayer of thanksgiving as she swallowed the aromatic, sweet spiced coffee.

"Where do you think we are?" Ed Doty asked as he looked down the table at the bedraggled travelers. "Anywhere near Los Angeles?"

"If the compass was correct, I think we're close," James answered, taking a sip of his drink.

"Who are these people, do you suppose?" Sheldon Young asked. "I thought the old gentleman would be angry about that calf we killed. But if I'm not wrong, he and his men are outside butchering another one for us."

He was correct. It wasn't long until the table was covered with clay platters of tender beef, mashed beans, flour tortillas, and golden squash. There were new greens from the garden and even a pitcher of creamy milk. James stood and said a prayer of thanks aloud. The señora and her servants stood respectfully by with their heads bowed. When he was finished, their Spanish chatter began again.

After the meal, the señora took Juliet's arm and led her from the table. In a separate small room with a low bed

covered by a clean white spread, the woman gave her a set
of clean clothing—a loose, white bodice and a practical, tan
skirt that covered her knees and ankles—and showed her a
washtub filled with warm water. The children were sent with
one of the servants to bathe in the pond. When Juliet saw
them next, their hair was brushed and trimmed, and they
were dressed in simple clean clothes. They napped under
fresh blankets on the floor near the table.

Later that evening, with her clean hair secured in a
neat bun, Juliet found James sitting on a long, low wooden
bench along the outer wall of the adobe buildings. He wore
a plain set of unfamiliar clothes, including brown pants
that buttoned from his ankles to his knees, and his hair and
beard were trimmed. He held out his hand to her as she
approached.

"Are you feeling better?" he asked as he moved over to
make a spot for her.

"Oh, yes, James. Clean and well-fed and so greatly
relieved."

"I've never witnessed such a fine example of hospitality," he said.

"I agree. All without exchanging a word. Have you
noticed the care they've given the children?"

"Yes. Even Big Jake has grain and plenty of water. I'll
repay their kindness one day. After we're settled."

"Yes."

The sun was setting in a fiery blaze of orange in the west. She moved closer to James and leaned back against the warm wall, still holding his scrubbed hand. She must thank the señora one last time before she collapsed onto the soft bed meant for her inside. Even if she spoke in English, perhaps her generous new friend could understand a thankful voice.

Sheldon Young, scholar that he was, knew a few words of Spanish. Juliet overheard him the next morning as, with gestures, diagrams drawn in the dirt, and his scant knowledge of the language, he ascertained that the name of this gigantic ranch was the Rancho San Francisquito owned by the Del Valle family. It was, *Señor* Del Valle indicated to him, an easy half-day's journey to Mission San Fernando and, from there, only a few miles farther to the pueblo of Los Angeles.

"For all our uncertainty, we ended up where we intended," Young told Doty afterward. "From what I can understand—and I wish they wouldn't speak so fast—the very canyon we followed is where the first gold was discovered. Now the bigger strikes are up north near Sutter's Mill, of course, but this was the first."

"No matter where we Jayhawkers scatter from here, I'll wager we'll never forget this place," Doty replied.

"That's right. I can hardly believe the extent of these people's kindness. Del Valle said we should take his horses the rest of the way. He'll send a cowboy along to bring them home again."

Ride horseback to Los Angeles! Juliet had never dreamed of finishing the journey in such luxury.

It would be a few days before they could go. Some of the men were ill with cramps, and a doctor had been called to see to them. The oxen needed more time to recuperate on the lovely rich grass and plentiful water. James would see the doctor about his dysentery, but for now, he walked straighter, as if a load had been lifted from his shoulders. The children were beginning to play games with the dark-eyed children of the rancho. Juliet busied herself beside the señora, trying in some small way to help with her work, and she slept.

Before they left, she would give Señora Del Valle her grandmother's sapphire brooch, the one she had secured inside her pocket all those long miles. It was a wonder it hadn't been lost. Today, it was pinned inside her clean new pocket, scrubbed and polished and sparkling again—a fitting gift, she thought, for someone to whom she owed her gratitude, and, very possibly, her life.

CHAPTER 58

There was a knock on the kitchen door. Juliet wiped her floury hands on her apron to open it. Every time she made bread for the hotel guests here in the pueblo of Los Angeles, she marveled over the abundance of flour, the wonderful smooth powdery feeling of the dough, and the yeasty fragrance of it.

She pulled open the door. There on the stoop was a wiry man with a trimmed brown beard, neat hair, and a new cotton shirt. His blue eyes beamed in his tanned face, and he smiled at her without speaking until she recognized him.

"Why, Mr. Manly!"

"Yes. I heard you folks made it through. Is everyone all right?"

"Yes. Yes, we are." She paused. "All but poor Mr. Isham and Bill Robinson, that is. We lost them back in the desert. And you, Mr. Manly? But you must come in."

He sat backward on a wooden chair, quietly taking in the swept clay floor, the large rough-hewn table that filled the center of the room, and the black stove radiating warmth in the corner. A kettle steamed on the stove, filling the air with the fragrance of hot chowder. April sunlight poured through the glass window, framed with starched white flour sack curtains.

"It looks as though you're comfortably settled."

"We are. And how we've appreciated a roof over our heads these past two months! James was able to find this little adobe hotel, and he traded our few remaining oxen for half an interest in it. We take boarders and I cook the meals. The people here have been especially welcoming to us since James is a preacher. He delivered the first Methodist sermon ever given here a few weeks ago."

"All the rest of the Jayhawkers made it through? Doty, Rood, Young, and all?"

"Yes. It took a few weeks for them to recover. We very nearly died out there. But now they've scattered to the gold fields up north."

"I suspected so."

"Young John Colton suggested gathering for a reunion someday. It's a nice idea. I feel as though some of those men are my brothers by now."

Juliet brought him a bowlful of thick chowder and a metal spoon. She quickly finished kneading her dough, divided it among six pans, and put it on a warm shelf to rise. Then she removed her floury apron and joined him at the table.

"I'm afraid to ask, Mr. Manly. But Sarah Bennett and her family . . . and the Arcans and Wades. What became of them?" In her mind, she could still see Sarah waving her handkerchief in farewell as the Briers left their group—and then burying her face in her hands. Juliet could see Abigail Arcan, too, dressed in her pastel silk dresses and fancy hats, defying the elements while stalled in that most deathly of valleys beneath harsh rock mountains. She envisioned Mr. Bennett and Mr. Arcan, tortured by their decision to wait for help instead of toiling on. And the children—little Martha, Melissa, George, Charley—ill from hunger and thirst, crouched under the blankets waiting day after day for rescue. Rescue that might never come.

She looked again at Mr. Manly. The prospect of going back for them would be too much for any man: the dreadful thirst, the torturous distance, the likelihood that the families would have already perished, and the overpowering need for rest and food and plenty of water.

Mr. Manly gazed back at her, his eyes level and calm, as if he knew what she was thinking. Then he said quietly, "They're safe, Mrs. Brier. They're recuperating just thirty miles up the valley. Safe. And well."

Juliet's eyes filled with tears and she couldn't speak for a moment. She swallowed.

"The children, too?"

"The children—all of them—made it through. We almost lost little Martha. She was malnourished nearly to the point of death, but we got there just in time, Mrs. Brier. She's fine now."

A tear slid down Juliet's cheek and she stopped it with a floury finger. "You actually turned around and went back for them . . . "

"Rogers and I. We decided neither of us would be much of a man if we didn't," he said simply.

The lump in her throat made a reply impossible. As Mr. Manly spooned his chowder into his mouth, she sat silently, thinking of the enormous self-sacrifice.

Finally she said, "And Sarah? Did she fare all right?"

"I'll never forget her gratitude, ma'am. Never, as long as I live."

James came into the kitchen then, followed by all three of the children.

"Manly! Is that you?" James strode to the table as Mr. Manly got to his feet and held out his hand.

"Yes, Reverend Brier. I've returned from the Valley of Death . . . " Manly's tone was light, but he looked seriously at James. "And you folks look as though you fared all right. The children seem strong and healthy."

"Yes, they are. We're all better," he said, looking at Juliet as he spoke. Then he returned his gaze to Manly and pulled out a chair for himself. "But what befell you, Manly? After you came across us near that red rock canyon? You were hurrying to get help for the others."

"It wasn't long after that when my knee gave out. It hurt like the devil, and I could barely walk. Rogers slowed his pace and we pressed on, and after days of limping and thirst and dreadful hunger, we finally reached civilization. The fine folks we encountered put together rescue supplies for us, including a mule and a couple of horses. We had to communicate in sign language, but the women who helped us knew what we needed. They fed us and helped us on our way."

"And you went back for the families . . . "

"Yes. It was utterly grueling, as you can well imagine, and it took us much longer than we anticipated. The horses never made it through, but in the end, the mule did. We cached some of the provisions along the way to lighten the poor fellow's load."

"And when you reached their camp?"

"At first we thought we were too late. When we came into sight of the wagons, there was no one in view, even after we hollered. We were expecting to find corpses, to tell the truth."

Juliet glanced at her boys, who stood quiet and wide-eyed beside Mr. Manly's chair. The three of them were filling out again, even Kirke. Their cheeks were rosy from play, and their dark hair was shiny. The shadows were gone from under their eyes. When they sat at the table with their lessons each morning, they fidgeted or swung their feet or poked each other. Juliet reprimanded them gently, but in truth, she welcomed their liveliness.

"Then one by one, they appeared, thin and weak as ghosts. Every one of the Bennetts and Arcans. Wade and his wife had gone down the valley to try to find their way out, and they encountered some prospectors who directed them to the Old Spanish Trail. They made it to safety, too. With all four children. So did Captain Hunt and the remnants of our old wagon train. And the Mississippians."

They were quiet for a moment. Juliet said a quiet prayer of thanks. Mr. Manly resumed his story.

"There was a scant bit of forage where we left Bennett and Arcan. Their oxen had had a long rest from hauling. We hurried to make some good nourishing soup for the families and we gave the animals a handful of oats apiece. I think the soup is what saved little Martha. The next day we started out. Left the wagons behind. Mrs. Bennett sewed some large sacks for the children from extra clothing, and we hung them from Old Crump's sides. That old fellow carried those children all the way to the settlements."

"Some of those oxen deserve a lot of credit," James said. "We couldn't bear to part with our own Big Jake, no matter how much we needed the money. How long did it take?"

"Long enough for Mrs. Bennett to stop crying," Mr. Manly smiled. "Those poor folks. The trip was complete misery for them. You should have seen Mrs. Arcan scrambling down the mountains with those ridiculous ribbons flowing down her back."

"And you and Rogers? No lasting ill effects?"

"No. My knee still pains me. But I've got a clear conscience."

"A clear conscience—and everyone's gratitude," James said. "The Lord will bless you for your courage, Manly."

"If I travel north to see Bennett and Arcan sometime, perhaps you folks would like to come along."

"Oh, yes!" Juliet answered. There had been a time when she thought she would never leave the safety and warmth of her new home. For weeks, she had jerked awake each night with her heart pounding as images of parched deserts and her skeletal family haunted her dreams, only to find herself curled cozily on a comfortable mattress with James in this snug little hotel. The salty smell of the ocean wafted in the open window. At first, she could not sleep until she placed a large cup of water within reach. She had hoarded the variety of delicious foods that came to them so readily in this generous village—blessed corn and beans, mutton and beef, and flour and vegetables—but she soon realized there was no need.

Now, she sat back in her chair and looked around at her family. James sat tall, and the old light was back in his eyes. His face, though still thin, had lost its ghastly pallor and sharp hollows. His trimmed hair was combed back from his face; like the children's, it was turning glossy again. He ate massive quantities of her hot soups and stews and warm cornbread with melted butter.

She looked down at her skirt—the one Señora Del Valle had given her. Its plain tan folds were clean and it was long enough to brush the ground as she walked. The waist fit better now that she had been eating. Her next goal—after she wrote a letter to her brother—was to sew each of the children new trousers. Then she could decide how she and James would show their gratitude to the Del Valle family. Perhaps she could learn enough Spanish to write them a kind note expressing her heartfelt thanks and inviting them to visit the hotel, where she could return a tiny portion of their generous hospitality.

James was right about California. Flowers bloomed and the afternoon breezes were pleasantly warm. The musical sound of chimes from the plaza church floated in through the open window. New gold seekers from the East and across the sea arrived daily, so the small pueblo they were expecting was nearly a city now. James found plenty of need for his preaching. Juliet had noticed that little Johnny, even young as he was, was captivated by his father's sermons.

For a moment, she closed her eyes, sending her thanks heavenward. Her stomach never clenched in fear here, and the terrible gnawing hunger and thirst were only memories. Even the lump in her throat was different. Now she felt its presence from gratitude instead of desperation. Here in their safe new home, she took careful note of the simplest of life's blessings: plain dry beans, shoes without holes, her husband's straight posture, a shoot of grass bursting from the soil.

She took a deep breath. During the harrowing journey west, even the stars had seemed cold and distant. Here they winked and sparkled in their old friendly way. She saw now what she couldn't see during those blackest of desert nights: There had been, after all, a kind star leading them home.

EPILOGUE

The Brier family thrived in California, where they lived for the rest of their lives. In the years following their arduous trek west, three daughters were born, two of whom survived to adulthood.

Historical records show that the family moved several times throughout southern and central California. James continued his work as a pioneer missionary for nearly half a century, helping to establish new churches in emerging towns and gold camps, working for social causes, and serving as a trustee for one of California's first colleges. He died at the age of eighty-four in Lodi.

Juliet raised her family and made certain that her three sons and two surviving daughters, Mary and Helen, received educations. Later in her life, she took part in the Jayhawker reunions that materialized, thanks mostly to the efforts of John Colton. The reunions generally were scheduled for February 4 to celebrate the day the desperate overland party was welcomed to the hospitable safety of the Del Valle family's Rancho San Francisquito.

Records indicate that Christopher Columbus Brier grew up to run a private school in the San Francisco area, while his younger brother, John Wells Brier, followed their father's example and became a pastor. Kirke White Brier was a popular educator in Sacramento. All three boys married and had children of their own.

The Bennetts and the Arcans, with the help of William Lewis Manly and John Rogers, did indeed make their slow way out of the deserts and bring their children to safety. Soon afterward, Abigail Arcan gave birth to a baby girl, whom she named Julia in honor of Juliet Brier. The Wades, too, successfully reached the end of the trail with all four of their offspring, who went on to live full lives in California.

Lewis Manly reportedly worked for the Briers for a short time and then traveled and prospected until he purchased a farm near San José. There he settled with his wife, Mary, whom he married in 1862. He published an autobiography, including an account of his trip west, in a book titled *Death Valley in '49*. John Rogers, too, lived a long and productive life. Their Death Valley rescue of the Bennetts and the Arcans is known as one of the most heroic deeds in California's history.

The Jayhawkers scattered to the gold fields. Some were successful in their prospecting; others had marginal luck. Many later bought land in California and established farms or ranches. Others returned home and lived out their lives in the Midwest.

Juliet Wells Brier died in Lodi in 1913, a few months short of her one-hundredth birthday. She is remembered for her remarkable strength and determination in bringing the Death Valley pioneers to safety.

ABOUT THE AUTHOR

Mary Barmeyer O'Brien was born and raised in Missoula, Montana, and earned her bachelor's degree from Linfield College in McMinnville, Oregon. She is the author of the western historical novel *Outlasting the Trail* and three non-fiction books about pioneers on the overland trails: *Toward the Setting Sun: Pioneer Girls Traveling the Overland Trails; Heart of the Trail: The Stories of Eight Wagon Train Women;* and *Into the Western Winds: Pioneer Boys Traveling the Overland Trails.* She has also written a biography for young readers, *Jeannette Rankin: Bright Star in the Big Sky.* She and her husband, Dan, have two daughters and a son. Mary works from her home in Polson, Montana.